VAN WHITFIELD

Something's Wrong with Your Scale!

Van Whitfield writes for the hit sitcom *Grown Ups*. His foundation, "Education Works!," encourages literary excellence among young people. Visit him on the web at www.vanwhitfield.com.

ALSO BY VAN WHITFIELD

Beeperless Remote

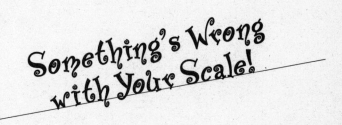

Something's Wrong with Your Scale!

A Romantic Comedy

Van Whitfield

Anchor Books
A Division of Random House, Inc.
New York

FIRST ANCHOR BOOKS EDITION, FEBRUARY 2000

Copyright © 1999 by Van Whitfield

Anchor Books and colophon are registered trademarks of
Random House, Inc.

The Library of Congress has cataloged the Doubleday edition
of this work as follows:
Whitfield, Van.
Something's wrong with your scale!: a romantic
comedy / by Van Whitfield.--1st ed.
p. cm.
I. Title.
PS3573.H4914S6   1999
813'.54 dc21   98-20279
CIP

Anchor ISBN: 0-385-48936-6

www.anchorbooks.com

Author photograph © Don Baker

Printed in the United States of America
10 9 8 7 6 5 4 3 2 1

"So you're going to let a little weight come between us?"
—*Sonny Walker*

The Top

5

Lame Reasons We Lose Weight

1. *Reunions*

2. *Weddings, Special Events*

3. *Seasonal Changes*

4. *To Get Someone's Attention*

5. *So We Can Say, "Look at Me Now!!"*

The Appetizer

Chapter 1

I can't believe it. I just can't believe it. Two years ago I had been the man. Don't get me wrong—it's not that I wasn't the man anymore, I was just more of the man. Or more accurately, I was two of the men. Extra large *used* to be a size. Now it had taken on a new significance for me—extra large was a way of life.

I hadn't had the nerve to step on a scale since Michael Jordan returned to the NBA. I even remember what I was eating when the newsflash came on TV proclaiming that the greatest player ever to bounce a basketball was back—I was waist deep in bones and drowning in the hickory-sweet sauce of my favorite food, my mother's secret-recipe barbecued ribs. Come to think of it, since I hit thirty, food seemed to be tied to literally every major event of the last couple of years. For instance, I was eating spiced shrimp marinated in lobster sauce when Magic Johnson came out of retirement. And, when Dominique Wilkins made it back to the NBA, I was pigging out on baked lasagna stuffed with turkey sausage. My buddy Chet says he usually remembers where he was when something important happened. He recalls the sights and sounds, and all sorts of useless details, but Chet's only twenty-nine. His memory is still fully functional because he hasn't hit the wall yet—the big thirty.

I even remember what I was eating when I hit the wall. Deviled eggs and a hot open-faced roast beef sandwich with lumpy gravy, fresh provolone cheese and a crisp Klausen dill pickle on the side. Actually it was two pickles. But who was counting back then? I had an incredible metabolism. It usually made my food digest magically, before it became a permanent part of my then well-maintained body. I could eat anything. I worked out, played tennis, and shed weight as easily as I gained it. But after I ate those sandwiches (and I'm not sure if it was after the sandwich or after the pickles), I didn't hit the bathroom for at least two days. The combination of supple, white Wonder Bread and tender, gravy-riddled roast beef drew me in like a narcotic. Over the next two days, I had six more of those sandwiches. Sometimes with three pickles.

That was, of course, just four days after my thirtieth birthday and two weeks before I met Marsha. We were introduced at D.C. Live, a swank new club on the trendy F Street corridor in the northwest section of the nation's capital.

Patsy, a mutual friend, told me an attractive girlfriend of hers was interested in meeting a nice guy. Despite the fact that Patsy had yet to find and keep a mate of her own, she was really good at hooking people up. And I was eager to become part of her track record. In the last year I'd been on too many really bad dates; they never quite measured up. In fact, they usually sucked. I essentially went in feeling anxious, left feeling bad, and I was almost ready to give up dating altogether after some of those dates. Somehow all the dates were the same. Each woman had been treated so badly by some other guy that I was rendered worthless before I even showed up. I'd have to listen to women talk about how men were dogs, how men couldn't be trusted and how they'd each get back at all men because of the no-good guy who'd screwed them over. Unfortunately for me, each woman's disdain for men fell right into my lap and made a beeline to my wallet.

I took the dates because Patsy was a decent lady who had a wide circle of friends. My friends felt that of all the single guys in D.C., I was truly the most single. I showed up at clubs alone and almost always left the same way. I went to Laundromats trying to meet women in spite of the fact that in my town house, I had a perfectly operable washer and dryer. And my visits to the ultimate meeting gallery, the grocery store, were hour-long adventures that had me jogging behind a half-full cart trying to place myself in the aisle of a woman I'd spotted earlier.

Unfortunately, I usually ended up in the wrong aisle and, of course, with the wrong women.

My buddies amazingly were able to date two, three or even

four women at the same time, while I struggled to meet just one who would take me seriously. The women I met were committed to friendship. At least until they met the guy they *really* liked. And on the rare occasion when I *was* that guy, it would work just long enough for them to find the guy they *really, really* liked.

But I always felt that Patsy would come through.

At least I knew her friends really wanted to meet a man. The women I met claimed they wanted to meet someone, but their actions didn't reflect their *alleged* intentions. They definitely had issues. They'd go to clubs and wouldn't dance. You'd say hello to them on the street, but they wouldn't speak. Maybe you'd open a door or hold an elevator. They wouldn't even say, "Thanks," they'd just order you to hit the button for the fourth floor and then stare off into space.

And these were the women who wanted to meet a nice guy?

It didn't make sense. But being alone made even less sense. I was in much better physical shape back then, so I played the game because I knew if I didn't I had no chance of winning. I saw Patsy's friends as rays of hope. She had so many friends that, considering the law of averages, one of them had to work out for me. But since I'd already spent a small fortune on dead-end blind dates, I now had a new rule: No more expensive first dates. I refused to spend a ton of money until I found out exactly how much a potential lady friend hated men. The night I was supposed to meet Patsy and her friend we decided to go to the city's latest hot spot, D.C. Live, because it was promising to stage the biggest singles mixer ever. I thought it was a good idea because if Marsha didn't work out, I'd at least have other options. Nine o'clock was the bewitching hour. But I decided to wait until ten *after* nine to make my appearance. I'd been burned so many times before, I wanted to make sure I could check her out *first*.

The deejay cued-up Eddie Kendrick's beat-thumping classic, "Keep on Truckin'." The mixer was rocking a seventies thing, complete with all the effects. Bright flashing red beacons and a piercing white strobe light made it difficult for me to see. Thankfully, a rail-thin guy in a big purple Afro wig with a matching bell-bottomed jumpsuit stepped to the microphone and the lights were turned up. To my surprise it was Chris Rock, the comedian who had skyrocketed to fame after his hilarious HBO special. I figured he was one of the surprise guests the club had advertised on the radio.

Sean "Puffy" Combs and his Bad Boy Entertainment hip-hop mob dominated one corner of the room while avant garde songstress Erykah Baydu, complete with a textured, spiraling headpiece and two beefy bodyguards, swayed about the room with a sense of style and elegance. Local basketball legends Chris Webber, Juwan Howard, Allen Iverson and Moochie Norris held court in another corner with a group of women who looked so good they probably would have passed up the chance to pose for the cover of *Glamour* magazine. Up-and-coming political movers Jesse Jackson, Jr. and Mark Thompson shook hands and chatted near the side of the stage. Local media stars like Lark McCarthy, Cathy Hughes, Monique Braxton, Jeanie Jones, Harry Evans and even D.C.'s top morning-drive radio guys, Russ Parr and Doug Gilmore, served as guest bartenders and slyly laughed while stirring drinks and exchanging the latest dirt on everybody else in the club. If the opening was any indication at all, D.C. Live was about to jump-start the city's near comatose nightlife. It would definitely be the place to see and be seen.

When nine-ten rolled around, I edged toward the bar and waltzed by several times. It was essential to catch glimpses from all of the appropriate angles. And when I saw her, I thought—*Wow!* She'd have been worth a meal and dessert. Marsha was wearing a tight-fitting, mid-thigh-length black velour dress. She had a wonderful smile and stunning brown eyes. Her jet-black hair was as shiny as a freshly minted quarter. It was done up in a semi-formal but very sexy after-six style. She had a petite, sassy figure like one of those eternally upbeat aerobics instructors. Nice legs. Shapely behind. Boobs to die for. She was definitely worth meeting.

Singles night wouldn't be a bust after all.

Patsy spotted me and yelled, "Sonny, we're right over here!"

"Hey," I replied, smiling. "What's happening?"

Oh no! I obviously was too caught up in the "oldies night" theme. *"What's happening?"* How could I have said "What's happening?" As an opening line, "What's happening?" was as dead as "I had to meet you, you made my mood ring turn blue."

"Nothing's happening. What's happening with you, cool dude?" Patsy said, smiling.

"I'm just hanging," I answered.

I was not making a good first impression. "What's happening," followed by the equally graceful "I'm just hanging" Marsha probably thought I was a complete idiot. Patsy had probably given her the big buildup and all I had come up with were the same lines my old man used to pull on my mom thirty-something years ago.

What was I thinking?

"Sonny, this is Marsha. Marsha, Sonny," said Patsy, her head going back and forth.

When Patsy smiled and slowly nodded before rushing off to the "ladies' room," I should have known what was up. I had been sized up and didn't even realize it. Thankfully, Marsha relieved the tension and started the conversation.

"Patsy tells me you're very successful."

"She does?" I asked, nodding my head and hoping it would make me look smooth.

"Yes," she answered casually. "She says you're a regional sales and distribution manager for Sports Authority."

"She said that?"

"Certainly. She told me you were in grad school and that you had control of forty stores."

"Forty stores?" I asked, stunned.

"I believe she said forty. That's a lot of responsibility. How do you keep up with forty stores?"

"Forty stores?" I repeated.

"Yes. You have forty stores in your region, don't you?" she asked.

"Yeah," I answered. "We may have more than forty in our region. It's a tremendous responsibility."

One problem. I had no clue as to exactly who had this awesome responsibility. I knew I didn't. I also knew I wasn't in grad school. I was thinking about enrolling in a certificate course on sales dynamics at Prince Georges Community College. That was a far cry from grad school. I didn't even have a degree. Not yet, anyway. I wasn't exactly a regional manager either. I wasn't even a store manager. I was team leader for the f-ing loose balls section. The worst section in the store. It was impossible to keep up with those stupid balls. Kids came in and threw them. Adults picked them up, decided they didn't want them and left them in some other section. I couldn't win. I wanted to work in tents and outdoor equipment. Nobody ever picks up a tent and leaves it in another section.

How was I supposed to tell a woman who was as sharp as Marsha *and* who I also wanted to impress that my level of responsibility was basically limited to ensuring that the labels on my stock were turned right side up?

The deejay must have seen the worry leaping from the top of my head; he helped me out by throwing on "Slide," the funky seventies hit by the soul-rock fusion group, Slave. I glanced toward the dance floor and took Marsha's hand. She was as smooth as she was sassy on the dance floor. She twirled, looked me dead in the eye and pranced about with more snap, crackle and pop than a bowl of Rice Krispies. Keeping up with her was useless. She was a real dancer and I felt like a guy who was just pretending to dance. Ultimately, we connected. As we bent at the waist, our shoulders rocked as we moved toward each other like we'd fallen into a Rosie Perez–choreographed video. She turned her back on me and threw her hands into the air while my arms slid around her waist. The beat was ours and we both knew we were on to something. The entire night was more perfect than even I had hoped for. We danced till three and toasted the grand opening of D.C. Live. Marsha called the next day and asked *me* out.

Patsy had come through! Marsha and I actually hit it off.

After we started seeing each other, I eventually told her I wasn't exactly a regional manager and she didn't even seem phased. By that time she was into me, and I had taken to her too (and the fact that she was a fantastic cook didn't hurt either). But our coming together was a prime example of what happens when you run into bad timing, or worse yet, how bad things can get when bad timing slams into you. I didn't need to meet Ms. Marsha Minor after I'd turned thirty and hit the wall. She insisted on feeding me even after my body elected to accept calories and store fat with the enthusiasm of a teenager who's just received his driver's license. As the weight first piled on I honestly didn't realize what was happening. Marsha was all up into me, things were going well at work, and I figured what was wrong with a few extra pounds? They would eventually go away. And even when the weight didn't leave (as I had repeatedly asked it to), I was certain I'd be able to lose it when I really felt like it.

But the wall had set in and I wasn't losing anything. Especially weight.

At least I thought I wasn't losing anything. . . .

After a year of regular dating, wall-thumping sex, and an additional fifty pounds that didn't bother to submit a request before joining my body, Marsha made me one last meal (teriyaki steak and mushroom potatoes with mambo sauce and Parmesan cheese), and a dessert I'd never even heard of (peanut butter cheesecake with some sort of gooey marshmallow glaze). As I reached for a second slice of the cheesecake, which was nothing short of magnificent, she walked into her bedroom and quickly returned wearing a silky seethrough red robe. To my delight, she hit me with a sexual experience that she must have uncovered in *Penthouse* magazine's steamy "Forum" section. Before I could fall asleep, an act I always felt was a man's right after sex, she poked me in one of the rolls of skin that was masquerading as my side and told me we needed to talk.

"Talk?" I asked, surprised. "About what? We already did it once."

"Not that," she said flatly. "I knew we were only going to do it once, because you can barely get done once."

"Funny, Marsha," I answered, smiling.

"No, Sonny," she shot back. "There's nothing funny about it at all."

I slowly sat up, cleverly pulled the sheet over my unsightly belly, and cautiously asked, "What's up, Marsha—what are you talking about?"

"I don't know exactly how to say this, Sonny," she said, before pausing. "But I just can't take this anymore."

I didn't know what she couldn't take. And I'm not certain I really cared, because at that particular moment I couldn't get her peanut butter cheesecake out of my mind, or off of my taste buds. For just a second it got quiet. She'd already said she couldn't take *something*, which I could relate to because I had reached my limit as well.

I had to have some more of that cheesecake.

"Hold that thought, hon," I said, interrupting our silence. "I'll be right back."

I wrapped the soft red sheet around me like it was a modern-day toga and hurried to the kitchen. My eyes widened as I spotted the cheesecake sitting majestically on a thick black plate. First I took a tiny slice, which I ate while standing in the kitchen. Then I cut a real piece and slid it onto a matching black dessert plate. I figured if the slice was big enough I could at least pretend to offer her some, which I knew she'd refuse. She may have been a master baker but she wasn't really pressed about dessert, which was cool. It just left more for me.

With fork and plate in hand, I walked back toward her bedroom. I didn't think I was gone long but apparently I was. When I got back she was completely dressed and was playfully styling her hair in front of the bathroom mirror. I plopped down onto the bed, and for some reason she just shook her head in disgust.

"I'm sorry," I said, holding the plate toward her. "You want some?"

"No, Sonny," she forcefully answered. "I've already had enough."

"You didn't even eat dessert," I reminded her.

"I'm aware of that," she slowly answered. "I've had enough of you."

"What do you mean you've had enough of me?" I asked, surprised.

"Look at you, Sonny!" she implored. "Roseanne would have had enough of you."

"So what are you trying to say?" I fired back, lifting the fork to my mouth.

"I'm saying I can't take you anymore, Sonny," she said convincingly. "I can't take your falling asleep at a moment's notice, your third, fourth and fifth helpings, and worst of all, Sonny," she told me, "I can't deal with your weight."

I was surprised because she'd never mentioned my weight before and I wondered why she chose to distract me while I was trying to finish that glorious peanut butter cheesecake.

"You've changed so much since we first met," she told me.

"You used to be in such good shape, and you were so much fun. But now all you do is eat, drink, sleep and then wake up to eat some more."

"And whose fault is that?" I asked, before wiping away the mustache that the strawberry-flavored Quik milk had left over my top lip.

"It's certainly not mine!" she exclaimed.

"That's crap, Marsha!" I yelled. "You always wanted to stay in and cook," I reminded her. "If I was going to play ball with the fellas you'd say, 'You don't need to go to a gym to play ball—you can come play with me.' "

I polished off the milk, let out an embarrassing belch (I tried not to, but it just came out), excused myself and quickly refocused on her problem with my perceived weight problem.

"Look, Marsha," I went on. "This is your fault because I wasn't like this when we met, and if it's that big a problem I can lose the weight."

"It's not so much your weight," she told me. "It's actually more you than the weight."

"You're not making much sense," I said, sliding another chunk of cheesecake over my teeth and into my happy mouth.

"Sonny, you have no control when it comes to food and it bothers me so much because my initial attraction to you was that you were so controlled without being controlling."

"I'm still in control," I quickly replied.

"Yeah," she said, grinning. "You're in control of any fork, knife, and spoon that you can get ahold of."

I had to laugh because I knew she was right. And because at that very moment, I was supporting her theory by expertly raising her silver-plated fork to my mouth and devouring the last bite of cheesecake that had decided to hang around on the tiny dessert plate.

"So what are you saying, Marsha?" I asked, concerned. "You're dumping me because I put on a few pounds?"

"A few pounds!" she loudly exclaimed. "Ten pounds would have been a few pounds. Twenty-five or thirty pounds may have been a few pounds. But look at you, Sonny!" She shook her head. "You have to be at least fifty pounds over-weight."

She then grabbed my hand and led me to the bathroom.

"Let's see," she said, pointing at a tiny black-and-white scale, which she slid to the middle of the cold tiled floor.

"Let's see what?" I asked, embarrassed.

"Let's see how much you weigh!"

"Why do we have to see what I weigh?" I asked nervously.

"Because we have to!" she demanded.

I dropped the sheet to the floor (as if it would make me lighter) and slowly stepped onto the scale. I would have rather seen the shark from *Jaws* jump out of her bathtub than witness the numbers on her scale climb off the chart.

"Sonny," she said, gasping and shaking her head, "I don't believe it. It's amazing."

I didn't want to believe it. She was right.

"Yo, Marsha," I said, not hesitating to step back onto the floor. "Something's wrong with your scale!"

"There is nothing at all wrong with my scale," she said, walking back into the bedroom. "But there is absolutely something wrong with you and I can no longer deal with it."

"So what you're telling me is that you're going to let a lit-tle weight come between us?" I nervously asked.

"No, Sonny," she said forcefully. "*You* let a *lot* of weight come between us. And like I already said, it's not as much the weight as it's your lack of control. I don't need a man in my life who is as lacking in the control department as you."

She'd made her point. I wasn't about to make a fool of myself and try to convince her she was wrong. Her message was clear. I wasn't about to be pressed about any woman. Even if she was as good in the kitchen as Marsha. But I was pressed about the rest of that peanut butter cheesecake, and I wondered if she would let me take the rest of it with me, even though she'd just dropped me.

I carefully squeezed myself into my sweatsuit, slowly rolled into my shoes and headed toward the door with my dignity intact. Though getting dumped was as awful as one of those fat-free chocolate bars, I took solace in the fact that I hadn't been reduced to begging her for a chance to work things out. I walked slowly, hoping maybe she would come to her senses and change her mind.

She didn't.

As I reached for the door, she stood by the kitchen and said, "I'm sorry it has to be like this, Sonny."

"I am too," I countered.

"Sonny," she softly added, "you're a beautiful man, and you have a lot going for you, but you have got to get it together, and you have to do it for yourself—not for me or for anyone else."

I just blankly stared at her. How the heck should you hit her up for the cheesecake? I thought, concerned.

"I understand, Marsha," I said, interrupting the silence. "You're just looking out for you. I guess it's just a woman thing or something."

"I don't know what that means, but I won't honor it with a response," she replied flatly.

"My bad," I told her, shaking my head. "That was a cheap shot," I said, trying to persuade my tongue to rid itself of the hypnotic taste of that cheesecake. "I'm sorry."

The only thing I was *sorry* about was the possibility of leaving without the cheesecake.

It was clear this was my last chance. And since it was obvious she wasn't about to offer up the rest of that incredible dessert, I had to make a move. I walked slowly in her direction (like I was one of those obviously fake, ultra-desirable guys in a grainy black-and-white Calvin Klein underwear ad), reached out for one last hug, and made a heroic swipe at the cheesecake, which was situated on the table directly behind her.

It almost worked.

But as she lay her head on the part of my body that once resembled a male chest, but which was now in need of a sturdy underwire training bra, my hand hit the table. She forcefully backed away and yelled, "What the heck are you doing, Sonny!"

"I'm not doing nothing," I answered, lying.

"If you're not doing anything," she said in disbelief, "then why is that big piece of cheesecake stuck on the side of your sleeve?"

"It just got there," I told her.

"It just got there?" she replied. "This is crazy, Sonny— you're sick!"

"I'm not sick, I just like your cheesecake," I said, worried. "What's wrong with that?"

She sighed, and without saying a word wrapped the entire

dish up in aluminum foil and handed it to me. "Take it and get out," she said forcefully.

"Thanks," I replied as she slammed the door behind me. "Do you need the plate back?"

I never found out if she needed the plate or not, but it didn't matter. That was the best cheesecake I'd ever had. As I finished it off that night I rationalized that Marsha was just another shallow woman who was looking for an excuse to get out of a commitment. She may have been right about my "lack of control," but blaming it on her made it easier to accept getting dumped.

It also made it easier to make a late-night trip to the International House of Pancakes (IHOP), where I ordered a Rooty Tooty Fresh and Frutti breakfast, which featured three huge pancakes with strawberry compote topping, three gleaming slices of bacon, three juicy sausage links, and a healthy mound of freshly grilled hash browns. When I ordered a second helping the buxom, stiff-haired waitress asked, "Are you okay—is something wrong?"

"Yeah, something's wrong," I confessed. "I'm hungry!"

That was over a year ago and I know it seems incredible, but it took me that year *and* another twenty-five pounds to realize that Marsha could have actually been right. I realized I might very well have a problem that I couldn't control. Most of the time, I felt the food was controlling me. I'd forced myself to believe that I'd hit the wall when all along the wall had come crashing down on me.

I looked and felt terrible and I was tired of feeling that way. That's why I was here. It felt weird being in the tiny white-walled room with this pathetic collection of clearly overweight overeaters, but I was as bad off as they were. I *never* thought it would get to this but, much like pictures, bathroom scales don't often lie. If I could have waved a magic wand to be rid of my weight, I would have. But this was no fairy tale and with a butt as big as mine, I was definitely no fairy. I was fed up, I'd had it and I simply couldn't take it anymore. I prayed this was the right move, and even though it seemed so desperate, my heart told me it would work. I just couldn't help but wonder what my buddies, player-hating Chet and too-tired Everett, would say if they knew their main man, Sonny Walker, was cooling his heels in a FutraSystem Weight Loss Center.

On second thought, I really didn't know what they'd think and I guess I didn't care.

I just wished the counselor would hurry up and start our orientation so I could get out of there, because I was hungry.

Chapter 2

I didn't think I got this. A cute little number who identified herself as our counselor (but who insisted she was our friend *first*) asked us why we were there. Everybody just looked around like second graders who didn't want to get called to the blackboard, but I knew (and I'm certain they knew as well) *exactly* why we were there. We were there because we were fat and because we'd probably tried everything else, and since nothing else has worked, we were giving FutraSystem a chance.

One of the problems with being overweight is that it's so easy to get sucked into every weight-loss scheme in the book. In the past six months I'd tried everything from crash diets to the patented Gut-Away waistline trimmer. I like to eat, so I understand why the diets never worked. But I couldn't figure out how the Gut-Away failed me. I made a point to use it at least once a week and I was certain it would work because it cost me $99 (broken into three easy payments of $33 each). I was watching an infomercial for the Gut-Away when I couldn't sleep one night, and as I recall, it was about two in the morning. My stomach was yearning for a late-night snack, so I heated up two meatloaf sandwiches with beef-stock gravy and thick, French-toast-style bread.

I would've had a pickle with it but I was all out, so I made a note to pick some up the next day.

When the Gut-Away ad hit the screen, I was amazed by the tiny waistlines and perfect smiles of the people who claimed they had used the product. Everything about them looked great, so I knew this was the ticket for me. The women wore revealing bikinis and the guys had abdomens that looked like they were on loan from the Mr. Universe contest. What impressed me most was that the celebrity endorser, a guy who was the bus driver for Panama's Olympic ski team, promised the Gut-Away would work for busy people like me.

"The Gut-Away is effective," he assured me with a spicy island accent, "because it works around your schedule, okay, mon?

"Best of all," he continued, nodding his head, "you can eat whatever you'd like. Just use the Gut-Away right after you've eaten, okay mon?"

That seemed easy enough. I hurried to the phone because they promised a copy of the top-selling *Buns of Gold* workout tape for the first one hundred callers (I even paid an extra ten bucks for express delivery). The *Buns of Gold* tape never made it, but that was okay, because the only buns I really cared about were the hot crossed buns I always purchased from Safeway. I sometimes had a box of eight with dinner, and at three boxes for $2.59 they were a bargain.

The Gut-Away never worked for me. It did fit into my schedule as promised (though I rarely used it), and I did follow the infomercial's advice when it came to eating whatever I liked. That wasn't a problem. But my waistline ballooned and I never started to look like one of those guys from the infomercial. I don't know if it failed me or I failed it, but it's now part of my museum of weight loss tools and gimmicks that never worked.

My collection includes the Ab-Buster; the Gut-Flexer; the Thigh-Melter; the Flab-Trimmer and even the patented chrome-plated Tummy-Tucker Plus. And the only thing all these items have in common besides the fact they didn't help me lose weight is the dust they've collected.

I was hoping that FutraSystem would be the answer to my prayers—I got the feeling they understood my particular dilemma. I had to eat. And if their ad bore any truth, FutraSystem would help me lose weight without starving to death.

When our group failed to give the counselor a conclusive reason for our attendance, she directed each of us to state our name and our reason for selecting FutraSystem. She obviously had her own take on our plight.

"At FutraSystem we're concerned about your futures," she said, pointing at no one specifically. "By selecting FutraSystem, you have enrolled in a program concerned not only with the out-of-shape you of today," she went on, her head shaking and finger waving. "We care more about preparing you for the slim-and-trim you of tomorrow and the future." She smiled. "So share with me how FutraSystem can help you with *your* future."

As heads dropped, everyone muttered their name and repeated a common theme. "Hi, I'm So-and-so, and I have a weight problem."

It was like a well-practiced drill. I imagined we had much in common. We all probably ate as if food would soon be outlawed. Most of us were probably on a first-name basis at several restaurants around town. And this I was sure of: we all avoided mirrors like the plague. Essentially, we were just plain tired of the weight. I'd heard this crap before. I'd said it to myself so many times even *I* had stopped believing it. I wanted this to be different. FutraSystem had to work. I had too much on the line and failure simply wasn't an option.

I had to tell the truth.

"I don't know what to say," I told them, standing.

"Why don't you start with our anthem," the counselor advised, nodding her head.

"Oh, yeah," I nodded back. "My name is Sonny Walker and I have a weight problem."

"Hi, Sonny," everyone replied together.

"Very good, Mr. Walker," she said, writing on her clipboard. "And you're with us because you'd like to change a few things, correct?"

"I guess you could put it like that," I answered. "But I really want to lose weight so I can attract a nice woman."

The room got quiet.

The counselor quickly stated, "That's an interesting goal, Sonny, it really is, but losing weight is ideally done for one's self."

"I know what you mean," I told her, shaking my head. "But I was fine with me until a woman I was dating dumped me because of my weight."

"That happened to me too," said a guy who was sitting in front of me.

"Same here," added a woman who looked as though her burgundy warm-up suit had been glued onto her flabby arms.

It was clear everyone had a "lose the weight or else" story. But our counselor, who was, of course, "our friend" as well, wasn't interested in hearing too much of it. She interrupted by yelling, "I understand, I understand, but this is not about your problems, it's about your weight!"

"Excuse me," said someone forcefully. "But this *is* about our problems, because our problem *is* our weight!"

Everyone applauded. We didn't dare try to stand and clap because we knew sitting back down would be an adventure unto itself. But, like everyone else in the room, I looked around to find just who had uttered this pearl of wisdom.

I was pleasantly surprised to see an intelligent-looking, bespectacled woman with long curly brown hair, a playful double chin, cheerfully chubby cheeks, and full, pouting lips that seemed perfect for kissing *or* eating. I placed her at about a size 24. Maybe a 22 on a good day, I thought. I couldn't help but notice that despite her weight, she was a real cutey. She told us her name was Kayla Jennings and that she had come to tonight's FutraSystem meeting because she wanted a change in her life. Kayla said she'd tried all sorts of gimmicks. She'd shared with us that she'd lost weight only to gain it right back. I quickly got the impression that Kayla was super confident, and under normal circumstances would *never* admit she was anything less than happy with herself, but since we were fat too, I guess she decided it was a safe place to reveal how she really felt. Her weight and her body had evolved into a social problem—it had taken a devastating toll on her psyche *and* her professional life.

She had a sultry, very feminine voice that stung each of us when she convincingly said, "I want to be happy with myself and I've tried to adjust to the weight, but I'm fed up because other people actually have more problems with my body than I do."

That remark hit home for all of us. We all knew the hardest things to endure were the perceptions and attitudes that others had about our weight. Kayla had hit the nail on the head and though I knew she was right, I didn't dare comment.

I just wanted to hurry up and get out of there so I could get some food.

Our counselor, who finally identified herself as Eleanor, told us we'd meet and weigh in every Wednesday at 7:00 P.M. She then directed us to individual rooms where our weight would be recorded and our goals and menus would be set. As far as I was concerned, that was a good sign, because setting menus meant getting closer to eating, and that was always a good thing.

A guy with HENRY stamped on his name tag came in and directed me to the scale before he sat down. He dispassionately said that if I set reasonable goals and stuck with my menus the program would work for me. He then handed me a long checklist of FutraSystem foods that supposedly met the requirements for the basic food groups. I gave it a quick glance and I noticed that it didn't include anything from my favorite food group, McDonald's, but it was a start. The list included snacks, desserts and an array of breakfast treats. I told Henry I wanted to lose about seventy-five pounds. I admitted I liked the fact that FutraSystem provided good food to help me reach what I thought was a modest goal.

He handed me a price list and explained that the average food cost was just $70 a week. He then walked toward the doorway, looked both ways down the hall and then carefully shut the door. He motioned for me to join him at the mirror, which was hung on the door, and told me to look at myself.

"A hefty guy like you ain't gonna make it on that little bit of food they give you," he whispered. "Slip me a twenty every week, and I'll make sure you get extras of the stuff you really like."

I turned my head sideways (as if it would make my blubbery body somehow fit into the slim floor-length mirror) and said, "I'll still lose weight?"

"You'll still lose it."

"Only twenty extra bucks a week?"

"Just twenty."

"Deal!"

As an incentive, I gave him forty bucks. I figured that it would land me more food than I bargained for. Luckily, I ended up having to spend just $120. That was chump change. I couldn't wait to get home to dig in and find out how everything tasted. Thanks to Henry, I had enough FutraSystem food to have at least three helpings at every meal. If I was lucky, I could squeeze out five helpings per sitting, but I figured that if I stuck to the program and ate only the FutraSystem food, reducing my consumption to just *three* helpings per meal would have me prancing in thin city in no time.

Henry handed me his card, wrote his home number on the back and told me to call him if I needed extra food or any FutraSnacks. He told me he'd have my extra bag ready every Wednesday and reminded me if I wanted to meet my goal I should eat only FutraSystem foods. We sealed our deal with a firm handshake and I thanked him for looking out for me.

I took one more look at myself in the mirror and couldn't wait to get home. I knew I'd soon fit into that FutraSystem mirror if I stuck to the program like Henry had advised. The whole thing seemed so easy and I was set. As I headed out of the room and down the hall a pleasant voice said, "*I* wouldn't have dropped you because of your weight."

I smiled, slowly turned around and jokingly said, "Look at you. You *couldn't* have dropped me because of my weight."

We both laughed before she extended her hand and said, "Hi, I'm Kayla."

"We all know who you are," I replied. "I'm Sonny."

We walked toward the door, and Eleanor, who noticed that I had five bags instead of two like everyone else, asked, "Will we see you at our next meeting, Sonny?"

"I'm not sure," I responded, lying and looking down at my bags, "so I bought enough to last me a month."

"That's good planning," she cheerfully acknowledged, "and good planning is the first step toward meeting your goals. You should be proud of yourself."

Kayla laughed and said, "Way to go, Mr. Big Stuff."

As Eleanor walked into her office Kayla took a long look at

her. "What does she know about good planning?" Kayla whispered. "She's never had a weight problem in her life."

Kayla was probably right. Eleanor was a striking little blonde. (Emphasis on *little*.) Not even her oversized white doctor's coat could hide her petite figure. She had sleek, slender features, and definitely couldn't relate to our struggles. Eleanor was our counselor and she may have wanted to be our "friend" as well, but she was nothing like us. She was so—how shall I say it?—unfat.

"No joke," I said, as I opened the hatch on my midnight-blue Chevy Suburban. "But being around people like her should help you."

"What's that supposed to mean?" asked Kayla.

"She's slim and trim and that may rub off on you," I casually replied. "She should be an inspiration."

"Oh, really," she scoffed. "And just who is supposed to inspire you?"

"Inspire me?" I asked. "I'll inspire myself."

Kayla laughed and then fired off, "Well, that should work just fine. It's certainly been successful so far."

"I haven't always been like this," I told her, "and I know how to lose weight."

"I do too," she told me. "That's why I'm willing to pay FutraSystem seventy dollars a week, because I've been so good at losing weight on my own."

We both laughed because she'd made a good point (even if it was at my expense). I offered her a ride home, but she said she lived only a few blocks away. She felt she needed the exercise anyway. I looked at her and knew she was right (about needing the exercise). I wished her well with the program.

She wished me luck and suggested we keep in touch to support each other.

"It's obvious our support systems have failed us thus far," she said, grinning. "Maybe we can keep each other honest."

I figured she had a point, so we exchanged numbers and she made her way to the corner. I looked in my rearview mirror, got an unflattering view of her abundant rear end, and pulled off toward my place. I opened a bag of the cheese-curl-style FutraSnacks and ate them on my ten-minute trip home. Not bad. I couldn't wait to unpack my food to get my first taste of a real FutraSystem meal and I could hardly believe I was actually going to lose weight while eating well at the same time. I was so excited that I stood in the mirror, attempted to suck in my gut and imagined the new, thin me in a red, skintight Speedo swimsuit.

It was the best I'd felt in over a year.

I was beginning to feel that the me I imagined would soon be a reality, and I was especially happy because FutraSystem was going to do it for me—all I had to do was eat their food.

Chapter 3

It took all of two minutes for me to come to my senses. I wasn't about to show up anywhere in anybody's red Speedo. As much as I wanted FutraSystem to get me to thin city, I knew I needed more than the type of support Kayla talked about. I couldn't just count on her. She was as wide as a glacier in December. Counting on her to help me lose weight would be like asking Stevie Wonder to help me drive.

Chet and Everett would have to help.

We've been buddies since I was little. I can usually count on them. But then again, that may be because I never really ask them to do anything for me. It's hard to figure Chet out.

For the last five years, he's been the loss-prevention supervisor for every Hecht's department store in the region. A few years after he graduated from Morehouse College, in Atlanta, he came home and hit the lottery. Literally. He played his kid's birthday, his ex-wife's birthday and his license plate number in the lotto one night. The next morning, he found himself in a new tax bracket.

He looks out for us if we need him, but we don't want to take advantage, because whenever we *do* ask him for help we never hear the end of it. Chet's a bright guy, though, and he's as funny as they come. At six foot two, 220 pounds, he's any woman's dream. He has the type of physique women dig. Barrel chest. Rock-solid arms and a trim waistline. A gleaming bald head, diamond stud earring and a tiny pit bull tattoo making him a poster boy for the machismo that has come to define the nineties.

And in typical nineties fashion, Chet is the ultimate "player hater." He doesn't seem to want anybody else to be particularly successful at anything. Especially dating. All in all, he's an okay brother, but he does have one significant flaw: Chester Melvin Stewart has absolutely no respect for women.

"Women don't have a clue," he often says. "They just don't get it."

Chet's ex-wife Yvette had run off with another man. His mom, Claudine, was an accountant who found herself on the wrong end of an audit. Claudine's company was $325,000 short the same year her bank account benefitted from an unexplainable $279,000 windfall. And now she's trying to figure it all out while sitting in the state pen. Chet never met his dad, and his baby sister, Pauline, was busted for eating grapes on the subway—and *everybody* knows that eating on the D.C. metro is illegal.

Chet rarely talks about either of them, though he did once confess, "They're two of the dumbest chicks on earth. You could unscrew their skulls and see their thoughts because they have no brains. But they're chicks, so what do you expect?" Whew! My man Chet definitely had issues, but even though I didn't share his opinions about women, he was still one of my closest friends.

My other buddy, Everett Steven Casey, is the exact opposite of Chet. He's a pushover when it comes to women. He's been a systems engineer with D.C.'s ever-expanding metro system since he came out of Johns Hopkins University, in Baltimore. We've called him "Easy E" since he was twelve years old. He earned the tag because he bought Carla Livingston a Good Humor toasted almond bar every day for two weeks. He used the money his father had given him to cover his registration for boys' club football. E never signed up because Carla had exhausted his bankroll. And when he didn't come home with a uniform, E was forced to lie to his old man. He told his pop that the coach cut him. E's dad was furious.

He was also the coach's boss. A big scuffle ensued and following a very messy situation, E's dad ended up working as a cop for the metro. To make matters worse, Mr. Casey was the one who arrested Chet's sister for eating grapes on the train, so there's some understandable tension between Chet and E. E's mom split when he was three, but he barely mentions her and neither do we. The fact that E is a white guy hasn't had an impact on our friendship. He's totally down with our slang and the way we communicate, he doesn't try to "play black" and accepts us just like we accept him.

Fortunately, our relationship with E didn't suffer from the usual strain associated with race in the United States. We grew up in Bowie, Maryland, which had become integrated almost by accident. When brothers and sisters first rolled in from D.C., the white folks in Bowie weren't going anywhere. They had established Bowie, built it into a comfortable upper-middle-class enclave and weren't about to surrender it to what they believed were a bunch of Cadillac-driving, big-hat-wearing black folks like the rest of Prince Georges County had. As Bowie got blacker, many whites left. But E's dad liked Bowie and he fit in well, just like E did with us. When E pissed us off, we never saw him as a screwed-up white guy, we just saw him as screwed up. I know he dealt with us the same way. Like all friends, we've had our ups and downs, but we're straight with one another and we have a real bond. We respect each other. Want the best for each other. And know exactly where we stand.

Chet is the rich and cocky one.

E is reliable and sensitive.

And after I hit thirty, I became the fat guy.

E is five nine, 175 on a good day. He stays in shape, but he more or less has the personality of a generic can of peach halves. But he is very intelligent. E moderates all of our disagreements. Chet usually starts them. I think E feels guilty about Chet's sister so he usually avoids any confrontation they may have. He puts up with Chet's crap just like I do, but we love Chet. Deep down, we know he's cool. He's just a little f'ed up because of his bad bookkeeping mom and his brain-surgeon, grape-eating sister.

At thirty-two, E was still stuck on Carla Livingston, who would soon be Carla Livingston-Holmes. Believe it or not,

Carla was engaged to E's first cousin, Donald, who also worked for the metro. We called Donald "Snake" because several years earlier he had snatched E's girl. The sad thing was that E was still letting Carla use him. It was kind of sad because E's such a decent guy.

I definitely knew E would help me with the weight. Chet would help too if only because he'd piss me off so much that I'd stick to my FutraSystem program just to shut him up. I wasn't looking forward to asking them for help, but I had to call. They couldn't help if they didn't know what's up.

I opened a pack of FutraPretzels (for emotional support) while the phone rang, and downed half of the ten-ounce bag by the third ring. I couldn't help it. I was hungry.

"E, what's up, dawg?"

"What's up, Sonny?"

"It's all good. Look, E, get Chet on the three-way."

"For what?"

"I got some news, Money."

"What's Chet got to do with it?" he asked, sounding annoyed.

"Man, just get him on the three-way. Why do we always have to go through this?"

"Because I don't feel like dealing with Chet unless I absolutely have to," E told me.

"Well, you absolutely have to, so get him on the line."

The phone rang three times, which gave me just enough time to finish off the rest of the FutraPretzels.

"Hey, Chet, how's it going?"

"Who dis?"

"It's E."

"E. What's up, fool?" Chet asked.

"Not much, Chet," E answered uneasily.

"It must be something if you calling. You don't never call me. What's up? Carla need some loot to buy Snake's birthday present or something?" Chet said, laughing.

"Chill on that, Chet," I said.

"Who dis?" he replied.

"It's Sonny, Clown."

"Chubbs. What's up, baby boy?" he asked.

"I told you about that Chubbs crap," I reminded him.

"I told you about it too. Your big behind needs to lose some weight."

"That's why I'm calling," I said.

"I should have known," Chet replied.

"You should have known what?" I asked.

"I should have known that E didn't call," Chet said sarcastically.

"Can't you just chill, Chet?" I said.

"What did you call about anyway, Sonny?" E asked.

"I'm about to lose my weight."

Chet, of course, broke out laughing.

"What happened, Chubbs?" he joked. "You run into Marsha and her new man at the Safeway or something?"

"Marsha's got a new man?" I asked, trying to sound cool.

"Heck, yeah," Chet said, laughing. "And she's probably boning Snake too. What you know about that, E?"

"Screw you, Chet. You need to get a life," E told him.

"You'ze a punk, E," Chet shot back.

"Your sister is your momma's punk in prison," E said, laughing.

I couldn't help but laugh. It was one of the rare occasions that E came back on Chet. Chet was stunned. He's not used to E striking out at him. And in that sense he's a classic bully. Hit him back, and he tucks in his tail like a wet puppy strung out on Alpo.

E got him.

Chet deserved it.

And I was still hungry.

"Look, y'all," I said, breaking the tension. "I joined FutraSystem."

"You did what?" they yelled in unison.

"I joined FutraSystem. I'm about to lose this weight."

"Have you lost your mind, Sonny?" asked Chet.

"Yeah, Sonny," E said. "That stuff is just a scam. You may lose some weight, but you'll just put it right back on."

"E's right, Sonny," Chet remarked. "That crap's for the birds. The big fat birds. You may be big and fat, but you ain't no bird. You don't need that. You need to pick your big behind up, stop eating so dag-on much and start working out or something."

"I *am* going to work out," I told them. "But I'm in this now and I need your help."

"You ain't gettin' no help here," Chet said, laughing. "You betta help your big tail away from the table and to somebody's gym."

"This ain't no joke, Chet," I stressed. "I need y'all to be there. I need your support. This weight is killing me."

"It's killing me too, Chubbs," Chet told me, laughing. "But if you're serious, I'm down."

"I'm down too, Sonny," E added. "You know I'll always be there for you."

"Check out Mr. Softee Ice Cream himself," Chet joked.

"You'll always be there for everybody, E. Carla can testify to that."

"Ease up, Chet," I said. "Y'all need to chill on that."

I was the one who needed to chill. I had just finished an entire bag of FutraPretzels and was already hungry again. Thankfully, Henry had hooked me up with extra food, so I popped open a bag of FutraNachos and started on them. A beep alerted me that I had another call. "I'm out," I told them. "I'll get back with y'all later.

"Hello," I said, answering the call.

"Hi, is this you, Sonny?"

"Yeah, this is Sonny. Who's this?"

"It's Kayla."

"Kayla?"

"Yeah, Kayla from FutraSystem."

"Oh, the big girl."

"Yeah, the big girl," she said, laughing.

"What's up?" I asked.

"You know when I said I may need some support?"

"Yeah."

"Well, I need it now. I just ate two bags of chips and I'm still starving. What do they put in this stuff, air?"

"I don't know," I said. "But it sure tastes like air. I just ate two bags of snacks myself and I'm starving too."

"What should we do?" she asked.

There was a long silence, but there was little doubt what would happen. Two overeaters who are hungry are going to do one thing. Eat. She gave me her address and we decided to go to Uncle Leon's Eat & Weigh Kountry Buffet. Leon's sold food by the pound. The server would weigh your food right at your table or you could trust them to weigh it in the kitchen. I preferred the kitchen. I never really wanted to know how much I'd eaten anyway.

The seductive aroma of freshly cut salted greens, soft-buttered sweet potatoes and crispy fried chicken kept the lines long and the crowds coming. Spacious cloth-covered booths lined the outer walls and were separated by a row of neatly arranged square tables. Shiny hardwood floors gave way to classic white walls adorning the "usual suspects" from the world of black art. The picture with people lined up at the funeral (You know. The one from the living room of the old *Cosby* show.), the ladies who were waiting to exhale and the picture that jumped across the screen at the beginning of *Good Times* in the seventies all found a home at Leon's.

Uncle Leon's was one of my favorite spots for a quick meal. Surprisingly, even though I'd never noticed her, Kayla was a regular there too. When we hit the register, we both pulled out our Uncle Leon's Frequent Eater's Club card and took advantage of our 10 percent discount and a free dessert. What a mistake, though, because Wednesday was "Free Dessert for Hump Day." So Kayla and I each got *two* free desserts for having made it halfway through the week. She had two pieces of strawberry cheesecake and I had a double strawberry shortcake. We were so excited to be eating real food, neither of us offered to share anything. When we were done she looked at me, smiled and said, "I am so embarrassed."

"Embarrassed about what?" I asked, wiping my face.

"I shouldn't have eaten so much."

"Yeah," I said, laughing. "You shouldn't have eaten so much."

"And what about you?" she asked.

"What about me?"

"I didn't exactly see you pushing away from the table."

"Look, Kayla," I said, reaching for a toothpick, "we don't have the same problems. You called me and said you needed some support. I'm here because you *asked* me to be here. It's not like I was sitting around waiting to come to Leon's."

"Oh, really," she said, smiling. "And just what were you doing, Sonny?"

"I'd just hung up with my boys and was about to call my ex and tell her I'd joined FutraSystem."

"Why would you do that?" she asked. "Do you really think it will make a difference?"

"Maybe it will," I told her. "Then again, maybe it won't. But I want her to know I'm doing something."

"And you think that will bring her back?"

"I don't know," I said. "But I won't know if I don't at least try."

"She must have been special."

"She was," I said, sighing. "She could really cook."

"She could cook?" she asked.

"Yeah," I said, slumping my shoulders. "She could *really* cook."

"No wonder you want her back," she said, shaking her head. "Good cooks are hard to find. And really good cooks are a godsend."

"Tell me about it," I said, reaching for a napkin.

Marsha was indeed special. She was as gifted in the kitchen as Tyra Banks was in front of a camera. I still spent many nights thinking about her. What she was doing. Who she was with. And more important, what she had cooked for dinner that evening. I had to call her. If she knew I was at least addressing my little food problem, she'd probably take me back. She dug me. I dug her. And she cooked. What else did we need?

"Look, Sonny," Kayla said, focusing me back on our conversation. "I don't know you that well, but I can't imagine why you'd want to be with someone who dumped you because of your weight."

"I can't say that I blame her," I admitted. "I'm a mess."

She looked at me, concerned.

"I put on so much weight she probably thought she was dating a completely different person. I don't even understand what happened. But I do know that I'd lose this weight in a minute if she would even consider taking me back."

"You got it bad," she said, looking at me. "I hope things work out."

"Yeah," I said, nodding in agreement. "I do too."

"Tell me something, Sonny," she asked.

"Something like what?"

"Tell me about yourself and why you're so concerned about someone who obviously can't accept you for who you really are."

"I'm not really like this," I said.

"Excuse me?"

"I'm not really this big."

"Well, how big are you?" she asked, laughing.

"I mean that I haven't always been like this," I told her. "Heck, not so long ago I was cut-up from the butt up."

"I used to be cut-up from the butt up too," she said, shaking her head. "But I wouldn't dare waste one minute worrying about some shallow a-hole who dumps me because I gained a few pounds."

"I didn't just gain a few pounds," I confessed.

"That's not the point, Sonny," she said forcefully. "I may not know you well, but I know people. Trust me," she added. "I've been dumped because of my weight. I know how screwed up that can be. But I would never be pressed about someone who isn't pressed about me."

Kayla was probably right. But I don't know if it mattered. She was a *before* picture. Most guys want an *after* picture. *Nobody* would be pressed about her, which I'm sure made it easy for her not to be pressed about anybody.

"Look, Kayla," I said, leaning back. "I'm not pressed."

"To hear you tell it, you're not big either," she said, laughing.

"That's messed up," I said.

"What's messed up is that you're hanging your head over a woman who didn't respect you enough to stick it out with you," she said with an edge. "You're doing something about it, but she's not around to see it or to support you while you're doing it. Do you really believe she's worth your effort?"

I didn't know what to say. Maybe she was right. As big as she was, she had to be right. I just didn't know if Kayla's rap was all that relevant. Marsha meant a lot to me. It had been a year and I still hadn't gotten over her. I wanted her back. But I couldn't believe Kayla was reading me as well as she was. Being exposed by a woman, especially one I barely knew, was not the ticket. I was squirming and she knew it.

I had to change the subject.

"So, Kayla. What's a big girl like you do for a living?" I asked.

"A big girl like me," she answered curtly, "is a computer systems designer and analyst."

"You're into computers?"

"Yes, Sonny, I design networks, I dabble a little in software, I even design web pages when I have a chance."

"How did you get into that?"

"I went to school, got a degree and started a business," she said, smiling. "Isn't that how it usually works?"

"I guess so," I answered.

"And what's a big guy like *you* do for a living?" she asked, playing with her napkin.

"Oh," I said, concerned. "I, uh, work for Sports Authority."

"You work for Sports Authority?"

"Yeah," I said, looking toward the door to the restaurant kitchen. "I work with them."

"Sonny," she said flatly. "You work for them, you work with them, which is it?"

"Neither one," I admitted. "I actually work at Sports Authority."

"Really, now," she said, nodding her head. "You must be in management."

"Kind of."

"Kind of?"

"Yeah," I answered. "I run the loose balls section."

"The loose balls section," she said, smiling. "I admire a man who knows how to manage his balls."

We laughed as I motioned for the waiter. He walked toward our table and slid the check under one of the six plates I had gathered.

"You must be rich," he said, while handing plates to the busboy who was standing behind him.

"What's that supposed to mean?" I asked.

"I don't mean no harm, big fella," he casually stated, "but y'all can eat."

"Do you know him?" Kayla asked, alarmed.

"I've never seen him in my life," I said, stunned.

"I seen you," he said, laughing. "Heck. I couldn't miss you if I tried."

"Whoa," I said, sitting forward. "You can't talk to me like that. I'm a big customer here."

"You'ze a big customer anywhere," said the busboy. "I ain't never took this many plates from one table. I problee took 'em from a party of ten or something, but you and big girl, y'all gots y'all's eats *all* the way on."

"Big girl?" said Kayla, her eyes tightening.

"Do you gots to axe?" said the waiter, laughing.

"Let me see the f-ing manager!" I demanded.

"I'm am the f-ing manager," said the waiter.

"You're the manager?" I asked, surprised. "I've never seen you here before."

"You ain't seen me 'cause you don't see nothing that you can't eat," he said, shaking his head. "Your waita lef when we closed two hours ago and you problee didn't know he was gone."

"You closed two hours ago?" asked Kayla.

"Pretty much," said the busboy.

"Well, if he's the manager, who the heck are you?" I asked the busboy.

"I'm the f-ing manager's brother," he said, batting his eyes. "And I wish y'all would pay y'all's bill. We tryin' to go home."

"This is unbelievable," said Kayla.

"It ain't as unbleeable as dat tab y'all ranned up," said the busboy.

I turned the grease-stained check over. He was right. Not only had we eaten well past their nine o'clock closing time, but we managed to amass a $126.38 bill in the process. Kayla wouldn't know it because I'd never show her the bill. But $126 for two people at a low-cost, family-style restaurant like Leon's was ridiculous. I hated to admit it, but the manager and his plate-toting brother were right. Our appetites were "unbleeable." Worse than that, we allowed ourselves to fall off the wagon without ever really getting on. I was ashamed, hurt and angry at myself all at once. Kayla didn't seem to care. She just smiled and jammed her abundant arms into the sleeves of her jacket as I paid the bill. The manager and the busboy walked away without even asking if I needed change. Then the manager turned around and said, "All right, big girl, it's time for you and your boyfriend to *leave!*"

"He's not my boyfriend!" she yelled.

"I wouldn't claim his big behind either!" said the busboy, laughing. "That fool's fatter than a first grader's pencil."

I didn't know what was worse. The way we were treated tonight, or having a size twenty-something chow-hound like Kayla making it clear that I wasn't her boyfriend. It didn't matter and I didn't care. I wanted to be out of Leon's just as much as I wanted to be out of my woeful body. I marched toward the door and slammed it as hard as I could. Neither of us said a word as we headed toward Kayla's place. When I pulled up to her place, she looked at me and, for some reason, smiled.

"We shouldn't have to deal with that," she said softly. "I can't believe they were so rude."

"They couldn't believe we were so big and that we ate so much," I said, laughing and doing a perfect impersonation of the busboy.

She laughed while reaching for the door handle.

"Let me get that," I said, opening my door. I always believed it was important to open a woman's door. Even if it wasn't a date, because this definitely wasn't a date.

"You know something," she said, searching her purse for her keys. "The things we have to deal with—being called heavyset, full-figured, lazy, embarrassments—we shouldn't have to put up with that."

"The flip side is that we shouldn't put ourselves in the position to *have* to deal with it," I told her.

"I've always been overweight," she confessed. "I was born big, was always the biggest girl in all my classes and I love to eat," she acknowledged. "I can deal with who I am and frankly, I get tired of people acting as though their opinion of me matters when they don't even know me."

"True indeed," I replied, nodding my head.

"It's true and it's wrong," she said, convincingly. "That's why jerks like those fools at Uncle Leon's really tick me off."

They pissed me off too, but we gave them all the ammo they needed. We ate too much, stayed too long, and even had double desserts to top it off. The way I saw it, if we wanted to eat that way, it was *our* business.

"Kayla," I said, helping her out of the truck. "Thanks."

"Thanks?" she asked. "Thanks for what?"

"Thanks for hearing me out about my ex. I appreciate it."

"You don't have to thank me, Sonny," she said, walking toward her porch. "I'm glad you felt comfortable enough to share that with me. Take care," she added. "Be in touch."

Ironically, I'd never really discussed wanting Marsha back with anyone. Chet and Everett knew we'd split up some time ago, but I never let on as to what really happened. I guess the fact that Kayla was a woman *and* a virtual stranger made me feel at ease. It was probably a plus that I knew there was no way I'd ever be attracted to her. Kayla was decent. She seemed to have a good sense of humor and appeared to be intelligent and well spoken. She said she had her own business, didn't mention any children, and probably wasn't on probation or parole. She'd be a good catch for the right type of guy.

But she was big and big would *never* work for me.

As I headed home I thought of what I'd say to Marsha. I wondered what it would be like to hold her again and to eat at her dining room table. I reminded myself that I had to stick with *the program* if I really wanted her back and promised myself that I would. I pulled into my parking space and sat for a minute. I thought about everything. Marsha's smile and of course, her legs. Her deep-dish apple pie and her barbecued chicken pizza. Her special way with pasta, and the seafood bisque she used to make just for me.

Kayla may not have known me but she was on target.

When it came to Marsha, I was pressed.

THE REASONS WE LOSE WEIGHT

Lame Reason

#1

Reunions

I could care less about losing weight for some-body's stupid reunion. Who cares about seeing a bunch of dumb people who you've been trying to duck for ten years anyway? Yeah, I gained weight. So what? Who hasn't? The only thing I care about is what's on the menu. As far as I'm concerned, good food means good reunion. That's the whole point, isn't it?

—Sonny Walker

Chapter 4

As I dressed for bed, it struck me that Kayla was probably right. I wouldn't be doing myself any favors by calling Marsha while I was still packing on the pounds. After
being called out by that no-good waiter and his brother at
Leon's, I truly knew *I* was indeed the problem. It was obvious Kayla wasn't going to help. She didn't even seem to care
about being fat. I, on the other hand, had had enough of it. I
figured a good's night sleep would put me in the right frame
of mind.

Sleeping was always an adventure. Besides the fact that I
usually made a minimum of two trips to the fridge each and
every night, I snored so loud that I often woke myself up. Be-

ing awakened by my own snoring was as bad as a bowl of melted Ben & Jerry's Chunky Monkey ice cream. But it also served as a workable excuse to eat. When I woke up, I had to do something. TV was usually the first option. TV without food was as useless as eggs without cheese. I would stuff my face while channel surfing and often fell asleep with my hand jammed in a bowl of overly buttered popcorn or stuck in a box of jumbo powdered jelly doughnuts. As I hit my knees and prayed, I asked God to give me strength.

I didn't just want FutraSystem to work. I *needed* it to work.

Thankfully, I got through the night with just one trip to the refrigerator. Even I was impressed when I reached for nothing more than a bag of unsalted FutraPretzels. The pretzels made a difference. It was the first time I'd had a late-night snack without really wanting seconds. I was usually plotting what I'd get next while I was just halfway through my first snack. This time was different. I didn't want or even think about seconds. I reasoned that the FutraPretzels were so bad, I just didn't want anything else. FutraSnacks would get me to where I needed to be. Back in shape and, of course, back with Marsha.

I knew breakfast would be a challenge. I usually had five eggs (grade A extra large, of course), three pieces of toast, four thick slices of bacon, five or six sausage patties, a mound of corned beef hash, a hunk of cheese, a tomato and at least one pickle. I figured adding a vegetable made the meal a little less fattening. Having a good first meal was important to me. If I could start my day off right, I knew good things were to follow. FutraSystem offered me some pretty interesting choices: French toast with some sort of low-fat spread, an English muffin with a meat substitute and microwave pancakes with a *gel* that faintly resembled syrup. I didn't know what to eat.

Everything was packaged in bright-yellow boxes bearing bold-red FutraSystem logos. The usual nutrition nonsense was scribbled on the sides in black ink: 90 calories this, 10 grams of protein that, fat, polyunsaturated fat. I didn't get it and I didn't care. I was hungry and I had to get to work. I finally decided to go with a box of powdered egg substitute. The serving suggestion picture on the box made the eggs look delicious. Almost delightful. Full and fluffy, just like I liked them.

I should have known that eggs, particularly substitute eggs in a stupid yellow box, would never stand up to the misleading serving suggestion featured on the box. You don't get a serving suggestion with real eggs. Have you ever noticed that a *real* egg carton doesn't have fancy pictures that titillate you and make you salivate? It doesn't bore you with stupid nutritional junk (that you don't care about anyway). Real eggs would never string you out like that. Real eggs, real, oval eggs, the kind that are objects of desire on Easter, don't need a fancy container. Especially a stupid yellow FutraSystem box.

But what choice did I have? I had to eat.

I ate the entire box. Powdered egg substitute in a stupid yellow box. The idea alone made me sick.

The sausage substitute that also came in a yellow box was just as bad. Eating is supposed to be a joy. It was always that way when I was with Marsha. But this FutraSystem food was about as joyful as electroshock therapy. I knew if I didn't get enough to eat, I wouldn't make it through the day. So even though I hated the way this food tasted, I kept eating. Before

I knew it, I'd downed three boxes of those dumb eggs, two boxes of substitute meat product (which had to have been produced by a Goodyear rubber plant) and four tall glasses of orange juice. The orange juice was the only thing that reminded me I was still alive. At least it was *real*.

I had a big day ahead of me. The bigwigs were scheduled to be in the store today and when they showed, promotions weren't far behind. I liked working at Sports Authority, but the loose balls section had worn me down. It felt like I walked five miles a day just so I could find some stupid ball that's been hidden, misplaced or partially destroyed. It was virtually impossible to keep up with all the balls, and when the regional managers came through they didn't miss anything. If a baseball was out of place, they knew it. If a Spaulding basketball had somehow found its way to the Wilson rack, they'd tell me about it. If a tiny blue racquetball was mixed in with a tiny black handball, I was done. But if my area was in top shape and I could impress the regional managers, I knew my boss would give me a shot in my dream department, the tents and outdoors section.

Getting dressed for Sports Authority was probably one of the pluses of the job (it's not like I had to get a wardrobe together or anything). Every day I put on the Sports Authority uniform—khaki pants and a bright-yellow knit collar shirt. Today would be no different. My trip to work was as uneventful as ever.

I didn't lose any weight on the way.

Couldn't stop thinking about Marsha.

And wondered what it would be like to land a spot in tents and outdoors.

After parking and checking my hair, I made my way toward the front door. Sports Authority was, in a word, huge. The store was divided into several large sections and each had a certain amount of rank and prestige for its team leaders and staff. Loose balls provided a reasonable amount of clout because it was such a difficult section to manage. But the big-ticket departments like exercise and tents and outdoors had major clout.

I walked into the store and made my way down one aisle and up another. I'd been in loose balls way too long. I was in loose balls when I met Marsha. Was in it when I fell in love with her. Was *still* in it when she left. And here I was a year later. Still in f-ing, stupid-behind loose balls. I had thought about it while I ate my FutraPretzels the night before and I made a decision: If I didn't get out of loose balls this year, I was through. They wouldn't have to worry about me. I'd go work at Foot Locker, Foot Joy, Foot Action or Foot something. I knew they'd appreciate me at any one of those spots.

"Mr. Walker, are you quite ready?" said a voice I wasn't interested in hearing. It was my boss's.

"Mr. Matthews," I answered, reaching for a rubber basketball that had been tossed in with the synthetic leather balls. "I'm getting it together."

"You should have done like Andrew over there," he said, pointing toward the row of perfectly centered, freshly polished exercise equipment. "He was here last night. He's already ready. His people are really hard workers."

I didn't need to hear anything about my least favorite coworker, the brown-nosing, poot-butt Andy and his hardworking people. He was everything I hated. Popular. Confident. And hard-bodied. The type of guy I *used* to be. Andy Martinez would do anything, kiss anybody's behind, wash anybody's car and mow anybody's grass if he thought it would give him a leg up on the competition. As far as I knew all he did was work out, eat Goya beans and figure out whose ego needed stroking or whose behind needed an imprint of his lips. He always called me "my man" because he thought I liked hearing that nonsense. I didn't like it and I definitely didn't need it. The only thing I *needed* was to get out of loose balls. And it was beginning to look like Andy could get in the way of that. He truly made me sick.

"This is a big visit we're having today, Sonny," Mr. Matthews said, reaching toward a price-tag faceplate. "There is plenty of room for opportunity here."

"I sure hope there is," I said, neatly arranging a row of Wilson peewee footballs. "I'd like to make a switch. Three years of loose balls is three years too many."

"It's been a good three years, Sonny," he told me. "We may have the best loose balls section in the region. You should be proud of that."

"I take what I do seriously, Mr. Matthews, but I can't say that I'm proud to have run the loose balls section for three years. I'd like to do something else. I'm really interested in tents and outdoors," I said, while ensuring that an Adidas six-panel soccer ball was not mixed in with a Nike six-panel ball.

"You want to move, I want to move, Andy over there wants to move; I understand how you feel," Mr. Matthews said.

"I don't have anything to do with Andy wanting to move," I said, dusting a row of brightly colored oversized kickballs. "Andy's only been here a year, and you gave him the exercise department as soon as he came in the door."

"Well, look at him, Sonny," he said, waving toward Andy.

"Andrew *is* the exercise section. People see him and they become inspired. They want to exercise, they want to *buy* equipment. It's that simple. He excites customers. They want to be like him. I don't mean any harm, Sonny, and I don't want you to take this the wrong way, but what do you suppose people think when they see you? Do you think they want to buy workout equipment? Do you think they run to buy spandex? Do you believe, perhaps, that you inspire them to hike, jog or even walk? These are the things that make Sports Authority, Sports Authority. This is why people like Andrew make the exercise section the profit center that it is. He inspires regular people to become faithful customers," he added, before walking away.

Matthews had struck a nerve. What *do* people think when they see me? I wondered. Food. Eating. Gorging out. Dessert trays. The same stuff *I* think about when I see myself. Why did he have to be so right and why did he need to do it today?

I quickly got ahold of myself and realized I couldn't think about that now.

Why didn't really matter; opportunity was knocking and I had to answer the door. The regional managers had arrived and my section was as ready as it was going to get. The drill never changed. Our region had four very picky managers who wielded a great deal of power. Once a year, this hapless quartet of tight-suit-clad, eye-glass-wearing, notepad scribbling busybodies would visit your section, quiz you about your inventory and tell you how great a job you were doing, even if they spent the entire time inspecting your section without cracking a smile. If they asked you to walk with them to the next section, that meant they were impressed. The very moment when a regional manager would say,

"Why don't you join us?" was exactly the moment each and every Sports Authority sales rep and section leader longed for. The next morning, there'd be a meeting, and you'd be introduced as the new manager or supervisor of something. You'd get a new shirt, a new name badge and a personalized clipboard. After that you were on your own. Maybe you'd become a store manager or even a regional buyer, but you'd be something better than a loose balls section leader like I was.

The regional managers hit the shoe section first. Team leaders of the shoe department usually quit from boredom before our annual inspection because there was so little involved in maintaining the area. Everything was in clearly marked boxes. People usually knew what they wanted and they could get it themselves, so in terms of actual work, it was a piece of cake. The tennis and bowling sections were next. Though I felt a little guilty, I was happy when they shook Helen's hand. She carried a 175 bowling average and could serve and volley on the hard courts with every guy in the store. But that handshake meant Helen wouldn't be taking a walk to my section. And with three departments left, exercise, tents and outdoors and, of course, my loose balls section, I knew my odds at a nice walk had jumped.

As they approached me, I tried to suck in my gut.

Moby Dick would have fared better.

They greeted me and went about my section like they never had before. I took this as a good sign. They inspected each row and smiled as they scribbled on their notepads. I even heard one of them whisper, "Impressive." Mr. Matthews looked toward me, nodded and hit me with a thumbs-up sign. This was exactly how I wanted it. The smiles. The nods. The whispers. These were all good signs. I'd made a good impression. I could feel it. I was about to be asked to join them on a stroll to Andy's department, where I would give new meaning to the word *gloat.*

"Well, Mr. Walker," said one of the managers. "You have outdone yourself. Your section looks fabulous."

"Really sharp," said another, wiping his glasses.

"Quite a job."

"Excellent."

I got their point. I was glad I'd thrown a little polish on my black Nikes because I knew I was about to walk.

"Gentlemen," said Mr. Matthews, standing beside me. "Mr. Walker here has indeed done a fine job and he's expressed an interest in upward mobility. I recommend him highly."

"Is that right?" said one of the men, peering over his glasses. "Well, we'll certainly consider that."

"We'll look into it."

"We most certainly will."

"That's always a possibility."

I couldn't believe what I was hearing. It *had* to be a mistake.

I'd been through this two years in a row. The first year I expected it. The second, I *accepted* it. But this time I was stunned. They shook my hand, told me to keep up the good work and reminded me I had one of the best loose balls sections in the region. Didn't they know I already knew I had the *best* loose balls section? I couldn't believe I'd let them get away without even muttering a word. I never backed down from anybody, but they caught me so off guard I just figured they'd made a mistake or something. As they walked away in what seemed like super-dooper slow-motion, I felt as if I were stuck in a bad dream. Only it wasn't a dream. It was a nightmare.

I was still in the stupid loose balls section.

The exercise section was next and I didn't even need to look. They greeted Andy like he was one of them. They stood around a weight bench and didn't even pretend to scrutinize Andy's section the way they'd scrutinized mine. It took all of three minutes. Although I had a feeling it was going to happen, I didn't want to accept it. Butt-kissing Andy was likely to be my next supervisor.

Andy Martinez was about to take a walk.

With Andy in tow, they headed toward tents and outdoors. I felt as bad as a Chia Pet looks. I couldn't believe it. Three years. Three screwed-up years in the loose balls section. I was lost in a daze.

I turned in slow circles and started to daydream. I stared at the huge rows of balls that were situated on the top racks some twenty-five feet over my head. One row of balls had big white letters that spelled out *A-N-D-Y S-U-C-K-S*. Another spelled out *L-O-S-E W-E-I-G-H-T*. Another was inscribed with *W-A-T-C-H O-U-T-!!!*

Watch out!!! I said to myself, concerned.

Before I knew it, every ball on the top and middle racks came thundering down on top of me. I was covered in a hideous assortment of basketballs, footballs, soccer balls and every other kind of ball that I had so neatly arranged for the regional managers. I did everything I could to free myself, but nothing worked. I'd been overcome, overtaken and overwhelmed by the entire loose balls section. What made it worse was knowing that that no-good Andy was probably going to pull me out and *then* make me clean it up because he was my new boss.

"Sonny. Sonny. What are you doing? Didn't you hear them?"

"Hear who?" I said, snapping my head back.

"They paged you to tents and outdoors twice."

"Who paged me?"

"Mr. Matthews and the regional managers."

"They paged me?"

"Yeah, I came to get you, and you were in a daze."

"I can't believe it, Helen," I said, shaking my head.

"Really, Sonny, they paged you."

"I believe that. I just can't believe they picked Andy."

"Are you kidding?" she said, laughing. "It was in the bag. Andy is Mr. Cooper's wife's personal trainer."

"Do you mean Mr. Cooper as in district manager Cooper?"

"You got it," she said, crossing her arms.

"Incredible," I said, while making a ridiculous attempt to tuck in my shirt.

"Sonny Walker, Mr. Sonny Walker, please report to tents and outdoors right away."

"That's your call," said Helen, smiling. "Knock 'em dead!"

"Helen," I said before leaving. "I'm sorry."

"Sorry?" she said, surprised. "Sorry about what?"

"When you didn't walk with them, I was actually happy."

"Don't feel so bad," she said, smiling. "I was pretty happy when you didn't walk either."

"Oh, really?" I said, nodding my head.

"You best believe it. But now you'll be my supervisor and I know you'll make me pay."

"Andy would make you pay. I'll just make you work over-time," I said, laughing.

"You'd better go," she said, smiling.

Helen was right. I couldn't wait to get there. Tents and outdoors. In that section nothing moved. Tents were station-ary and nearly every item in the department was in some kind of box or bag. Mr. Matthews spent a year in tents and outdoors before he moved up, and every manager in the re-gion had done a stint in this section. Being selected for tents and outdoors meant almost as much to me as getting Marsha back. It would be a sign that my luck had changed. My mo-ment had arrived. The daydream I'd just had seemed worlds away. I was no longer stuck in loose balls. I was out and I was up. My hard work had paid off. All I needed was my new shirt, name badge and clipboard to seal the deal.

I arrived at tents and outdoors, and Mr. Matthews said they were considering rearranging the section. Great! They actually wanted my opinion before they retooled *my* new de-partment.

"The regional managers think we should put our new jumbo, family-size-tent line right over here," he said, point-ing beside me.

"Okay," I said, nodding my head in approval.

"But Mr. Martinez feels they should be over here," he said, pointing behind me.

"Excuse me, sir," I said, concerned. "Mr. Martinez?"

"Of course," he said, walking toward me. "Mr. Martinez. Andrew."

"Oh, yeah," I said, shaking my head. "Andy."

"We need your assistance," said Mr. Matthews.

"Well, I agree with the regional managers," I said, hoping to solidify my new position.

"That's very good," said one of the managers.

"Intelligent young man."

"He's quite a guy."

"Good management material."

That's how they talked. If one of them said something, the others had to respond.

"Okay, Sonny," said Mr. Matthews. "We do appreciate your opinion, but this *is* Mr. Martinez's new department. And since he'll have to live with it, it's his call."

"I don't get this," I said, startled. "What do you mean this is Andy's new department?"

"Mr. Martinez is the new manager of tents and outdoors," he said, smiling.

"He's the one," said one of the managers.

"Mr. Martinez himself."

"He's Mrs. Cooper's personal trainer, you know."

"The boss will be very happy."

I couldn't believe it. Andy. No-good, rotten Andy. No good, rotten, behind-kissing, personal-training Andy actually took my department.

"I'm sorry, sir," I said, trying to maintain my composure. "I told you earlier I was interested in this department. I thought that was why you had me paged here."

"Please do accept my apologies," he said, looking at me. "But since you're already here we could use your assistance."

"And what might that be?" I asked.

"If you could just stand right there for just a second," he said, rubbing his chin. "That's perfect."

"Perfect, sir?" I asked, confused.

"Perfect," he answered.

"Now, as you can see," he said as Andy walked toward us, "the area now occupied by Mr. Walker would be perfect for our new jumbo, family-size tent. Given the proper spacing, I think we could erect an authentic campground-style display."

I couldn't believe what was happening.

"Sonny, *mi amigo,* would you mind spreading your arms so we can get a more accurate feel for the space, my man?" asked Andy.

I shook my head no, but my arms apparently weren't paying attention. Slowly, they went up.

"Outstanding!" said Mr. Matthews.

"Great!" said one of the managers.

"Fantastic!"

"Wonderful!"

"He makes a great tent!"

That did it. My arms plopped to my sides and I stormed away. I didn't even bother to punch out. It usually took me twenty minutes to get home. Today it took just seven. I didn't know what to do. There was no way I was going back to that store. I'd be without a job first. Andy Martinez as the manager of *my* department. *Me* as a tent. And a *jumbo, family-size* one at that. I'd had it. In the past, this was all I needed to go on a wild binge. One wrong move and bam, I'm pigging out. And though times have changed, I hadn't. It's ten-thirty, I'm hungry, and I've got a house full of food.

I walked right past one of my neighbors who was outside enjoying the summer sun and stormed into the house. I couldn't believe what had happened. They actually wanted me to be a tent. A f-ing jumbo, family-size tent. How could they think that was fair? What the heck was on their minds? Then as I walked through the hall on the way to the living room, I caught a reflection of myself in the mirror, and what happened earlier suddenly and painfully seemed to make sense. I saw what they saw and sadly, I thought it too. I looked terrible. I really hated the way I looked. But it didn't much matter. As I parked myself on the sofa, my mind begged for answers to questions I'd asked a million times.

How did this happen? I wondered. How did I get like this?

I don't think I was feeling sorry for myself; that wasn't the problem. But everything had gotten totally out of control. My life had no balance. My weight had gotten the best of me. It had probably screwed up my health and most likely taken years off my life. And the terrible irony is that the more weight I gained, the more I lost in other areas of my life.

The pictures Marsha and I had taken together haunted me from the top of my television. When we were together we were the king and queen of Kodak moments. In the first picture our smiles said it all. In each other, we felt we had found the right person. In later photos, the smiles seemed strained, almost forced. I usually had some kind of food in one hand and a dessert in the other. As I looked around the room at all of the pictures, I noticed that eventually there was more of me in each shot than her, if only because as I grew out she seemingly grew in.

There were shots of us at picnics and cookouts. Photographs of us at dinner parties and at brunch. There was even a picture of us at Chet's place during a Halloween party.

We were standing in front of the buffet table. Marsha was decked out in a sexy white nurse's outfit with a huge plastic thermometer and I was Bullwinkle the cartoon moose from Frostbite Falls, South Dakota. But no matter what, Marsha and I always managed to end up exactly where I didn't need to be. Around food. Our entire relationship could have been told through those stupid pictures. We started out right, but somewhere, things went terribly wrong.

I don't even know why I still had those pictures. Marsha had been out of my life for so long, they should have been gone. It just didn't make any sense. I never felt more alone in my life. It hit me. It really hit me that Marsha was gone.

What made matters worse was despite everything I wanted and worked so hard for, the job I really wanted had gone to someone else. It would have been easier to accept had I lost it because I hadn't earned it, but to miss out because they wanted me to be a jumbo, family-size tent? How did they expect me to handle that?

Sometimes one of those stupid sitcoms where nothing seems even slightly real works when you're down in the dumps, so I decided to turn on the TV. I grabbed the remote and hit the power button. My timing couldn't have been worse. A guy about my size was in a dressing room trying (unsuccessfully) to button a pair of pants. The audience was cracking up and while they laughed, I clicked off the TV.

And then I proceeded to do something that's *definitely* not my style.

I got choked up; the tears started rolling and I cried.

I knew the sight had to be awful. A guy as big as me with tears running down my face like a little baby—this couldn't be happening. Me crying? I don't cry. Especially about something that doesn't involve food.

The tears were coming as fast as the pain. And the pain was as fast and as hard as a six-car pileup on the back turn at the Charlotte Motor Speedway. I never really stopped to think about how I felt about a lot of stuff. I don't know if that's a big-guy thing or if it's just a guy thing.

When you feel like everything's all your fault it's easy to sidestep the pain. It almost seems natural to take all the blame and never deal with anything that's affected you. It was easy for me because most of the time I refused to accept that the problems were really mine. I was obsessed with being happy-go-lucky Sonny. I couldn't admit I *had* any problems. When crap went wrong my solution was simple: I hid inside the food. But one good look at me made it painfully clear—the food had all but hidden inside of *me*. And because of that, I'd heard it all.

Fat boy.

Fat wheels.

Fatso.

Heavyset. Big-boned. Chubby.

My nickname was even Chubbs.

Why did anybody think I wanted to hear that nonsense? People I didn't even know would say totally insensitive stuff to me like "Were you big when you were a baby too or are you just lazy?" . . . "Do you have a thyroid problem or do you just like being big?" . . . "Hey, you've put on some weight, haven't you?" . . . "Have you ever tried stapling your stomach?" . . . "What about the grapefruit diet . . . the rice diet . . . the Beverly Hills diet . . . the Scarsdale Plan . . . Fen Phen . . .

Redux ... Weight Watchers ... Slim Fast ... Herbalife ... Jenny Craig ... Nutri/System ... Richard Simmons ... Susan Powter?" ... "How about wiring your mouth shut?"

Most of the time I would just smile and pretend it didn't bother me, even though it almost always did. There were times I didn't care because in the back of my mind, I knew one day I'd lose the weight and show everybody I wasn't the lazy, fat, ignorant, underachieving slob they'd made me out to be.

Despite everything my common sense told me, I had convinced myself things would work out. Marsha would come back. The weight would go away. And I would know what it felt like to be happy again. More than anything else, that's what I missed. Just being happy. Being truly happy with who I am and where I am in the world. I hadn't been happy since the day Marsha dropped me. I wanted food to make me happy and I thought it had.

But it hadn't.

I wanted my life back and had no plan and no clue as to how to make it happen. I truly, truly wanted things to be like they once were. I hoped, wished and even dreamed things would return to normal, but the steady stream of tears said something I'd ducked and dodged for far too long.

Maybe things would never be right.

Maybe things would never be the same.

Maybe they never would.

Soup and Salad

Chapter 5

When I woke up from my long nap, I was starving. I had all I needed to binge, but this time I couldn't do it. I just couldn't do it. As much as I hated what had happened at work, I couldn't fall off the wagon again. Food had always been the answer and that's exactly why I was in the position I was in. I needed willpower much more than I needed food. I'd cheated at Leon's last night and felt so guilty I was able to force myself through those terrible FutraPretzels.

Excuses? I didn't need any.

It was time for me to face facts: I was fat. And I was finally fed up with everything that went with it, so I *refused* to binge.

This was a crisis point. If I were in one of those anonymous groups (AA, NA, or even GA), I'd have a buddy. They'd assign me someone who could get me past painful times like this. In a strange sort of way, I knew Kayla could very well be that person for me. But it was hard to figure out who failed whom last night. She called me and said she was struggling, but I'd been the one who jetted over to her place and drove us to Leon's.

I screwed up. It was late in the afternoon, so I decided to call.

"Hello."

"Hello."

"Kayla."

"This is she."

"Hey, Kayla, it's Sonny, from FutraSystem."

"Oh, you, the big guy," she said, laughing.

"Funny, Kayla."

"Well, this is a pleasant surprise," she said.

"Really?" I asked. "What's so pleasant about it?"

"It's nice to hear from a decent man who's not after me for my body," she said slyly.

We both laughed.

"So what's up?" she asked. "To what do I owe this pleasure?"

"Well," I hesitated. "I've had a totally screwed-up day. I got passed over for a promotion at work. I wanted to work in the tent department, but instead they told me that I'm as big as a tent."

"*O-k-a-a-a-y?*" she said. "So, they think you're as big as a tent."

"Okay?" I repeated.

"Okay."

"Okay what?" I asked.

"So you got passed over for a promotion at work and they think you're as big as a tent. Do you still have a job?"

"Yeah."

"Do you still have your place?"

"Yeah."

"Have you lost any weight?"

"No."

"Well, two out of three ain't bad," she said, laughing.

"You're a real riot," I said flatly.

"I'm sorry, Sonny," she said, still laughing. "But it can't be that bad."

"It *is* that bad," I told her. "I haven't felt this bad since Marsha left me."

"Not her again," she said with an edge.

"What's that supposed to mean?"

"Sonny, you seem like such a nice guy," she said. "I could see myself really getting into a man like you, but you really need to let that Marsha thing go," she added. "How do you expect to get anywhere with another woman if you're always whining about Marsha?"

What did she mean, "whining about Marsha"? And what made her think that I was even slightly interested in her "getting into me"?

"First of all, I don't whine about Marsha," I insisted. "And secondly, I don't even know what makes you think that I'm interested in you getting into me."

"I never said I could get into *you*. I said I could get into a man *like* you," she shot back. "Believe this, sweetie," she added, "I couldn't get into you because you're stuck on Marsha like burned eggs on a hot pan."

"Burned eggs on a hot pan?" I said, dismayed.

"You're so stuck that if she did come back you'd never be able to reach her because you wouldn't be able to move."

"Burned eggs on a hot pan?" I repeated. "You couldn't come stronger than that?"

"You got my point," she said. "You know if she said she'd take you back, you'd starve yourself just so you'd be acceptable to her. You're pressed."

"Oh, I'm pressed," I said.

"You are most definitely pressed."

"Well, you're jealous," I told her.

"Please," she said, laughing.

"You're trippin'," I said.

"I'm not 'trippin',' whatever that means."

"You're jealous," I said again, trying to stay cool.

"Look, Sonny," she answered. "You really do seem like a nice guy, but don't flatter yourself. The next time you get such a ridiculous notion, just remember this."

"Remember what?"

"I don't *even* need to be jealous because you called *me*, not Marsha."

"I called you because you're as fat as I am."

"I don't know if it matters why you called me," she said sharply, "but you did. So believe me, I'm not jealous."

It didn't matter that she wasn't jealous. I could have cared less. But for the second time in as many days, she was right. I *was* pressed and I would absolutely starve myself to get Marsha back. I got Kayla's point. If Marsha wouldn't accept me for who I am, if she saw me only for *what* I am, then she was the one who had a problem.

Yeah, right.

But if Marsha had the problem, why was *I* so miserable?

"Look, Sonny," Kayla said softly. "I don't know you well enough to argue with you. I just hate to see you down on yourself because of her."

"You're right, Kayla," I confessed. "I just need to let it go."

"You sure do," she told me.

"Look, Kayla, what are you up to?" I asked.

"I'm taking care of some business. Why do you ask?"

"I was thinking that maybe we could hook up."

"What do you mean when you say 'hook up'?"

"You know, like get together, watch some TV, pop some popcorn."

"FutraSystem popcorn?" she asked, joking.

"Yeah," I said, sighing and shaking my head, "FutraPopcorn."

"I'm game," she said. "When are you talking about getting together?"

"In about an hour if that works for you."

"An hour works for me," she said.

"Good. I'll pick you up at five-thirty."

"If we're going to watch movies and pop popcorn, we can do that here," she told me.

"Actually I figured we would hang at my place."

"You figured wrong," she said, laughing. "You can come here."

"What's wrong with my place?" I asked, concerned.

"I didn't say anything's wrong with your place," she said. "But if we're at my place, I'll feel more comfortable."

"You can get comfortable at my place."

"Maybe I could. But if *you* try to get too comfortable, I can't do anything about it."

"Anything like what?" I asked.

"Like put you out."

"Put me out?"

"Yeah," she said, laughing. "I can't put you out of your place, but I can sure enough run you out of mine."

"It's not like that, Kayla," I said.

"You don't know what it's like because you haven't had the *real* pleasure of my company yet," she told me. "So I think it's best that we hang out here."

"Okay," I said, reaching for a bright-yellow bag of Futra-Chips. "I'll blow through in about an hour."

If we were going to eat popcorn later, I at least needed a snack to hold me until I got to Kayla's house.

"Excuse me, you'll blow through?" she said.

"You know. Like I'll get by there."

"You'll blow *through*, you'll get *by*," she said, sighing. "I imagine you're telling me you'll be here in an hour."

"Exactly," I said, tearing open the bag of chips.

What the heck was I doing? What was I thinking? Why in the world did *I* suggest that we hook up? Was I *that* pressed?

Thankfully, my ringing phone didn't give me time to worry about it.

"Yeah, what's up?" I said, swallowing a handful of chips.

"Sonny, what's up with you, buddy? Why are you home? I thought I'd get your machine."

"What's up with you, E? I'm off today," I lied.

"What's going on, Sonny?"

"I'm chillin', dawg."

"As usual," he said. "Look, Sonny, what you doing later on?"

"I ain't got no plans," I told him.

"That's a bet," he said.

"What's a bet?" I asked.

"We're gonna meet up over your place."

"We?" I said, downing another handful of chips.

"Yeah," he told me. "Me, you and your boy Chet."

"*You* want to meet with Chet?" I asked, surprised.

"I'm not really trying to meet with Chet," E said deliberately. "But he's your partner and all, so I figure he needs to get with this."

"Get with what?"

"Later, buddy," he said. "If you're not there, I'll let myself in. I'll blow through there 'bout eight-thirty."

"It's on, playa," I said, tossing the empty FutraChips bag in the trash.

Though I truly, and I do mean *truly* had no clue as to why I was going over to Kayla's, I *was* going. I hadn't actually blown through a woman's place since the day Marsha put me out of hers. I'd been with Marsha for such a long time that I'd stopped worrying about how I looked and what I wore. My Sports Authority wardrobe, or lack thereof, didn't help me with my plight. I was one sweatsuit-wearin', blue-jean sportin', slip-on sneaker havin' brother. When I met Kayla, if you can call it "meeting," I was wearing my favorite black-and-white Nike sweatsuit. Chet once saw me in it and laughed out loud; he told me I looked like a police SWAT van. Kayla had seen me twice, and both times I had on the same thing. It's not like I was trying to impress her, but I might very well run into another honey while I was riding over there, so I had to be prepared.

I didn't understand why I was making this such a big deal anyway. I knew there was nothing and could never be anything between me and Kayla.

She was fat.

I opened my closet and found a black blended-knit T-shirt and my favorite pair of black pleated slacks. The shirt was a triple X, so it hung, instead of clung, off my flabby chest and arms. The pants were just plain big. They were my favorite pair because I didn't have to squeeze into them.

As I dressed, I thought about what cologne I'd wear and what shoes I would sport. There was little doubt that this was a Tommy Hilfiger day. Clean and crisp. Light and refreshing. Just as I liked it. Heck, I liked anything that made me feel light. I hadn't splashed on cologne in over a year and since it didn't come with a "born-on" date like a bottle of Budweiser, I hoped it still would do its job.

I looked in the mirror, took care of the essentials (the whole brush the mustache, eyebrows and hair routine) and wondered why I hadn't bothered to even attempt to look so decent for such a long time. It hadn't taken me too much time to get myself together. But I knew why. Like Kayla said, I had to put things behind me.

Maybe she was right. I never wasted time looking into the floor-length mirror that hung behind my bedroom door because I stopped fitting in it some time ago, and as far as I could tell my shoes were in passable condition (but I wasn't *about* to bend over to find out) and my clothes flowed. As I walked by my kitchen I reached for a yellow bag of Fu-traCurls and headed out the door.

On the way over to Kayla's I thought about that no-good Andy and then wondered what excuse I'd use to get out of

Kayla's place in time to hook up with E and Chet. I chuckled as I thought I'd tell her I had to break out because I had a date. That way, she would *know* I wasn't interested and that I was off limits.

Even if she could get into a man like me, I thought while parking, I couldn't get into her. There ain't that much gettin' into in the world.

Kayla lived in a comfortable single-family-home development with tidy lawns and well-manicured trees and bushes. She had a brick-covered A-frame with a cleanly swept walkway and a tiny porch that had two shiny green ceramic flower pots. A smoked-glass storm door swung open to an impressive oak-paneled front door that had a shiny brass knocker. I knocked and waited just a few seconds.

"Yes," said a voice, which came from a tiny speaker.

"Yo, Kayla, what's up? It's Sonny."

"Yo?" she asked, obviously annoyed.

"Yeah," I said, inching my head back. "Yo, what's wrong with that?"

"It's as bad as 'blow through,' " she said, laughing.

"Well, I'm here," I said, sighing.

"Be right down," she answered.

She's a trip, I thought. I can't stand no woman who thinks she has to correct me. Like I ain't got good English or something.

"Hi, Sonny," she said, opening the door. "Glad you could blow through."

I was glad I blew through too. What a big-time surprise. Kayla's spot was laid.

Chapter 6

"Wow," I said, stepping inside.

What a place! I'd been in some pretty impressive homes before, but nothing like this. Kayla's spread was awesome. *H-i-g-h* ceilings. Spirited African prints with bright, splashy colors. A real sunken living room. Plush carpet. Hardwood floors. Furniture that looked way too good to sit on. And the smell. When I was at Marsha's, food permeated the air. But Kayla's place was potpourri down. It was as sweet and as fragrant as a hunk of freshly baked carrot cake.

"Your spot is like that," I said, impressed.

"My spot is like what?" she said, shaking her head.

"Like that," I told her, my eyes going all over the place.

"Is it safe to assume that 'like that' is okay?" she asked.

"It's like that," I said, nodding my approval.

I never dreamed Kayla would have a spread. I figured she would have a joint. Clothes all over the place. A color scheme from Wal-Mart. Two-day-old pot of greens on the stove. A dusty cat or ratty dog. And cheap, beat-up furniture straight from The Hub. I didn't know what to make of it. Kayla's spread had the type of flair, style and pizzazz that's usually reserved for drop-dead beauties in the movies. Plus she had an exotic bamboo cage that housed a bird with more colors than the opening ceremony at the Summer Olympics.

"You want to go downstairs?" she said, walking toward a set of fashionable French doors.

"Sure," I said, following her lead.

"Have a good time, fat boy," snapped a voice I didn't recognize.

"Who the heck was that?" I asked, alarmed.

"Have a good time, fat boy," the voice repeated.

"Who *is* that!" I said, looking around.

"KJ, stop that," said Kayla, annoyed.

"KJ," I said, concerned. "Who the heck is KJ?"

"KJ is my cockatoo," she said, smiling.

"Your cockatoo?"

"Yeah," she said, walking toward him. "Sometimes I take him downstairs with me and he watches infomercials or videos while I work out. He picks up lots of 'fat this and fat that' language," she added, stroking his head. "So he doesn't mean any harm. Try not to hold it against him."

"Try not to hold it against him?" I asked. "Your bird called me fat boy."

"He calls everybody fat boy, Sonny, so don't take it personally. Why don't you come meet him."

This was ridiculous. Here I am at a woman's house I barely know—who I'm not even *slightly* interested in—and she wants me to meet her stupid bird.

What the heck was I doing?

I walked toward the cage and didn't know exactly what to do. I've done a lot of crazy stuff in pursuit of a woman (and I was *not* pursuing Kayla), but this took the cake. *I'm meeting a bird. And not just any bird. I'm meeting a bird who seconds ago called me fat boy.*

"Come a little closer, Sonny," she said, reaching for my hand. "He's a nice bird. He won't bite."

If he's so nice, why did he call me fat boy? I wondered.

"KJ, meet Sonny. Sonny, KJ," she said, her head moving back and forth.

I just stood there. What did she expect me to do? I'd never been introduced to a bird in my life. She acted like I was supposed to shake his wing or something.

"Say hello to him, Sonny," she said, poking me in the side.

"Say hello to him?"

"Just say hi."

"Say hi?" I asked.

"Just say hi, fat boy," said KJ.

"Who you calling fat boy, you stupid bird!" I shot back.

"He's a fat boy, he's definitely a fat boy, he's as big as a tent!" the bird quipped.

"KJ!" yelled Kayla.

The bird quickly rotated on his perch and turned his back on us as if *he* was insulted. I couldn't believe it.

"KJ, apologize," Kayla demanded.

He just ruffled his wings and stared out the window.

"*K-k-k-k-J-j-j-j,*" she urged.

"It's all right, Kayla," I said. "You already said he didn't know what he was doing."

"No, Sonny," she said, walking to the other side of the cage. "Turn around and apologize right now, KJ."

"It's cool, Kayla," I said, hoping to avoid another confrontation. "I don't need no apology from no bird."

"KJ, be nice," she said, again stroking his head.

Surprisingly he turned around and Kayla moved beside me.

"KJ, tell Sonny you're sorry," she demanded.

He looked toward her and then looked me up and down as if he was disgusted and then focused back on her.

"KJ," she said, nodding her head.

"KJ is sorry," the bird quickly stated.

I couldn't believe it. She actually got a bird to apologize. I was totally impressed.

"Come on, KJ," she said, nodding her head toward me. "Apologize to Mr. Sonny."

He just looked at me like both of us were crazy.

"KJ!" she ordered, clapping her hands.

"Sorry, fat boy," he blurted out.

I rushed toward the cage but KJ was quicker than I was. He leaned his beak out and bit into my hand. I screamed in pain and Kayla, in an attempt to push my hand away, accidentally opened the cage. KJ jetted out and flew around the room, yelping, "He's a fat boy . . . He's as big as a tent . . . He's a fat boy . . . He's as big as a tent." I held my hand in anguish, but I wasn't about to let that crazy bird get away with biting me *and* calling me a fat boy. It made no sense, but I ran in circles trying to catch him, while at the same time ducking when he actually got close enough for me to get my one good hand around his scrawny neck.

"He's a fat boy . . . Y'all sure can eat," he said, reminding me of that no-good waiter and his brother at Leon's.

"I'll kill you!" I told him, still running and ducking. "I bet you taste just like chicken!"

"White men can't jump, fat boys can't run," he said, swooping about like an F-14 fighter pilot.

"This fat boy can run!" I yelled.

"Sonny!" yelled Kayla, pointing toward me. "Look out," she said, her voice dropping.

Look out? I wondered.

I shouldn't have wondered. Before I knew it, I slammed into a white leather ottoman, slid face first on a soft white border rug, and ended up knocking over a bowl of fluffy white popcorn, which of course found its way onto my unsuspecting head.

"Sonny, are you okay?" Kayla asked, running toward me.

Jeez, I thought, chomping down on the popcorn, some of which had landed into my mouth and stuck to my lips. This is f-ing FutraPopcorn.

"Are you okay?" she said again, laughing and wiping popcorn from my shirt.

"This is whack, Kayla," I said, shaking my head. "What's up with you and your maniac bird?"

"What do you mean, Sonny?"

"Yeah, whatta you mean, fat boy?" KJ said, returning to his cage.

"Where does he get this stuff from?"

"What stuff?" she said, picking up more popcorn.

" 'He's as big as a tent' . . . 'Y'all sure can eat'?" I said, rising to my feet. "Where did that come from?"

"Oh," she said, turning toward the cage. "He probably overheard me talking on the phone."

"Oh," I said, sighing.

"Anyway," she said, locking the cage. "I apologize and I'm certain KJ is sorry as well," she stated, turning toward me. "Why don't we go downstairs and catch a movie?"

"The bird stays up here?" I said, wiping the front of my shirt.

"The bird stays here, fat boy," said KJ.

I pretended to lunge toward him and couldn't help but grin as he ruffled his feathers and backed away in his cage. Kayla just shook her head, reached for my hand and then led me down the stairwell.

Her basement was as tight as her living room. An inviting red leather sectional couch rested on the super-plush, bright-white shag carpet in the center of the room. In front of it was what looked to be a fifty-inch Mitsubishi big-screen TV, encased in a customized white lacquer multimedia unit with Yamaha stereo components. There were four Bose speakers situated on the side walls, which I imagined produced an incredible surround-sound effect. On the other end of the room was a mirrored wall and a neatly arranged row of high-tech exercise equipment. As I looked at Kayla, I wondered how she evolved into such an abundant woman while she had a Nordic track treadmill, a Bally's stair climber and a Solo Flex weight bench *with* the butterfly attachment sitting in her basement.

She probably doesn't use them, doesn't know how to use them or doesn't even know they're there.

"Have a seat," she said, directing me toward the sofa.

I plopped down and nearly sunk into the couch.

"Anything in particular you want to see?" she asked, reaching for a remote.

"It doesn't really matter," I said, hoping she would turn to some type of sports event.

"Why don't we watch *Sounder*," she said, pointing the remote toward the entertainment center.

"*Sounder?*" I asked, surprised.

"Of course," she said, smiling, "I think it's about to come on BET's new movie channel. It's a classic."

"*Sounder?*" I whispered to myself.

She flipped a switch and her entertainment center took over. Lights were lit, gears went into motion and the screen glowed. The sound was as awesome as I thought it would be. A gun shot flew from one wall right into another. I thought I could feel Sounder's fleas buzzing around *my* head. Kayla was slouching and munching on a snack (that she didn't need), which I guessed was FutraPopcorn.

After just a few minutes, I realized I needed to hit her with a reason for breaking out.

"Yo, Kayla," I said.

"Yo?" she repeated, sitting up.

"Yeah, yo," I answered. "I can't hang out too long."

"That's good."

"That's good?" I asked, concerned.

"That's good," she said, smiling. "Because I'm actually expecting company."

"Okay," I said, looking toward her.

It didn't make sense, but I wondered what she meant when she said "company." I knew it couldn't have been a guy. But when a woman says "company" you can bet she's referring to a man. Otherwise, she'd just come out and say, "One of my girlfriends is dropping by." I couldn't figure why it mattered or why I was thinking about it in the first place, but I had to know. What was she doing with a "friend"? I don't even have a "friend." At least, not one who was coming to my place.

"Yo, Kayla," I said.

"Yo?" she again asked.

"Yo, check this out," I said, turning toward her. "Who's coming over?"

"Why do you ask?"

"I was thinking maybe it would be a little honey you could hook me up with," I said.

"That's a joke," she replied, laughing. "I don't think you're quite ready to be hooked up."

"I've *been* ready," I told her.

"The only thing you're ready for is Marsha to run back into your life."

"Yo, Kayla," I said.

"Yo?" she asked, her eyes glaring at me.

"Yo, Kayla," I repeated, smiling. "You need to let that Marsha stuff go."

We both laughed and she passed me some popcorn. That would have been cool if it weren't that god-awful FutraPopcorn.

"You know something, Sonny?" Kayla said, looking toward me. "You're something else."

"What do you mean 'something else'?" I asked.

"You come by to see me and before you even get comfortable, you're working your way out the door," she said, removing her glasses. "I let you drop by because I sensed something was bothering you and because I thought you could stand a little company. I don't want anything from you, I can't think of a thing you could do for me, and though you seem like a really nice guy, quite frankly, Sonny, you're not my type," she said bluntly. "So why don't we both relax?"

"That's cool," I answered.

"I hope it is," she said, slipping her glasses back on.

Though it shouldn't have, it stung when she said I wasn't her type. I wasn't interested in being her type, but *I* wanted to make that decision. *I* wanted to turn *her* down. *I* wanted, needed and deserved to have that say.

I couldn't believe she beat me to the punch.

She was, however, right on target. Because after we "relaxed" we had a wonderful time. We talked about how truly bad FutraSystem food was and why we both desperately needed FutraSystem to work. Kayla put up a pretty brave front about being comfortable with her weight, but she was as concerned about hers as I was about mine. Though her focus was her overall health and the way folks perceived her, and mine was getting slim and trim, we essentially wanted the same thing: to be rid of the fat. We told jokes, played cards, ate that terrible FutraPopcorn and chatted about everything from sports to religion. We even played charades, which is always a little more interesting when people our size play. I don't recall ever feeling so good about being with a woman I'd just met and wasn't interested in. For several hours it seemed as though I were somewhere else. I didn't think about Marsha once and began to see Kayla for who she really was, an attractive, intelligent woman who seemed to really have it going on.

It was perfect. Until the doorbell rang.

She walked to the wall and pushed the intercom button.

"Yes?" she said.

"It's me, sweetie," replied a voice that was definitely male.

"Be right up, honey," she answered.

I stood up. I wasn't about to let her dismiss me. I wanted to leave on my own terms.

"I'm going to break on out," I said, looking at my watch.

"Break on out?" she asked, smiling. "Is that like leaving?"

"Yeah," I told her, "I'm about to break out."

"Okay," she said, walking toward the stairs. "Give me a call later."

"All right," I said, following behind.

As we went up the stairs, I wondered just who "honey" was. I couldn't believe it even crossed my mind, but I was curious. Kayla was big, but she was so nice and seemed to be so complete. She showed me the best time I'd had in over a year and though it shouldn't have, it bothered me that "honey" probably scooped her up while fools like me reasoned she was too big. At the very moment her doorbell rang, for a split second, I was seriously considering what move to make. I thought I would ask her out on a real date. But "honey" showed up and crushed that. I was reduced to pretending like I had to leave. As if I actually had something or someone to go home to. I was supposed to hook up with Chet and Everett, so I guess I had them in a strange sort of way.

But she had "honey" and that was real.

We got to the top of the steps and KJ blurted out, "See ya, fat boy!"

"Later, stupid," I said, walking toward the front door.

Kayla opened the door and a surprisingly fit, bronze-colored man with a beautiful bouquet of mixed flowers and roses walked in.

"Hi, baby," he said, kissing her on the cheek.

"Hi, honey," she answered, smiling.

"You do look good," he said, handing her the flowers.

"Thanks, honey," she replied, reaching for a hug.

They embraced as if I weren't even in the room. He whispered something to her and she giggled. A giggle like that is the most nauseating act a woman can pull off. Especially when she's not giggling at something *you* said. He backed away and looked at me. I hated that look. It was one of those "I am clearly better than you" looks. With his crisp linen slacks, coordinating vest, sharp, gleaming shoes and bulging, sculptured arms, he was probably right.

"Who is this gentleman?" he asked.

"He's the fat boy!" said KJ.

"Stop it, KJ!" demanded Kayla.

"Don't yell at him, he doesn't know any better," said honey. "How are you, sir?" he asked, reaching to shake my hand. "I am Kayla's friend Jonathan James Leslie."

"What's up, playa?" I asked, squeezing his hand as hard as I could. "I'm Sonny."

"That is indeed an interesting name," he said, squeezing my hand so hard that it nearly made my knees buckle. "Sonny. Is it a nickname of some sort?"

"Hardly," I said, tightening my forearm and squeezing even harder. "I'm my old man's oldest son, so they named me Sonny."

"Well, Sonny," he said, tilting his head and squeezing my hand with the tenacity of a power vise, "it is indeed a pleasure to make your acquaintance."

"Dagonit!" I yelled, snatching my hand away and waving it in pain.

He (of course) politely nodded before again kissing Kayla on the cheek. He then said, "I need to change. I'd like to work out before we leave, sweetheart."

"Go on ahead," she said, blushing. "I'll be right there."

"Won't you join me, Sonny?" asked Jonathan, smiling. "A brisk jog on the treadmill wouldn't hurt."

"Fat boys can't run!" quipped the bird.

"That's enough, KJ!" said Kayla, sternly.

She was right. It was enough. I was still waving my hand as if the air would somehow make it feel better. Jonathan made his way upstairs and KJ again turned his back on me. I didn't know what to do. Kayla made it easy for me to decide. She opened the door and I walked out. Before I reached the end of the walkway, she said, "Sonny."

"Yo," I said, turning around.

"Yo?" she again asked, shaking her head.

"Yeah," I said, frustrated. "What's up?"

"I'm sorry about Jonathan and KJ."

"Not as sorry as me," I said, rubbing the hand that had been bitten by that no-good bird *and* squeezed half to death by Jonathan.

"Yo, Sonny," she said, laughing.

"Yo?" I asked, surprised.

"Yo," she said, whispering and looking behind her, "I had a wonderful afternoon."

I had a wonderful afternoon too. But I wasn't about to tell her. She was about to hang out with Mr. Honey himself and I was rushing home to Chet and Everett.

Something was very wrong with this picture.

I rode home in complete silence. No radio. No CD. No tape. No nothing. I thought about Sports Authority and that no-good Andy. I thought about that stupid bird, how he bit me and how I made a complete fool of myself chasing him around and winding up covered in that terrible FutraPop-corn. And to top it off, I couldn't believe I lost the last safe macho battle, the handshake challenge, to her fly-guy honey, Jonathan James Leslie. What a day.

Maybe it wasn't so bad, I told myself as I pulled into my parking space.

I sat and considered it. For one afternoon I felt safe. No fat jokes. No wicked stares. No comments about my weight I wasn't trying to hear. When I was one-on-one with Kayla, everything was great. She was funny, she was smart, and in the midst of it all we connected. I didn't know exactly how it happened and I didn't know what to make of it, but some-thing definitely clicked. Maybe it was her gentle smile or the way she just listened while I rambled on. It was the first time in a long, long time that I felt like a regular person. And not just a regular person with an embarrassing weight problem, but a regular person with plain old regular problems.

Kayla was able to do what no one had done since Marsha. She made me feel like a man.

THE REASONS WE LOSE WEIGHT

Lame Reason

Weddings, Special Events

If I had *to lose weight for a wedding,* I doubt that I'd get married. Don't get me wrong, I truly, truly want to be married, but I'm not about to starve to do it. If I'm a size ten on my wedding day and size twenty a year later, what have I proved? Besides, I sincerely believe that a good marriage beats a good wedding any day of the week.

—Kayla Jennings

Chapter 7

"Sonny—what's up, Sonny!" yelled Chet as I opened my front door.

E sprung from behind the sofa. Around his neck was my Polaroid camera.

"Smile, big fella!" he exclaimed, setting off a bright flash in my face.

Chet ran behind me and grabbed the whistle that was hanging around his neck and blew as loud as he could. "Drop and give me twenty!" he yelled. I instinctively dropped and, just as instinctively, gave him two of the most pathetic push-ups ever before sprawling out on the floor. Chet then rushed toward me, kneeled down and placed his face directly in mine. "What are you doing, big fella?" he yelled. "I said give me twenty!"

I hurried to turn my head.

Unfortunately, E had planted himself on the other side.

"Smile, Sonny!" he said, setting off another flash.

As the tiny motor that kicks out the picture churned, I lay in a complete daze exhausted from those two push-ups. I didn't know where I was, who was there with me, why they were there or even why *I* was there. I don't even think I knew who I was.

"Sonny!" they yelled in unison. "Get up, Sonny."

I shook my head and rose to one knee.

"Yo, big fella," said Chet, standing over me. "You ready to work out or what?"

"What the heck are you talkin' 'bout?" I asked, still hazy.

"He's talking about you losing your weight," E said, snapping another picture.

"What are *y'all* talkin' bout?" I asked, annoyed.

"You called us yesterday," Chet said, chomping on his whistle.

"Yeah," E said, waving a picture around to dry it off. "You said you needed our help, so we're here to help."

"That's why we did all this," Chet said, spreading his arms.

"Did all what?" I asked, finally gathering the strength to rise to my feet.

I couldn't believe what I was seeing.

"What the heck?" I whispered, my eyes racing about the room. "How did y'all manage this?"

"Happy Birthday, Chubbs," Chet answered, smiling. "I

know your birthday ain't for another few months, but the way I see it, you need help now."

It was incredible. E and Chet had pulled off a minor miracle. They had transformed my crowded though completely intimate living room into what appeared to be a high-tech, fully functional fitness center. In one corner was a sleek black Precor treadmill. In another sat a Schwinn bow-flex workout station. A Bally's recumbent Lifecycle rested in another corner and a StairMaster stair climber with a magazine rack *and* a cup holder was situated across from it. My television and VCR had been moved to one wall, and in front of them was a huge blue exercise mat.

"What's all this stuff doin' here?" I asked, turning around.

"We have a plan," Chet said, walking toward me.

"Yeah, Sonny," E said, holding a clipboard.

"Let's move this to the dining room," Chet quickly added.

We walked into the dining room, which had been completely rearranged. Moved against the wall was my maplewood dining table and upholstered chairs. In their place was a white Precor rowing machine.

"Have a seat," Chet said, directing me toward the rower.

I eased my too-large behind down into the tiny plastic seat and huffed when the rest of my body caught up to me.

"You can warm up while we talk," E said, moving the rowing machine pull bar toward my outstretched hands.

"What the heck is goin' on!" I yelled as the bar recoiled and jerked my unsuspecting body forward.

"This is what will get the weight off you," said Chet, pointing toward an easel-bound flip chart.

On it read:

FAT GUYS DON'T HAVE FUN
FAT IS AS FAT DOES
HOW SONNY GOT HIS GROOVE BACK
SONNY'S PLAN TO BE THE MAN

E pushed me in the back and I lurched forward on the rower while Chet turned the page.

"This is your exercise program, Sonny," said Chet, pointing toward a diagram of what was once my living room. "This here is the pit," he said, drawing a circle around the fitness area.

"You'll spend most of your time there," E said, aiming the camera toward me while I continued to row. "Smile, Sonny," he stated. "That's a good shot."

"Before you enter the pit," said Chet, flipping to the next page, "you'll warm up for ten minutes on the rower."

"Ten minutes?" I said, gasping from barely a minute on the rower.

"Ten."

"After you warm up, you'll give me fifteen minutes on the steps."

"Ten minutes?" I repeated, still gasping and just barely rowing.

"Not ten. Fifteen," he corrected me.

"I'm still stuck on the ten from the rower," I said, shaking my head.

"After that, I'll give you a break," he said, turning to a page that pictured the bicycle. "I want fifteen here."

"Fifteen minutes," I said, huffing. "That's a break?"

"You get to sit on the bike," said E.

"After that," chimed in Chet, "you can get a nice pump on the bow-flex."

"Fifteen minutes?" I asked, worried.

"Ten different exercises, eight to ten reps apiece," E said, snapping another picture.

"What happened to fifteen minutes?" I asked, still rowing.

"Fifteen minutes is history at that point," said Chet, turning another page. "You'll do twenty minutes on the treadmill and then you'll wrap it up."

"Wrap it up?" I asked, panting.

"Yeah, Sonny," E said, flipping another page. "You'll do fifty sit-ups, fifty push-ups and then you can cool down."

"It's an ambitious plan, but you can handle it," Chet said, turning back to the front page.

"You have to handle it," said E, walking toward a bright-yellow poster board with BEFORE pasted across the top.

"Can—we—get—back," I asked, desperately gasping, "to—the—cool-down part?"

"Sure we can, big fella," Chet answered, pointing a remote toward the TV.

"As soon as you do your workout," said E, plastering the Polaroids he'd taken of me all over the huge BEFORE poster.

"When does the workout start?" I asked nervously.

"Good question," Chet stated, pulling out a chrome-plated stopwatch. "Your ten minutes on the rower is just about up. You can hit the pit after this and *then* you can work your cooldown."

Before I knew it, Chet blew that nerve-racking whistle and ordered me toward the pit, where I clumsily mounted the step machine.

"Fifteen minutes, Sonny," he reminded me, before starting his stopwatch. "Your routine is on the wall over there."

"We'll be upstairs checking out the game," E said, walking toward the refrigerator. "Watch the tape we put in the VCR while you work out," he continued. "It should help."

I wasn't about to watch anybody's stupid workout tape. That was out of the question. I couldn't believe Chet and E left me down there while they were upstairs watching the game. Didn't they know the ten minutes on the rower were all I'd be able to handle? I was pooped. I took exactly seven steps on the stair climber and then somehow managed to make it to the bike. I plopped down, did about ten revolutions and then dragged myself to the bow-flex machine, where I lay down and "pumped out" two ridiculous bench presses. After that I crawled to the treadmill. I turned it on and listened as the track ran itself for the twenty minutes Chet and E had assigned. I left the treadmill running as I rolled onto my side and then over again to the big blue exercise mat in the middle of the pit. Chet told me I *owed* him fifty push-ups.

Well, I was about to go into major debt.

After the very first push-up, my arms gave way and I became one with the mat. I bonded with the pit like I never imagined I would. I turned over, placed my hands behind my head, lifted my blubbery torso halfway up, exhaled, and ended up flat on my back before I could knock out one complete sit-up.

One thing left, I happily thought. Cool down!

In their haste Chet and E forgot to tell me what the cooldown was. I decided to pop in the video. As I stretched out on my back I stared at the television, which was airing some tape with a group of serious hardbodies flinging weights around like I fling Twinkees into my mouth. It looked so easy. I imagined I was in the video and the women, who looked as strong as I looked fat, surrounded me.

My body was totally cut up, but my head and face were still large. I had on the same tiny red Speedo I imagined I was wearing when I first came home from FutraSystem and a pair of cool Oakley shades covered my eyes. I was curling a seventy-five-pound dumbbell with one arm while balancing on the other a buxom brown-haired beauty clad in a shiny silver metallic string bikini. She was holding a yellow mug of Gatorade in one hand and a cherry pie with Cool Whip topping in the other. Ironically, the Goodyear blimp flew overhead and flashed repeatedly: "Something's Wrong With Your Scale! . . . Something's Wrong With Your Scale! . . . Something's Wrong With Your Scale!"

That's the same thing you said to Marsha the day she dumped you, I recalled.

Strangely, at that moment, Marsha strolled by and gasped when she saw me.

"Hi, there, Mr. Sonny Walker," she said, smiling and extending her hand. "I can't believe how good you look."

She then paused.

"But what happened to your head?" she asked.

"What do you mean?" I asked, still curling the dumbbell.

"It's still big like you used to be," she answered.

"And you're still a jerk like you used to be," said a voice from behind my back.

"You do look great, Sonny, but your head."

"I know, I know," I said, looking toward the ground.

"Who the heck are you!" Marsha yelled, snapping her head back.

"The name is Kayla," said Kayla, walking toward Marsha. "But it's Miss Jennings to you."

"Oh, really," Marsha said, looking toward me, "and who is Miss Jennings, Sonny?" she asked. "Is she your new girlfriend or something?"

"I'm not his girlfriend, we're just friends," Kayla said, reaching toward my arm.

I couldn't believe it. This was the second time she felt a need to point out to someone that we were *just* friends.

Suddenly, Kayla jerked the cherry pie from the metallic string-bikini lady who had been on my arm. She threw it and the pie landed flush in Marsha's face. Marsha screamed and backed away while wiping cherries from her face and hair.

She grabbed the huge mug of Gatorade, which had been left on the ground by the metallic string-bikini lady, and hurled it toward Kayla. Kayla ducked quickly, which surprised me—her reflexes were pretty good for a big girl—and the cup struck me on the square of my right temple. That really shouldn't have surprised me. My head was so big, it made a perfect target. My eyes then rolled inside my head like the spinning faceplate on a slot machine, which made the whole act official.

I was out.

"Wake up, Sonny, wake up!"

"Are you all right?"

My eyes opened slowly. I figured it was Kayla and the metallic string-bikini lady.

"Get your big behind up!"

"Hey, Sonny! You're not supposed to fall asleep during a cooldown. You're just supposed to cool down."

It was Chet and E.

No Kayla. No metallic string-bikini lady. Just arrogant as heck Chet and boring old E.

I took one look at them and wished I was back in that stupid dream.

"What the heck is going on?" I asked, still groggy.

"You must have passed out or something," said E, handing me a glass of water.

"Yeah, big fella," Chet said, smiling, "you probably worked your big behind too hard."

"Did I have a choice?"

"You made the choice when you called us, Sonny," E said.

"We're just trying to help like you asked," added Chet.

"I asked you to help me with FutraSystem," I told them. "I didn't need this."

"Oh, you definitely need this," said Chet, laughing.

"You sure do," E added.

"Yeah, I guess I do," I admitted. "But what I really need is your support. I need y'all to help me with the diet."

"That's all about control, big guy," said Chet, sitting on the floor beside me. "You don't need me, E or nobody else to help you keep your big behind away from food. That's gotta come from within."

"And FutraSystem isn't a diet anyway, Sonny," E said, shaking his head. "It's just a gimmick. You still eat food; you just eat their food, and I'm not convinced that's in your best interest."

"Why ain't it my best interest?" I asked, concerned.

"Because if you don't stop stuffing your face, regardless of what you eat, you ain't never gonna lose no weight," Chet said, again reminding me of the scene at Uncle Leon's Kountry Buffet.

"Yeah, Sonny, think about it," E said. "If you lose weight on FutraSystem's food, but you're still overeating, you'll gain the weight right back as soon as you get off FutraSystem because you'll still be overeating."

Now I was getting annoyed. *What the heck do they know anyway? They've never been fat.... But what if they're right?*

Chapter 8

I thought about it. Maybe E and Chet knew what they were talking about. If I didn't adjust my behavior, if I didn't make a real change, and if I didn't stop *eating* so dagon much, as Chet, the waiter and his brother at Leon's and many others had told me recently, I really might be doomed.

But what about what Kayla said?

Am I really okay like I am? Is being overweight that bad? Am I less of a friend because I weigh more than I ever have?

"Look, fellas," I said, sitting up. "Y'all are my boys and all, but it seems like all we talk about lately is my weight."

"Yo, big boy," Chet said, looking toward me. "You called us with this FutraSystem nonsense. I ain't really trying to talk about you or your fat behind, because I believe you *like* being big."

"I wouldn't go that far," E chimed in. "But you're the one who's obsessed with your weight. It's not like we sit around and talk about how to help you or anything like that. You're our man and we blew through because we wanted to support you."

"Don't try to blame your big, bloated behind on us!" exclaimed Chet.

"I'm not trying to blame y'all, I'm just saying that maybe I was wrong to bring you guys into this. It's my problem and I'll deal with it."

"So what's up with you, Sonny? You heard from Marsha?" E asked.

"Marsha who?" I answered, laughing.

"Don't even go there, Chubbs," Chet said, waving his forefinger at me. "You ain't never gonna get over that fine Miss Marsha."

"Marsha is toast," I said, slapping Chet five.

"I should have known," E said, laughing.

"You should have known what?" Chet and I asked together.

"I should have known that you'd compare Marsha to some kind of food," E said, laughing at himself. "Toast," he said, still laughing, "you said she was toast."

"You need to get a f-ing life," I said, looking at him. "What are you wearin' to Carla and Snake's wedding anyway, fool?"

"I guess that's supposed to be funny?" E asked, obviously annoyed.

"That crap *is* funny," Chet said, laughing.

"Whatever, Chet," E said.

"Don't get mad at me, E," Chet replied. "Chubbs fired on you."

"I didn't do nothing," I said, sipping some water. "I just asked my man what he was wearin' to his true love's wedding to his clown of a first cousin."

"I'm wearin' the same thing you're wearin' to Marsha's wedding," E told me.

"Now, that's f'ed up," Chet said, laughing.

"What would be so bad about that?" I asked, sensing a major insult was in the offing.

"That little fool in your big clothes," he answered, still laughing. "That crap's criminal."

"It's not as criminal as your jailbird mother and sister," E fired back.

"Yo, Chubbs," Chet said, picking up the remote to my TV and VCR. "What *is* up with you? You still pressed about Marsha?"

"I was never pressed," I answered, shaking my head. "I was into her, but that was a long time ago. It's not like she was all that, she was just there at the right time," I went on. "Quiet as it's kept, I bet that Marsha's the one who's pressed."

Chet and E looked at each other and then slowly turned their heads in my direction.

"You must have lost your mind, Sonny," E told me.

"I know you don't think Marsha's trippin' over you," Chet added.

"You never even told us what happened, Sonny. We just know that after you broke up, you got even bigger than you already were," E reminded me.

"Yeah, Chubbs," Chet said, pushing buttons on the remote. "Marsha took your big behind all the way down the drain," he continued. "She worked on you like Liquid Drano."

"Extra-Strength Liquid Drano," E chimed in, laughing.

"It wasn't *even* like that," I told them. "Marsha was okay, but it's not like I lost any sleep over her."

"You oughtta stop, Chubbs," Chet answered with a grin. "Marsha blew your mind like you blow through food. She housed your big bottom."

"Whatever, Chet," I said, sounding very much like E.

"You're talkin' pretty bold, Sonny," E said. "If I didn't know any better, I'd say you've met someone."

"That chow-hound ain't pushed up on nothing that he couldn't digest," Chet joked.

"You betta ask somebody, fool," I said with an edge.

"I ain't got to ask nobody nothing," Chet said, glaring at me, "'cause I *know* you ain't pushed up on nothing."

"You met somebody?" E asked.

"Kind of," I answered, half nodding my head.

"Kind of?" E repeated.

"Yeah," Chet interrupted. "That's the same as him being *kind of* fat. It's a new thing. It would be like you spending the night with your ex-girlfriend Carla and her telling you she's pregnant two months later," he said, looking toward E.

"What the heck are you talkin' about now?" asked E.

"I'm saying that if you spent the night with Carla, and she told you she was pregnant, you'd know she was *kind of* pregnant because you'd know you ain't hit it."

"That's f'ed up, Chet," I said, trying to laugh under my breath.

"What's f'ed is that your big behind is tryin' to front like you done square business pushed up on somebody," said Chet.

"I'm trying to tell y'all," I said, taking another sip of water.

"You tryin' to tell us what?" E asked, looking at me.

"I'm tryin' to tell y'all that I got something in the works."

"You ain't got nothing in the works but food, Chubbs," Chet told me.

"I'm tellin' y'all I met a hottie," I said.

"Who?" they asked within seconds of each other.

"Y'all don't know her," I told them.

"So tell us," E requested.

"She's blind," Chet said, laughing.

"Wrong," I said, shaking my head.

"Crazy?" E asked.

"Not," I told them.

"Crippled, a crackhead, married?" Chet said in rapid succession.

"Nope," I told them, smiling.

There was a silence. They looked at each other, started nodding and big smiles jumped across their faces. It was obvious they knew.

"She's fat!" they yelled, high-fiving each other.

"Kind of," I said, nodding back at them.

"Chubbs, don't do it, Chubbs," urged Chet.

"You can't go out like that, Sonny," E told me.

"A fat chick ain't gonna do nothing but make a big fool like you even bigger," lamented Chet.

"You don't need a fat girl, Sonny," E added.

"Whoa!" I yelled. "What happened to 'Is she nice, Sonny?'

. . . 'Does she treat you well, Sonny?' . . . 'Does she make you happy, Sonny?' . . . What happened to *that?*"

"Is she *fat*, Sonny?" asked Chet.

"I already told y'all she's fat."

"Well, that's what happened to *that*," he told me.

"What's up with y'all?" I asked, frustrated. "I don't believe this."

"I don't believe you actually feel like you have to hook up with a fat chick," E said, shaking his head.

"Look at me, E," I said, spreading my arms. "What do y'all think I am? I'm fat too."

"Ain't no doubt about that," Chet said, laughing.

"You may be fat, Sonny, but you're our buddy, and we don't want to see our boy dating a fat girl," E told me.

"And what if her friends don't want her to hook up with me because *I'm* fat?" I asked.

"Her friends are probably fat girls too," Chet said, laughing.

"You know fat girls run in packs," E told me.

"Fat girls run in packs?" I asked, concerned.

"Fine girls hang with fine girls, dumb chicks run with dumb chicks and fat girls definitely wobble together," Chet said.

"Y'all are sick," I said, shaking my head.

"You the one who's sick, Chubbs," Chet replied. "Just because you went and got all big on us don't mean that you have to be a Chubby Chaser."

"Yeah, Sonny," E added. "If you date a fat girl, that's like giving up. It's like you're saying that you can't do any better, like you can't lose your weight so you're just throwing in the towel."

"I ain't throwin' in no towel and I can't believe y'all are

this petty," I said. "It makes me wonder what y'all really think of *me*."

"We don't have to think about you," Chet said, casually flipping channels. "We *know* you're fat, but it's cool 'cause you're our boy."

"So if I wasn't your partner, I'd just be another fat boy, right?" I asked.

"Right," Chet answered, laughing. "But you're *our* fat boy so you're down."

"Y'all can kiss my big fat behind," I said, disgusted.

"Naw," Chet said, looking toward me. "That ain't happenin'." He shook his head. "You can get your fat-behinded girlfriend to kiss your big fat behind."

We all laughed. Chet had a weird way of totally insulting you while at the same time forcing you to laugh at yourself.

"Yo, Sonny," said E, smiling. "Why don't you fill us in on your big girl?"

"It's not like she's my girl or anything," I told them. "We just met, but there's definitely something workin'."

"She got a job?" asked Chet.

"Yeah," I answered.

"Got a place?" E asked.

"Got an awesome place."

"Car?"

"I ain't sure about that."

"How did y'all meet?"

"FutraSystem."

"She's smart, nice, decent-looking, single?"

"I don't know about that," I cautiously answered.

"What do you mean 'you don't know'?" asked E, concerned.

"I don't know if she's single," I replied.

"You don't know if a fat girl's single and you're pushing up on her," Chet said, looking toward me. "You can't be that pressed, Chubbs."

"I ain't pressed," I said, taking another gulp of water. "I just said I liked her."

"Why are you interested in a big girl who's not even single?" asked E.

"It's like you still liking Carla even though she's with your cousin Snake," I answered. "She's a woman. I don't see her as a big woman or a fat woman or even as a woman with a weight problem like mine. I just see her as a woman."

"Both of y'all fools are sick," Chet blurted out. "I don't know who's worse." He laughed. "Your big tail and your chubby girlfriend who may not be single, or E, who's gonna be in his cousin's wedding when his cousin marries *his* girl."

"Whatever, Chet," we said together.

"Look, Sonny," E said, before pausing. "You're our partner regardless of how much you may weigh. If you like somebody, I guess that's all that counts."

"Thanks, E," I said, reaching for his hand.

"My man," he replied.

Chet being Chet just stared at the TV. He wasn't about to do or say anything that even came close to being sentimental.

"Whatever, fools," he said, flipping channels.

"Gimme a shout later," E said, slipping on his jacket. "I'm out."

Chet stood up and walked toward the door.

"I'm out too, Chubbs," he said, slapping me five. "Good luck with the big girl. And look, Chubbs," he added, nodding his head, "stick with your workout. It ain't about your big, bloated body, it's all about your health."

Typical Chet. Even when he's *trying* to be decent, he has to take a swipe.

"Thanks, dawg," I said, walking behind him. "I'm definitely gonna be workin' out in the pit."

"All right, Sonny," he said, as I closed the door behind him. "Chill out, big fella."

Chapter 9

As I dressed for bed, I recalled what Chet and E said about fat people. It was totally screwed up that they thought Kayla was somehow unacceptable because of her weight. All I could think about was what they *really* thought of me. Did they just see me as an oversize mound of bones, flesh and blubber? Had we lost any real connection we had to one another just because I'd gained weight? Why did Chet continue to call me Chubbs even after I'd told him how much it bothered me? And why did he and everybody and his momma seem to find it necessary to remind me that I had a weight problem? Was it anybody's business? What if I liked being fat? What if it were okay with me?

And why was I so dag-on hungry?

My mind was swimming with a zillion questions, but I couldn't answer any of them. I was really hungry, but I wasn't about to eat. Not tonight. As much as I loved my late-night snacks, even I finally realized they were like land mines. Eating, falling asleep and waking up later to eat some more was like begging to be even fatter than I already was. I hated admitting it, but Chet and E were right. Working out wasn't about losing weight, it was about my health. When E told me I needed to change my habits, I listened. Even if FutraSystem worked, it wouldn't mean much if I was still a big-time pig. And if I didn't give up my late-night (meal-size) snacks, I knew one day I'd be enshrined into the fat guys hall of fame.

But it was eleven and I was starving. Maybe I could just have a little snack. The FutraPretzels would have to do. As far as I was concerned, they were the perfect snack. I hated them so much that they simply weren't a threat. I got out of bed, grabbed a bag from the kitchen and headed back to my room. As I sat down on the side of my bed and popped open the bag, the theme to ESPN's *SportsCenter*—da, da, da—da, da, da—played in the background. Then the phone rang. I figured it was Chet or E. I knew there was no way they were going to let me forget passing out during the cooldown and I knew I'd hear more about Kayla. I leaned over and grabbed my tiny black portable phone, which was nestled in the middle of my comforter.

"Yeah," I answered, after clicking the talk button.

"Yeah?" repeated the caller.

"Yeah," I said again.

"Yeah?" she again asked. "Is that how you answer the phone, yeah?"

"Yeah," I told her.

"This is Kayla," she said.

"Hey, Kayla," I said, swallowing a pretzel. "What's up?"

"Nothing's up," she answered. "What's up with you?"

"Just chillin'."

"Just chillin'?" She chuckled. "You do have a way with words."

"I'm hip," I replied, reaching for another pretzel.

"That you are," she said, still laughing.

"So what's up?" I asked.

"Does something have to be up for me to call?" she asked.

"No," I answered. "But if you're calling me, I figure something's up."

"Well, actually, I wanted to invite you over for dinner one evening."

"Why?"

"I just think it would be fun," she told me. "I had a good time this afternoon. There was a nice vibe."

"It was pretty cool," I said. "Next time why don't we chill over here?"

"Chill over there?" she said, pretending to be *ultra*prissy.

"Yeah, maybe we can eat a little, work out a little, you know, just kind of chill."

"Can you cook?" she asked.

"You think I got this big from breathin' or something?" I asked, laughing.

"I know I didn't. Look, Sonny," she said cautiously. "I am really sorry about this afternoon. KJ was a mess and Jonathan was . . . well, he was Jonathan."

"He was Jonathan James Leslie, to let him tell it," I said, impersonating him.

"*Mr.* Jonathan James Leslie," she said, topping my mimic.

"So what's up with you and Mr. Jonathan James Leslie?" I asked, downing another FutraPretzel.

"He's just a friend."

"Women always use that crap," I said sarcastically. " 'Oh, he's just a friend,' " I added, trying to sound like her. "He's just a friend when you're talkin' to another guy. But when he's up in the house, he's *'honey.'* "

"That's very perceptive, Sonny," she said, giggling.

"So what's up with you and honey?" I asked.

"Honey is honey," she said, still giggling. "Jonathan is a really nice guy. He's very attentive, he has a good heart and he really means well."

"He means well?"

"Yes, he means well."

"Is that the best you can say about a guy you call 'honey,' that he means well?" I asked.

"Yes," she answered. "Jonathan has some issues he needs to resolve, but all in all, he's a nice guy with good intentions."

This sounded strange to me. I couldn't imagine dating someone and feeling that they "meant well." If someone were dating me and she told a girlfriend, "He has good intentions," when asked to describe me, I'd know our time was limited.

Good intentions?

He means well?

Those are words you use to describe a parolee or something.

"Yo, Kayla," I said, reaching for another FutraPretzel. "What's this 'He has good intentions' crap? What's the deal . . . are y'all dating or what?"

"Or what," she replied, laughing.

"What does 'or what' mean, exactly?" I asked.

" 'Or what' means that we do date," she said, laughing. "But I wouldn't say we're dating."

That answer was as ridiculous as "He has good intentions." How can you say we date but we're not dating all in the same sentence? I thought.

"So you're really not that involved?" I asked, chomping on another FutraPretzel.

"I don't know what 'that involved' means, but I guess you could say we're not that involved," she told me.

"This ain't making much sense," I said, frustrated.

"I guess it ain't," she answered, laughing. "Look, Sonny," she said, pausing. "Jonathan is my friend. We don't have a commitment, I doubt that he's even capable of a commitment, and he has no ties to me as I have none to him."

"Okay."

"It is okay," she said. "So let's leave Jonathan out of our discussion."

"He's out," I said, swallowing.

"Good," she answered. "So when do you want to get together?"

"Whenever you want," I replied.

"What are you doing tonight?"

"Sleeping," I told her.

"You want to do something?" she asked.

"Like what?"

"Like go get something to eat," she said, chuckling. "I'm hungry."

"I'm not really hungry," I said, lying. "But I guess we could go for a ride or something."

"Well, it's about eleven-fifteen," she said. "You think you can be here by eleven-thirty?"

"How about a quarter of?" I asked, looking at my watch.

"Works for me," she answered.

"I'm out," I said before clicking off the phone.

"See ya," she said.

What the heck was I thinking? Maybe Chet and E were right. I must be pressed. Why would I agree to go out at midnight? I guess I felt it gave me a chance to see where she was really coming from. It seemed like something was going on with Jonathan, but I'd figure that out later. But it seemed like Kayla definitely had a spontaneous side to her and I like that. When a woman calls out of nowhere and wants to hook up, that's spontaneous. If she calls and wants to get together at midnight, that's another issue.

When it struck me that Kayla had just made a booty call, I hurried to get myself together.

I jumped from my bed, brushed my teeth, threw on my black-and-white Nike sweatsuit (again), splashed on some cologne, grabbed a bag of FutraCurls and dashed for the door. I hadn't been with a woman since Marsha lowered the boom on me. The corner 7-Eleven was open and ready for business. You can't answer a booty call without the proper equipment.

I needed some protection.

I zoomed to the 7-Eleven and parked in a hurry. It was getting close to 11:45 and I didn't want to be late. Even *I* knew you had to answer a booty call immediately—before the sheets got cold.

"Can I get a pack of blue Trojans?" I asked the older man behind the counter.

He looked at me like I'd asked him to loan me a million bucks.

"You sure you want the blue ones?" he asked, peering over his glasses.

"Yeah," I told him, "I want the blue ones."

"I don't know if you want the blue ones," he said, looking me over. "They for you?"

"Of course they're for me," I answered, taken aback. "Who the heck else would they be for?"

"I can't say I rightly know," he said, rubbing his chin. "But, if they are for you, that could very well be a problem."

"Why would that be a problem?" I asked.

"I could be wrong, young man," he said, shaking his head, "and I don't mean no harm, but I'm not sure the blue box would work for a big fella like yourself."

"It problee would," said the woman in line behind me. "One of the guys I date, T-Bird, is big and fat just like you. And he don't hardly have nothing," she added, shaking her head. "I had to teach T-Bird how to use his tongue."

I didn't know what to make of her. She had full, round lips oozing with bright-orange lipstick that faintly matched her terribly bleached blond braids. She had an earring planted in the side of her nose, and appeared to have at least five tiny hoop earrings in each ear. She had a different "gold" ring on each finger, and her nails were air-brushed with flowers and birds. This "lady" was wearing a pair of baggy black jeans and a red Fubu sweatshirt. Her gray New Balance 570's didn't exactly match her outfit, but they were in style, which I guessed worked in her favor. I imagined T-Bird learned to like using his tongue. That way, he wouldn't be forced to actually look at her when they were together.

"Well, I guess you do need the blue box there, big fella," the cashier said, smiling.

"I know he do," said the woman, between pops of her gum.

"I don't think you know nothing," I said, looking toward her.

"Could be she knows what she's talking about," the cashier said, sliding the pack on the counter. "I ain't never been with no big fella myself, so I wouldn't rightly know. But she said she's been with a big boy—what did you say his name was, T-Bone, wasn't it? Anyway, it sounds like she knows about this kind of stuff."

"Keisha, what you doing, girl?" said a man, poking his head through the store's front entrance.

"This man don't know what he want," said Keisha, rolling her eyes. "I be right there, T-Bird."

I'd had enough. I looked at both of them and shook my head. I then stomped toward the door and reached to push it open.

"Hey, big fella!" yelled the cashier.

I turned around.

"You want the red ones?"

"He ain't gonna need them either," Keisha told him, shaking her head.

I looked at T-Bird and shook *my* head before hopping in my truck. He was a bigger fool than I was. And his being with Keisha, who was buying some Pampers, a honey bun, a Welch's grape soda and a scratch-off lottery ticket didn't help. She was ghetto with a capital *G* and he was sporting her like she was Jada Pinkett.

Being unprepared for a booty call was bad business, but I couldn't buy a condom after the old guy from 7-Eleven had totally humiliated me.

I pulled into Kayla's well-lit development and parked near the edge of her driveway. I then checked myself in the rearview mirror (at least what little of me actually fit in the mirror) and opened the door. Why I even checked myself was a mystery to me. When it was booty-call time, a woman didn't care what you looked like. She called late, you showed up, took care of business and you left. When a woman made a booty call, it was about the only time she'd have sex and then allow you to leave without a fuss. In most cases, she *wanted* you to leave.

I rang the doorbell.

"Yes," she said through the intercom.

"Yo, Kayla," I answered. "It's Sonny."

"Yo, Sonny," she said, laughing. "I'll be right down."

I hoped she had some rubbers since I was blown away by Keisha, T-Bird and that old man at 7-Eleven. I couldn't help but wonder what her move would be. Marsha would sometimes answer the door in a super-see-through teddy and I'd know it was on. What would Kayla do? I figured big girls had to use big robes. I couldn't imagine someone as big as Kayla in a teddy. If they even made teddies in her size, they would be so big that they'd probably call them Theodores, I thought, amused.

"You ready?" she said, stepping onto the porch.

"I guess," I said, stunned.

"Well, let's go," she said, closing the door and locking it.

"Yeah," I said, looking at Kayla and suddenly realizing I wouldn't be needing the blue Trojans or the red ones, she was way overdressed for a booty call.

We hopped in my truck and pulled off into the night. I felt like a fool. And not just any fool. I felt like a big, fat fool. Kayla sat beside me, looking like she'd just stepped off the cover of *Essence* magazine, while I looked exactly like Chet described me. A black-and-white police SWAT van. Kayla was decked out in a beautiful bronze pantsuit that was made of more silk than a Dumpster full of Chanel scarves. A row of elegant medallionlike buttons was positioned at the center of her blouse, which (thankfully) was long enough that it draped over her ample behind. She had on a simple gold herringbone neck chain and gold hoop earrings. Her shiny leather sandals perfectly matched her outfit, right down to the three tiny gold medallions that sat across the front of each shoe. A stunning diamond tennis bracelet hung on her right wrist and a sleek black Movado museum watch graced the other. It was obvious she had curled her hair and her perfectly shaped nails were as bronze and as silky as her outfit.

"Yo, Kayla," I said, turning onto New York Avenue. "Where we goin'?"

"A friend of mine owns a nice little spot," she told me. "A little food, a little dance, nice wine list. It has atmosphere; you'll like it."

"Sounds nice," I said, just barely beating the light at Florida Avenue. "What's it called?"

"Republic Gardens."

"Republic Gardens?" I asked, concerned.

"You've never heard of Republic Gardens?" she asked, looking toward me. "It's the hottest club in the city. My buddy Marc owns it."

"I've heard about it," I replied. "I hear it's a decent spot."

It was decent, all right. Marsha and I met at D.C. Live and we spent hours there dancing, laughing and setting the course for our relationship, but we also spent lots of time at Republic Gardens. The food was good, the service was great and the music was thumping. The Gardens, as it came to be called, was thought to be one of the best places to meet a truly decent woman in D.C. It wasn't your classic meat market or sleazy meet 'em, take 'em home, screw 'em and never call 'em pickup spot. The classy cherry-wood decor, upholstered chairs, comfortable sofas and shiny hardwood floors set a tone where spirited dialogue and light, unimposing mingling upstaged pretentious opening lines and stale, overbearing raps every night of the week. Upscale, professional brothers and sisters throughout the metropolitan area called The Gardens their spot. On any given night you'd see groups celebrating birthdays, promotions and even graduations from Howard University's law and med schools. On those very same nights, it would be easy to run into Chet, E or, worse yet, Marsha. They all hung out at Republic Gardens from time to time. I hadn't been since Marsha dumped me.

I couldn't believe I was about to blow through The Gardens after such a long time. I just hoped I wouldn't run into Chet, E, Marsha or, worse, all three of them.

"You sure you want to go to Republic Gardens?" I asked, hoping she would change her mind.

"You'll like it," she said. "Have you ever been there?"

"I've been a couple times," I told her, knowing full well that I used to hit The Gardens at least twice a week.

"Good," she said, touching up her lipstick while looking in the lighted visor vanity mirror. "Because we're almost there."

"I don't know if that's so good," I said as we crossed Rhode Island Avenue.

"Why isn't it?" she asked, lightly dabbing her cheeks with a black cosmetic brush.

"'Cause I ain't really dressed for The Gardens," I said.

"I'll take care of that," she told me, brushing her hair. "I told you, the owner is a good friend of mine."

I didn't even have a good cop-out. I didn't want to stand in line and later walk through Republic Gardens with *her* on my arm. Suddenly, Chet and E were making sense. Kayla may have been all right for a booty call, and she certainly was good for a nice ride around town, but The Gardens? I couldn't do The Gardens with her. She looked good, but she didn't look Gardens Good. She was too large. The Gardens was filled with tiny women in tight dresses, spiked heels and stylish hairdos, not big girls. I was going to The Gardens since we had to go. But I wasn't about to sport Ms. Kayla Jennings around.

"Why don't you drop me off here?" she said as we pulled in front of the entrance. "I'll talk to Marc and he'll save us a table near the kitchen."

"Cool," I said as she opened the door.

"See you inside," she answered, closing the door.

That would work. The kitchen was at the back of the club. Nobody hung near the kitchen. I should've known *Kayla* would want to be near somebody's kitchen.

I parked at the Reeves Building, which once housed the mayor's office, and headed back down Florida Avenue toward Republic Gardens. The warm summer night air had seemingly coaxed many women out on the town. In a city like D.C., where hair is as important as some women's next meal, the ladies were out because they probably felt comfortable knowing that their hairdos, hairstyles and hair weaves would stand up to tonight's unusual, near-zero humidity.

Walking in front of me was one of them—a very shapely woman who most likely wasn't worried about her hair and who had been blessed with legs that would have made Jackie Joyner-Kersee green with envy. She dropped her tiny black purse and several coins rolled in my direction. Her date, a short guy in a sharp-looking shiny gold vest, hurried to retrieve the coins and she turned to help him. I wasn't about to bend over to pick up any amount of money that wasn't real cash. It's a big-guy thing. When bills slip away they usually float, so it's easy for me to catch them in the air. When coins get loose, they roll and I'd be forced to reach toward the ground, and with the load I'm carrying, I wasn't always sure I'd be able to get back up. That always made it an easy decision; I'd let the change go and try for the cash.

It also made it easy for me to get a clear face shot of Ms. Legs as she reached for her purse. I couldn't believe it. For a second I froze and my eyes tightened as I focused in on her. I didn't want to believe who I was seeing and definitely didn't want her to see me.

It was Marsha!

Here I was, wearing the very same sweatsuit I wore the night she dumped me over a year ago, and she was looking twice as good as she was looking back then, and back then, she already looked twice as good as any other woman I knew. If I could have disappeared into thin air I would have. Since that wasn't an option, I did the next best thing.

I spotted two mailboxes and jumped between them. Marsha and her date, Mr. Gold Vest, looked in my direction, but it was so dark that not even the flickering streetlamp provided enough light for them to make out who I was. Marsha's date handed her the coins he'd picked up and they turned and headed toward Republic Gardens. I just shook my head and sighed in relief. That sigh came too soon. I may have felt relieved but I needed relief.

I wiggled, squirmed, twisted and tried desperately to suck in my stomach, but nothing was working. This definitely wasn't my day: I leave the house to respond to a booty call, get called out by Keisha, T-Bird and that old coot at 7-Eleven, run into Marsha and Mr. Gold Vest while walking into a club that I'm not trying to go to in the first place, and now this.

I was stuck between two stupid mailboxes!

How the heck am I going to get out of this? I wondered, trying to find something to hold on to. I gasped for air as I wiggled more and made the situation even worse. At least, I *thought* I was making it worse. It didn't really get worse until a tiny dusty brown dog, who looked to be equal parts Scottish terrier and cocker spaniel, made his way toward the mailbox.

"Hey, little doggie," I said, worried, as he circled the mailboxes and sniffed away at my leg. "The fire hydrant's over there," I told him, trying to point.

Either he couldn't see, couldn't hear or didn't care about what I was telling him. He slowly raised his leg and my shoulders hunched and my eyes clinched as I prepared for the worst.

"Biscuit!" yelled someone from a distance. "Get your stinking hips away from that stinking mailbox!"

The voice drew closer and it was quickly apparent that it belonged to an older guy who was bundled up in a hodge-podge collection of colorful robes, stale blankets and a red, floor-length overcoat. And it didn't help that he smelled like he was allergic to any possible combination of soap mixed with water.

"Hey there, big fella," he said, walking toward me. "It's kinda late for the mail, don't you think?"

He smelled so bad, if my nose could have cried, it would have.

"I'm not mailing nothing," I told him, still trying to squirm my way out.

"If you are it doesn't look like it'll get there," he said, shaking his head.

Biscuit stood beside him and wagged what little tail he had. I was already embarrassed by just being stuck in the first place. My big, fat, bloated behind did me in again. I didn't need any help to make me feel worse. Being the meat in a mailbox sandwich was as bad as a tube of empty Pringles chips. And now I had a blanket-covered wannabe comic with a built-in stump-wagging audience reminding me how bad off I was.

Why does this crap have to happen to me?

"You wanna buy?" the man said, rolling up several sleeves to reveal a row of truly cheap-looking watches.

"I don't think I need a watch right now," I told him, still trying to free myself, but making absolutely no progress. "I could use a hand, though."

"I know what you mean," he replied, placing the watches near his ear, and obviously not caring one bit about my plight.

"You know what I mean about what?" I asked, panting.

"I know what you mean about needing a hand," he told me. "Me and Biscuit here, we haven't eaten since this afternoon and I haven't been able to move a watch all evening. So I understand what a man means when he says he needs a hand, 'cause I need a hand too."

"Well, maybe we can help each other," I told him, trying to catch my breath.

"Guess that means you want a watch," he said, smiling and rubbing his hands.

"It's not like I want a watch, but if it means you'll give me a hand, I'll buy one from you," I said, drawing another breath.

"What kind of watch you looking for?" he said, waving his arm in my face and nearly triggering my gag reflex from the smell. "I got a Roflex here, even got a real nice Bolivia," he said, pointing toward his forearm. "Of course, if it's basic time that you want, this here Time-ix is what you need."

"I don't need no watch," I reminded him. "I just need a hand."

"I can relate to that," he reminded me. "Did I tell you that Biscuit bit the mayor once?"

"He bit the mayor?"

"Yeah," he said proudly. "Old M.B.—he was standing right there." He pointed toward the sidewalk. "And he told me he didn't want to buy no watch just like you said, so old Biscuit, he just opened up, you know, and wham, he bit him like he was a juicy old T-bone."

"You let your dog bite the mayor?" I asked, surprised.

"The mayor wasn't trying to buy no watch," he said, shaking his finger at me.

"What happened when your dog bit him? Did he kick him or something?"

I must have said something very wrong because Biscuit growled and lowered his head like he was ready to attack.

"Heck, no, the mayor didn't kick him," the man said, suddenly smiling again. "He bought hisself a watch."

"I think I get the picture," I said, worried. "I guess I'll have to buy one too."

"Which one you want?" he asked, again waving his arm in my face.

"I think I'll take the Timex," I told him, coughing.

"Already sold."

"How about the Bulova?

"Holding it for Biscuit's girlfriend's owner," he said, patting him on the head. "Figure if I give her the Boliva, it'll give Biscuit a paw up on the other dogs."

"He's luckier than me," I admitted. "I guess I'll have to take the Rolex."

"That's a good choice," he said, smiling. "You need a batt-tree?"

"Naw," I said, still trying to work my way out, "I just need a hand so I can get outta here."

"You ain't paid for your watch yet," he told me.

"I can't reach my wallet," I told him. "But I promise I'll pay you as soon as I get outta here," I said. "Believe me, I'm a man of my word."

"The mayor said that too," he replied, obviously not impressed.

"He said that?"

"All politicians say that," he said, laughing.

Biscuit stood there wagging his little stump of a tail like he knew what we were talking about.

"Look here, big fella," he said, shaking his head. "I don't know if I can trust a man who went and got hisself all stuck up between some mailboxes at one in the morning. What were you doing anyway, you lose something?"

"I dropped some coins," I answered.

"That's a lie," he replied, again shaking his head. "Now I know I can't trust you."

"What makes you think I'm lying?" I asked, worried.

"Look at you, big fella. A big, ole boy like you ain't about to bend over to pick up no coins," he said, laughing. "Maybe a roll of quarters or something," he added. "But you'd probably let those go too."

Of course Biscuit just stood there wagging his stump like he'd won Dog of the Year on David Letterman's Stupid Pet Tricks.

"How much for the watch?" I said, frustrated.

"I like you," the old man said, looking at the watch. "So I'll let you get off for a hundred this time."

"A hundred bucks!" I exclaimed. "Are you crazy?"

Biscuit growled again and lowered his head.

"I don't appreciate you saying that, especially after I said I liked you," the guy told me. "I don't do business with people who don't appreciate me," he said, walking away. "Let's go, Biscuit."

Biscuit growled at me again before turning to join his blanket-covered master.

This wasn't going to work. I had to make a move.

"Hey!" I yelled frantically. "Hey! C'mon, my man!"

He just kept walking. And Biscuit just kept wagging his stump.

"I wasn't saying that you were crazy. What I was tryin' to say is that you must have been crazy to think that I'd cheat you. It's a Rolex. That's gotta be worth at least one twenty-five!"

"How about one fifty!" he yelled, turning around.

"You got a deal!" I answered, hoping he'd accept.

He walked in my direction and asked where my wallet was. He then reached for it, struggled to pull it out and slowly counted out $150.

"Hold this," he said, dropping the wallet into Biscuit's slobbering mouth.

"Give me your hand, big fella," he said, reaching toward me and grabbing my beefy arm. "Here we go! One—two—three!"

I don't know how he did it or exactly what he did, but I popped out of the mailboxes and landed on the sidewalk, where I was quickly greeted by Biscuit, who dropped my wallet by my side and then started slobbering all over my face.

"That's enough, Biscuit," the man said, calling him and walking away. "Let's see if we can find any other fools out tonight."

"Hold up!" I yelled. "What about my watch?"

"I thought you said you didn't need no watch."

"I didn't need one," I told him. "But since you got your one fifty, I want my watch."

"I guess you're right," he said, turning toward me. "Here goes." He tossed it to me.

He and Biscuit hurried up Fourteenth Street and disappeared into what looked to be a dark alley. As I glanced at the watch and sized up my investment, I saw why they were so quick to get away. The old man and his stump-wagging dog had beat me out of a hundred fifty bucks for a brand-new, shiny *Roflex,* not a *Rolex.* At least the time was right. I'd wasted nearly twenty minutes all because I wanted to duck Marsha and now I was going to have to face her in Republic Gardens with a Roflex timepiece. I was doomed. Everything had gone wrong tonight.

This wasn't how a booty call was supposed to work.

I edged toward Republic Gardens and wondered how I would duck Marsha and her date, Mr. Gold Vest. As was usually the case, there was a line that was nearly half a block long for those waiting to get into the club. I spotted Marsha holding hands with the short guy near the back of the line, but they were so caught up in each other that she didn't see me. Thankfully, Kayla was standing at the front door. She called out and motioned for me to come in. I walked toward the door and felt like a complete fool. Everyone was decked out looking either very fancy or very cool.

I still looked very much like a police SWAT van.

A burly doorman waved me through as he checked the crowd for ID's. I tried not to, but as I passed, I couldn't help but hear him whisper, "Check him out, y'all, that fool's bigger than me." The funky hit "Award Tour" by hip-hop mainstays Tribe Called Quest played as we walked toward the kitchen, which was located on the first floor of the two-story club. A waiter directed us to a corner table near the kitchen and then hit us up for drinks.

"Perrier with a twist," Kayla said, looking over the menu.

"I'll have some water," I added.

"Would you like Perrier?" he asked, smiling.

"Nah," I told him, shaking my head. "I just want some water."

"O-k-a-a-y," he said, turning toward the kitchen.

"So, Sonny," Kayla said, looking toward me. "Find anything you like on the menu?"

"I see a bunch of things that I like," I answered, laughing. "But I don't see any FutraSystem stuff."

"How about that," she said, looking back at the menu. "But we're out, so we might as well go for it. By the way," she said, focusing back toward me. "What took you so long to get here?"

"I kind of got stuck in the parking lot," I said.

"Yeah," she acknowledged, nodding her head. "Parking can be tough sometimes. Look," she urged. "The food is really good so you might as well take advantage of it."

"You can take advantage of it all you want," I told her. "But I've already cheated once this week, and I'm only cheating myself. So I'll stick with the water."

"How impressive," she said, placing her menu on the table. "What brought this on?"

"I was talking with my buddies earlier, and they made me realize one thing," I told her as the waiter slid my water and her Perrier on the table.

"And what might that be?" she asked, dropping the twist of lime in her glass.

"Losing weight ain't necessarily about losing weight." I lifted the glass to my mouth.

"If losing weight isn't about losing weight, what exactly is it about, Sonny?" she asked.

"It's about being healthy," I answered.

"That makes sense," she said, sipping her Perrier. "But is that really why you want to lose weight?"

"Of course that's why. Why else would I want to lose weight?"

"I can think of one reason," she told me.

"And what might that be?"

"Marsha," she said, smiling. "They probably told you you could get Marsha back if you lost weight."

"Check this out, Kayla," I said, downing my water. "This ain't about Marsha or nobody else. It's about me. I have a chance to actually make a big change, and I'm going to do it. Getting back to what I used to be, a healthy, happy guy who loved life, that's important to me. It may not mean nothing to nobody else, but it means everything to me," I added, my voice rising. "If I don't take myself seriously, if I don't want the best for myself, if I don't take responsibility for looking out for my own health," I paused, "then who will?"

"I know I won't," said the waiter, laughing. "I guess you two will be ordering from our lite fare menu after that speech."

"That won't be necessary," Kayla said, staring him down. "I'll have some buffalo wings, a basket of chili fries and a burger."

"With or without cheese?"

"With."

"Well done, medium, rare?"

"Medium."

"Anything for you, sir?"

"Just give me a house salad," I said, frustrated.

"Dressing?"

"Yeah," I answered.

"What kind, sir?"

"Uh, Ranch, I guess."

"Low-fat okay?"

"Yeah, that's cool," I told him.

"Anything to drink?"

"Water," I answered.

"I'll take a shake," Kayla said, flipping through her menu.

"Vanilla, chocolate or strawberry?"

"Chocolate," she said, smiling. "Double chocolate."

"Will that be all?" the waiter asked, probably expecting her to order a cake or something.

"That's it for now," she told him.

If that's "it" for now, I wondered, worried, what's for later?

Chapter 10

The waiter brought out her food and my salad a few minutes later. We talked about FutraSystem and she told me she thought it was a terrible waste of her time and money. "When I'm ready to lose weight, I'm sure I will lose it," she said while downing her chili fries. I slumped in my seat hoping no one, especially Marsha, would spot me. Kayla told me more about her computer programming company, and then joked that she could have landed a job at her dad's sports management firm had she slimmed down.

"He offered me a six-figure salary, a six-figure signing bonus and a six-figure luxury coupe if I lost weight," she told me, biting into her cheeseburger.

"Why didn't you do it?" I asked, surprised.

"I wanted a job because I was good at something," she said, sipping on her *double* chocolate milk shake. "I didn't need that type of incentive to lose weight." She dipped a buffalo wing into a tiny cup of blue-cheese dressing. "Like I said, I don't need a push from anyone; when I'm ready to lose weight, I'll lose it."

What type of incentive does she need? I wondered. Six-figure salary, bonus and a ride. She must be out of her mind.

When she finished, she ordered a slice of cheesecake with extra whipped cream and strawberries. Understandably, I nearly choked when she asked for a second slice.

"I was starving," she said, sipping on the second glass of Diet Coke she'd ordered.

"That's obvious," I said, shaking my head.

"You hardly ate," she commented, looking at my salad.

"How could I?" I asked. "I couldn't stop watching you."

What really got me was that watching Kayla pig out totally disgusted me. I never before had been in the company of someone who blazed through their food like her, besides myself. It was painfully clear that in Kayla, I saw myself and it was not a pretty picture. Being out with someone who placed a complete and disproportionate premium on food and eating was rough. It definitely made an impact. I now saw why Chet and E were so pressed to help me. They must have seen me like I was seeing Kayla right now, as a living, breathing, high-volume human food processor. I was glad I didn't buy the blue Trojans *or* the red ones. A booty call would have never worked with someone who ate like Kayla.

"Now I have some energy," she said, looking toward me. "Why don't we dance?"

"I think I'll pass," I said, as the Notorious B.I.G.'s "Love It When You Call Me Big Poppa" played in the background.

"You don't like to dance?" she asked.

"I just don't like that record," I told her, lying.

"I don't care for it myself either," she said, her fingers bouncing.

Good, I thought.

"How about a game of pool?" she asked, moving her head and shoulders with the music.

"I don't really like pool," I answered, wanting to keep her trapped near the kitchen and away from the slightest chance of running into Marsha.

"I can understand that," she said, laughing. "You're probably afraid I'd beat you."

"What?" I said, surprised. "I may not like pool, but it's not like I can't play." I sat up. "I don't think you're really tryin' to see me wear your big behind out on no pool table."

"Don't talk about it," she said, standing up. "Come on. Let me see you wear this big behind out!"

"Let's do it," I said, standing up.

We pushed our way to the steps, which really wasn't that difficult. One of the advantages of being big is that people will jump to get out of your way.

As we walked through the crowd toward the poolroom, I pushed the sleeves of my sweatsuit up toward my elbows and looked around, hoping that I'd spot Marsha before she spotted me. I felt a bit guilty because I didn't exactly like taking advantage of a woman on a first date, especially when I had an unfair advantage. I practically grew up in pool halls but had recently tired of the game because I couldn't find any real competition.

"What would you like to play for?" she asked, selecting a cue stick from the rack.

"I ain't tryin' to take nothing from you," I said, picking out a cue.

"You *couldn't* take anything from me," she said, laughing.

"This is a man's game, Kayla," I said, reaching for some chalk. "Let's just get this over with."

"Let's make it interesting," she said, walking toward me. "You win, we leave and go to my place. I win, we dance."

I lose either way, I thought.

"If that's the case, we can leave right now," I told her, laughing. " 'Cause I'd dive into a pool full of cactus before I'd lose to some girl."

"You won't lose to some girl," she said, leaning over the table. "You're going to have your tail kicked by *this* woman because there's no way we're going to end up at my place."

"Break," I said forcefully.

And break she did. After she quickly sank two solid balls, it felt like everybody in the club found a spot around us. The women crowded around Kayla's side of the table and I kept a lookout for Marsha. Thankfully, she wasn't there. The crowd was pumped and primed and was very pro-Kayla.

"You go, girl!" they shouted. "Run the table, boo!" they exclaimed, clapping and whistling. I even heard one woman yell, "Wear his big behind out!"

She blew her third shot, which gave me an opening.

I quickly dropped two striped balls.

"Woof, woof, woof, woof!" chanted the group of men who'd

gathered behind me. "This is your house, baby boy!" they said, amid applause. "Big Drawers is gettin' ready to set that thing out!" said one guy loudly.

I was so worried about running into Marsha that my concentration failed me. I scratched when the cue ball flew off the solid yellow one-ball into a side pocket. Kayla then took her turn, and ran three more balls before barely missing a breathtaking corner-pocket push shot. I made four difficult shots look easy, but her purple two-ball separated me from my final ball. She took advantage of it and sank her last two balls, leaving a clear corner shot for the black eight-ball that would hand her the game. Fortunately, she blew it and the white cue ball left me with my easiest shot of the match. I quickly tapped it in, chalked up and smiled. All I needed was to drop the eight-ball with a straight-ahead side-pocket shot, and the game was mine.

"Could you go get the car, James," I said to a short guy with dark shades. I nearly passed out when I realized who he was. Mr. Gold Vest himself.

"You got it, cuz," he said, slapping me five. "You and big girl gettin' ready to roll up outta here," he said, patting me on my back. "Y'all about to go to her place so you can get your swerve on."

Get my swerve on, I thought, worried. I'm about to get my swerve on with her and this midget's gonna be rolling out with Marsha—this ain't no justice.

I looked around. Everything was moving in slow-motion like the final race in the movie *Chariots of Fire*. The dance music slowed to a snail's crawl. Women shaking their heads in disbelief looked like robots programmed to move at quarter speed. Men pumping their fists in celebration appeared to have their arms stuck in midflight. And thankfully, Marsha still wasn't around.

Get my swerve on? I thought, turning my head slowly toward Kayla.

My cue stick hit the table with a loud thud and when I drew back, it felt like it took a full minute for the chalky tip to make contact with the cue ball. The white ball crashed into the black eight-ball, which rolled straight toward the right corner pocket I had called. I turned slowly to the short guy with the shades and he slapped me five in slow motion.

"G-o-o-d . . . s-h-o-t . . . c-u-z," he told me.

It felt like it took me all of thirty seconds to wink at him. And maybe it did, because when I turned back to the table the ball was *still* rolling. My bad day suddenly didn't seem so bad. I imagined that eight-ball rolling right over Andy and those fools at Sports Authority, the waiter and his brother at Leon's; Jonathan James Leslie and that wacky bird, KJ; the old man in the blankets and his senile canine, Biscuit; and every single bright-yellow bag of FutraPretzels that ever existed. It was perfect.

Well, almost perfect.

The ball stayed straight, but it ran out of gas and stopped right at the edge of the pocket. It was so close to falling that a baby on a respirator could have blown it in.

Kayla walked toward the table, sized up the shot and gently tapped it in.

"Game!" she yelled, bringing the entire room back to regular speed. The women screamed, the men dropped their heads and edged away from the table and Kayla dropped her cue stick and headed toward me. The brothers made a quick exit, but I didn't feel totally abandoned. Because even though Marsha was nowhere to be found, her tiny date, Mr. Gold Vest, was still here. I turned and reached for one last five.

"You suck, cuz," he told me before walking away.

Kayla reached for my hand and said, "To the dance floor, James," as TLC's booty-call anthem, "Ain't Too Proud to Beg," blared from the sound system. We found a spot toward the middle of the floor and Kayla moved about with ease. She was a great dancer. Had she been thin, everyone in the club would have stopped in their tracks to check her out. But because of her size, she was relegated to being a fat chick who was light on her feet. I, unfortunately, didn't have her gift. I was pretty good with a one-two, finger-popping side step, but I didn't actually move too much. I gave up trying to dance some time ago. Even *I* thought that the sight of big guys on the dance floor was comical.

Fat folks aren't supposed to dance, we're supposed to eat.

Kayla obviously didn't see it that way. She moved around like she was five three, one hundred fifteen pounds. She circled around me, turned her back toward me, went down, up and back down again and shook her stuff (and it was a lot of stuff to shake) with an ease and passion that amazed me. She even had the energy to mouth the words with the other women on the dance floor.

She pointed at me, swung her head and sang louder with each verse. I didn't know what to do. The music bounced off the walls like kangaroos on crack. Kayla jumped, sang and jumped even more, just like everybody else in the club.

I just two-stepped, tried to stay out of the way and kept looking around for Marsha.

When she turned her back toward me and sang, "Join the paddy wagon," I realized that joining her paddy wagon would be an ambitious undertaking. Ironically, it was the first time I seriously considered what it would be like to be with a big girl like Kayla. I knew I thought she was pretty interesting earlier, but I'm not sure I actually considered what being with her, kissing her or even holding her, would be like.

The next record didn't give me much of a chance to work out the details.

As the deejay blended in Luther's soulful "Make Me a Believer," she gently grabbed my hand and drew toward me. I had never before slow danced with a woman the size of Kayla. Because we were slow dragging, my initial reaction was to reach for her waist. But I soon discovered she didn't have one. In fact, it was more like she had two. I thought I would wrap my arms around her. That wasn't happening either. And slipping my leg alongside hers would have been like trying to fit the Macy's Thanksgiving Parade into a one-car driveway.

Thankfully, though, the music moved us and everything just fell into place. Amazingly, I no longer thought about, worried about or even considered what Marsha and her pint-size date were up to, though I had to smile when I looked up for a moment and saw him across the room dancing with another woman while Marsha fumed just a few feet away. With our hands at our sides Kayla and I moved slowly with the melody. And when Luther sang, "And forever keep you here," I knew just what he meant. Because at that moment, I wanted Kayla in my arms. And had she not been as big as I was, I would have made certain she was actually in my arms.

When the song ended we slowly pulled apart and exchanged a long, wonderful glance. It was one of those goofy "Who's going to say it first?" stares. We sized each other up, which for people of our girth took a while. As my eyes moved over her, I wondered what it was like to lay with a woman who was as large as me.

Do big girls feel it like little girls? Do they move like smaller women? How do you actually fit it past their thighs when there's no room between their thighs? Would it be safe to let her be on top? I wondered.

I didn't know what she was thinking. She sighed and then smiled. "I was hoping this wouldn't happen."

"You were hoping what wouldn't happen?" I asked, concerned.

"I didn't think I'd actually start to like you," she said, turning away.

"What's wrong with liking me?" I asked, reaching for her hand.

"I didn't say anything's wrong with liking you," she said, leading me toward the stairs. "It's just that you have so many issues."

"So many issues like what?"

"You know what I mean, Sonny," she said, smiling. "You know the whole thing with Marsha and all that."

"No," I told her forcefully. "I don't know what you mean. I already told you that Marsha's history. You were the one who said I needed to let it go and now that I have, *you're* the one who keeps bringing her up."

"I know, I know." She sighed, shaking her head. "But I don't want to see you making a move you're not ready to make. I don't want you to take a big leap if a big leap really isn't in you," she said, reaching for a chair. "You can't drop what you feel for Marsha because of something I said. You have to do it because your heart tells you to do it."

"It didn't hurt that you opened my eyes a little," I answered, smiling. "But my heart's not with Marsha."

"Oh, really," she said, obviously unimpressed.

"Really," I said, looking toward her. "What if I told you that Marsha was here tonight?"

"She's here?" she gasped.

"If she was and I didn't even mention her or make my way to her, wouldn't that say something to you?" I asked.

"It sure would," she answered. "It would tell me you were ashamed of me and that you didn't want her to see us together."

"That's not exactly it," I admitted, smiling. "I'm ashamed of myself and I didn't want her to see me and this extra seventy-five pounds I'm carrying."

We both laughed.

Then, even though it seemed like she tried to avoid it, our eyes met again. We connected like a hungry wide-mouth bass meeting with a well-placed spinner bait. I reached for her hand, which was already open and waiting for mine. The deejay slipped on Maze's "Happy Feeling" and the moment was ours. When the song ended she held on to my hand, and we walked out of the club and headed for the seclusion of the garage at the Reeves Building. I opened the door to my Suburban and she stepped up and into the front seat. I'm certain the springs screamed in agony as she sat down and the truck drew closer to the ground. It was cool, though, because I knew my shocks would be equally affected when I jumped in.

We headed down Florida Avenue and back into Prince
Georges County, Maryland. Kayla held my hand and nodded
her head with the music. The Isley Brothers' "Fight the
Power" rocked through the speakers and her head stayed
with the beat as she mouthed the words. I stayed quiet and
wondered exactly who was going to hit on who first. If
I made a move I would look too anxious. It would be as if I
were doing the typical guy thing—taking a wonderful
evening and reducing it to sex. If I didn't make a move and
she was expecting or even wanting me to make one, I'd be a
chump.

I was screwed either way.

As I turned into her driveway, she slowly eased her hand
away from mine. It was as if she were saying, "Ain't nothing
happenin' here, big fella." I parked and turned the engine
off. Stevie Wonder's "Super Woman" was on the radio and I
looked toward her. Our eyes again made contact and she
leaned her head on my shoulder. We stared at the moon and
gazed at the stars. I sighed when I thought of the crazy day
I'd had. Kayla made it right, though. Being here with her allowed me to feel like a real man and not like a fat guy.
Though I knew in the back of my mind she had Jonathan
James Leslie waiting in the wings, and that the only thing
awaiting me was a kitchen full of FutraSystem crap, tonight
it didn't matter. I raised my head at the very moment she
lifted hers and it was as if our lips were calling each other.

We kissed.

Though the earth didn't stop and high tide didn't roll in,
the kiss was special. It was soft, wet and just plain wonderful.
It was the first time I'd tasted a woman in over a year and it
hit me as hard as the aroma of Marsha's fresh-baked carrot

bread once did. Our kiss was great and I was glad she'd popped in a Certs so I wouldn't have to taste the burger, shake and chili fries she'd devoured at Republic Gardens. My shoulders twitched as she ran her hand across my back. We pulled apart for just a second and then embraced and kissed again. It didn't matter that our arms couldn't fit all the way around each other and I didn't care if our first evening together wasn't the booty call I'd earlier hoped for. In fact, I was glad it had evolved into more than a hit-it and quit-it romp in the bedroom. Sharing a special evening meant much more to me than jumping her bones would have.

We walked toward her door. She reached for my hand and whispered, "I really had a good time."

"So did I," I answered.

"Yo, Sonny," she said, doing a near-perfect imitation of me.

"Yo?" I asked, mocking her.

"Yo, Sonny," she repeated, opening the door. "Let's do this again."

"Yo, Kayla," I said, just before she closed the door. "Let's do it again soon."

As I drove home, I smiled and hoped her version of soon was somehow closely related to mine, because I wanted soon to mean *real* soon. As I opened my door and made my way past the pit and up the stairs, I realized I couldn't wait to see Kayla again. She'd made her mark. I chuckled as I looked down at my new Roflex, which had already stopped running, and thought about the old man offering me a "batt-tree."

I still felt a little foolish about being stuck between those mailboxes, and though my weight and my body had again put me in a position that both embarrassed and humiliated me, I couldn't help but smile. Biscuit hadn't used my leg to relieve himself on. I'd seen Marsha and survived. And for once, food wasn't dominating my thoughts. I was exhausted but it was okay. I knew I'd sleep well because things were suddenly as clear to me as a bottle of fresh springwater.

As I lay in the bed about to fall asleep, it hit me. For the first time in almost a year, I wasn't lost somewhere in Marsha-land. And, for the first time in years, I wasn't thinking about food. My battle with the pit seemed like a distant memory, and not even Chet and E could make me feel bad about hanging with a "big girl"—not after what had happened tonight with Kayla.

Chapter 11

My mind was racing when I woke up the next morning. What was going on? I hadn't done the late-night-snack thing. It was 8:00 A.M. and I *wanted* to hit the pit. And to top things off, Andy had called and offered me the day off to "get my head together." He said my skills in the loose balls section were far too valuable to lose. All I could think of was how to call Kayla so we could get together. Calling would be easy. I just didn't want to look as pressed as I really was. Last night was decent. In fact, it was better than decent; it was everything a good first date was supposed to be. Good company. Good time. And moments to remember. But what if she didn't see it as a good date? What if she was just looking for a break from Jonathan James Leslie? What if I wasn't her type?

I didn't know what to do.

I brushed, flossed and then headed down the stairs before sinking my teeth into some powdered FutraEggs and an English-style muffin with some kind of bland no-fat spread. Seconds weren't an option anymore. I had weight to lose. I walked toward the pit and knew what I had to do. Sit-ups were first. It wasn't easy but I did eight, which was a major improvement from the two I'd done yesterday. This time I managed seven push-ups before introducing my face to the mat. I was already exhausted, but I knew I had to go on.

I did five very difficult minutes on the bike and four equally exasperating minutes on the rowing machine. The bow-flex was next and though I didn't think I would last, I made it through the entire routine. Who cared if I only managed one set of everything? That one set was more than I'd done in the past two years combined! I was pooped, but I never really knew that feeling so horrible could actually make me feel so good. I was pumped, psyched and ready to take on the day.

I had to call Kayla.

A quick shower and shave gave me time to work on my approach. My goal was to have Kayla believe *she'd* made the pitch to get together. Sometimes a guy has to coax a woman into making the move even though he's the one who actually wants to get together. Women do it to men all the time. They call, pretend to want to talk and eventually get the guy to think that he's somehow missing something if they don't get together. She may be just looking for someone to pass time with, and he may have his own agenda, but if they don't get together nobody gets anything done, so they hook up. I needed a scam like that for Kayla. Last night, she let on that she was interested, which was perfect. She just needed to understand how truly interested she was.

When *my* phone rang, her level of interest was clear.

"Good morning, Sonny," she said cheerfully.

"What's up," I said, trying to sound as if I were still half asleep.

"I was wondering what you were up to today," she said.

"I'm just kind of chillin'," I answered.

"Kind of chillin'?" she asked, laughing.

"You know," I said, sitting at the edge of my bed. "I'm gonna do a little bit of this and little bit of that."

"A little bit of this and that?"

"Yeah," I said, feigning a yawn. "I'm gonna do some of this and some of that. I'll probably take a walk, read the paper, catch a movie, check my e-mail, maybe mow the grass, drink a glass of water. I got a few things working."

"That's very interesting, Sonny," she said. "It sounds as though you're trying to tell me you're busy."

My move was working. I hit her with everything but the kitchen sink. Unfortunately, she had the sink and I was the one who was hit.

"I'm sorry you're so busy," she told me.

"Why's that?" I asked.

"I actually was hoping you could stop by this morning," she said.

Nothing beats a woman who gets right to the point, I happily thought.

"But since you're so busy," she said, chuckling, "I guess I'll just have to make other arrangements."

Nothing's worse than a woman who gives up without a fight, I thought, concerned.

I had to clean things up in a hurry! She needed to know that I wasn't *busy* with anything besides trying to get her to get us together.

"If you want me to come by, I can," I told her.

"Are you sure?" she asked.

"Yeah," I answered.

"What time can you make it by?" she said.

She must be pressed, I thought, smiling. I should play hard to get.

"I'm already dressed," I replied in the midst of a sudden reality check. "What time you trying to hook up?"

"Hook up?" she asked, sounding surprised.

"Yeah, you know, like get together," I said, anxiously.

"I know what hook up means," she told me. "But I wasn't talking about hooking up."

"If you weren't talking about hooking up, what were you talking about?" I asked, worried.

"I wanted you to house-sit for a second."

"House-sit," I said, annoyed.

"Yes," she answered. "I have a delivery coming and I have to meet with a client. I really won't be too long and we can have lunch afterwards if you're not busy," she added.

Jeez, I thought, frustrated. She played *me*.

"So how about it?" she asked. "You think maybe you can handle it?"

"What's there to handle?" I countered. "I can house-sit

with the best of them. Just make sure the TV remote is in plain sight."

"I think I can handle that," she said, fumbling with some papers. "See you in a few."

I wasn't really dressed when she asked me about coming by so I threw on a pair of floppy Tommy Hilfiger jeans and a blue Fubu sweater. My look was casual-cool, which was a *major* step up from the SWAT-van sweatsuit I was sporting last night.

I was at her house in just a few minutes, and while I rang the doorbell I caught myself smiling as I thought about surprising her by making lunch while she was at her meeting. She answered the door in a beautiful navy-blue two-piece suit. Kayla definitely had a way with clothes. She was plenty big, but her clothes somehow made her look sleek, refined and classy. She looked important, confident and in control. Qualities that folks never expect to find in people who are overweight. She asked me how she looked and I immediately replied, "You look sharp!"

"You look nice too," she said, smiling. "I'm glad to see you own something besides a sweatsuit."

"Funny, Kayla," I said, shaking my head.

"I'm ready to go," she told me as we stepped inside. "KJ's new cage should be delivered in about an hour," she added. "The driver should make the switch, and just ask him to leave the old cage out on the deck."

"Wait a minute," I said quickly. "You asked me here to wait for a cage for KJ?"

"That's right, fat boy."

"Shut up, you stupid bird!" I yelled.

"KJ!" she said, scolding him.

I couldn't believe it. Talk about getting played.

"I'm sorry, Sonny," she said, reaching for her keys. "I didn't think it would bother you, plus I think you and KJ could stand some quality time together."

"Quality time?" I asked, annoyed.

"Once you two bond I think you'll get to like one another," she said, smiling.

"Bond?" I said, staring blankly.

"That's what she said, Big Wheels," blurted KJ.

"You stop that, KJ!" she said, pointing toward him.

I knew this was going to be a l-o-n-g afternoon. I looked at the cage—that stupid bird had turned his back on us!

"I won't be long," Kayla said before kissing me on the cheek. "The television is on in the basement and if you're hungry, the kitchen is all yours," she said, reaching for the door. "Have a good time."

Have a good time? How did she expect me to have a good time? She wanted me to bond with KJ and I wanted to bond with her. I couldn't believe she had actually called me to sit with her whacked-out bird. She might as well have asked me to shine Jonathan James Leslie's shoes while she was at it. This wasn't how I planned on spending my day off from work. Being stuck in Kayla's pad with a maniac bird that called me fat boy was worse than catching a cold at the beach in July.

I looked at KJ and thought, You make me sick. . . . I hope your birdseed gives you mad cow disease. . . . I wonder if you taste like chicken. . . .

Before I could figure out exactly how to work him into a nice stew or something, the delivery guy showed up with KJ's new cage. He was a well-groomed older man with a bushy head of white hair that was almost as bright as the ultra-white jumpsuit he was wearing. KJ's new spot was about twice the size of the cage he was in, which as far as I was concerned was twice as large as he needed in the first place. All he did was sit on his perch and occasionally turn his back on people after he had insulted them. He didn't need too much space to pull that off. Kayla could have put him on a Popsicle stick and thrown him under a clear colander, as far as I was concerned. There was no way KJ was worth the near-palatial digs the delivery guy was carrying through the door.

"A custom A-1000," he said, handing me an aluminum clipboard. "Please sign here, sir," he said with near-perfect diction.

I looked it over quickly and scribbled my name like I really knew what I was accepting. As I handed him the clipboard, I couldn't help but notice that he reeked of liquor. It really surprised me because I didn't think that a guy who spoke like Mr. French from *Family Affair* would show up to his job smelling like Otis the drunk from *Andy Griffith.*

"This is our top-of-the-line model, sir," he told me, walking toward KJ. "Titanium alloy bars, spring-loaded door, deluxe feeder, perpetual fresh water supply, sterling-silver perch with Astroturf, custom-grip padding," he said, shaking his head. "It doesn't get much better than this."

"How about that," I said, looking toward KJ. "The nice man is going to move you into your nice, new cage."

"We don't move birds from cages, we transfer inhabitants to new environments," he scoffed, walking toward KJ. "And the nice man doesn't execute transfers. Policy does not permit me to engage in the relocation process. That experience is reserved for the owner and/or his or her ward."

The relocation process . . . his or her *ward*, I thought, amused. *KJ ain't no ward, he's a stupid bird.*

"Well, the owner ain't here," I said, crossing my flabby arms. "So you can just leave it out there on the deck and I'm sure she'll move her *ward* when she returns."

"I am afraid that an arrangement of that sort will not accommodate our agreement," he told me. "Ms. Jennings traded in her A-500 for this new A-1000, so the A-500 will have to leave with me."

"That's cool," I said, smiling and looking toward KJ. "You can take the A-500 *and* the stupid bird that's in it."

"Well!" said the delivery guy in a huff.

"That's not funny, fat boy!" squawked KJ.

"Funny," I said, laughing. "What's funny is this guy calling you a *ward* when you're nothing but a stupid bird."

"Really," scoffed the delivery guy, turning away from me.

"Really," repeated KJ, who followed suit and also turned his back on me.

This was one ridiculous sight. The white-haired delivery guy in a bright-white jumpsuit with his back toward me on one end. Technicolor KJ with his back toward me on the other. And big ole me in the middle wearing my royal-blue Fubu sweater and still wondering if that dumb bird tasted like chicken.

"Sir, I must insist that you relocate the inhabitant," said the delivery guy, turning back toward me. "I do have several stops to make this morning. Nothing quite like this," he added, "just a few A-750's and an A-250. I would very much like to proceed. So if you could, sir, please transfer the winged ward."

"The winged ward?" I asked.

"Look, big fella," he said with an edge. "Could you just move da frickin' bird already!"

That got my attention.

"I guess I could move him," I said, looking toward the cage.

"Transfer, not move, transfer, not move," squealed KJ, spinning on his perch.

"Shaddup, ya stupid bird," said the delivery guy.

"Can you take the new cage out to the deck?" I asked.

"It's a custom A-1000," chirped KJ.

"I'll A-1000 your frickin' head if ya don't shut your beak!" yelled the delivery guy. "The name is Max," he said, reaching to shake my hand. "I hate these stupid birds, but delivering these overblown, overpriced cages pays the bills."

Amazingly KJ went silent. As I picked up the cage he edged closer toward me like I would help him. It was then that I realized he *was* a stupid bird.

We walked past the living room and out onto the deck. The weather was nice and moderate. Not cold and not hot. I guess it was just right for transferring a ward to a new environment.

"Okay, you stupid bird," I said, reaching toward the cage. "Big daddy's gonna move you into your brand-new cage."

"It's a custom A-1000," KJ reminded me.

"I told ya, shaddup already!" exclaimed Max, pulling a chrome-plated flask from his back pocket. "I bet ya taste just like chicken!"

This guy is a maniac, I thought, worried. He's scaring KJ to death. KJ's a maniac himself and the one thing a maniac fears is another maniac.

"It's okay, little buddy," I said as he backed away on his

perch. "Just hop on my finger and you'll be in your A-1000 in just a second."

"Hurry up and jump on his big, fat, finger, ya dingy bird!" said the delivery guy, wiping his face.

"It's okay, KJ," I reassured him. "We're just gonna relocate you to your new environment."

"Relocate, my ass!" said Max, before downing another swig from his flask. "I'll relocate his scrawny little neck if he doesn't hurry up and jump on your big, fat finger!"

"C'mon, KJ," I urged, keeping a worried eye on Max. "Why don't we hurry and transfer you to your new habitat?"

"Habitat, smabitat!" yelled Max, throwing his flask to the ground. "Get outta da way!"

He then rushed toward the cage and crashed into me. I quickly yanked my hand away before KJ could bite into it like he'd done just a day earlier. Max reached into the cage and flung his hand about like the drunk that he was. KJ couldn't wait. He bit into Max's hand like *it* tasted like chicken.

"Dag-on it!" Max yelled, grabbing his hand and falling to the deck. "I'll kill ya, ya crazy bird!"

"Ya have to catch me first, stupid!" KJ answered.

And with that he ruffled his feathers, ducked his head and flew out of his cage and high into the sky away from Kayla's house. Watching KJ romp into the clouds was like seeing Olympic champion sprinter Michael Johnson fly down the backstretch of the 200-meter dash. It was quick, it was awesome and it was a blur. Max was on the ground groaning. KJ had literally flown the coop. And it struck me that when Kayla came back home, I'd be in big trouble.

As Max laid sprawled on the deck, the phone rang. I

walked inside and headed toward the kitchen. The answering machine kicked in and a familiar voice came through the speaker.

"Hi, Sonny," she said cheerfully. "It's okay to pick up. This is Kayla."

"Hello," I answered, retrieving the shiny black handset.

"Hey," she said enthusiastically. "My client didn't show, so I'm on my way home. I forgot to tell you that I traded in KJ's old cage, so the delivery guy won't be able to leave it out on the deck."

"I'm hip," I answered.

"You're hip?"

"Yeah, I'm hip," I repeated. "He's here right now."

"Oh, my goodness," she said, alarmed. "I'd better get a move on. I'd like to talk with him before he leaves. I'm in the car so I'm not going to talk long, Sonny," she added. "I'll be there in just a second. Ask him to keep KJ's cage inside the house."

"It's already on the deck," I said, worried.

"No, Sonny," she said forcefully. "Tell me that KJ's cage is not on the deck."

"I can't tell you his cage ain't on the deck because it *is* on the deck."

"I don't think you understand me," she said, obviously annoyed. "Reassure me that KJ is nowhere near the deck."

"Now, that I can guarantee," I said, looking toward the backyard. "KJ is nowhere near the deck."

"Good!" she exclaimed.

"I think I need to tell you something, Kayla."

"Tell me when I get there," she said before hanging up.

I rushed back to the deck, stepped over Max and searched the sky for KJ.

"K-k-k-k—J-j-j-j— K-k-k-k—J-j-j-j!" I yelled nervously. "Come back, you stupid bird!"

"What the heck happened?" said Max, shaking his head and standing.

"KJ flew out of his cage," I told him, still hoping to locate Kayla's long-gone bird. "And his owner is on her way home."

"The bird flew the coop?" he asked, brushing himself off.

"You *let* him fly the coop," I reminded him. "You reached in his cage, and he bit your hand and he jetted."

"That's a bunch of crap! I would never do such a thing. A maneuver of that sort would violate policy," he said, standing back and quickly recovering the perfect diction that had escaped him just moments earlier. "As a matter of record, we are not permitted to assist in transferring an inhabitant to a new environment."

"I ain't tryin' to hear that," I told him, walking to the other end of the deck in search of KJ. "You f'ed up, Max."

"With all due respect," he said, shaking his head, "I feel it is necessary for me to report this unfortunate incident to my home office."

"Report what incident?" said a chilling voice that froze both of us.

"Kayla," I said, slowly turning around.

"What's going on here?" she snapped.

"Good day ma'am," Max quickly answered. "It appears your acquaintance here has somehow misplaced your ward."

"My ward?" she said, surprised.

"Yeah," I interrupted. "He's talking about KJ."

"Where is KJ?" she said, walking toward his cage.

"He left?" I answered, half asking and half responding to her question.

"What do you mean he left?" she fired back.

"You see, ma'am," Max eloquently stated, "your inhabitant departed his A-500 while this gentleman was attempting a transfer to the A-1000. He clearly resented the inhabitant and your winged ward sensed that. At some point during the attempted transfer the inhabitant elected to vacate the A-500."

"Inhabitant . . . winged ward . . . he elected to vacate?" Kayla said, stunned.

"Indeed," Max replied.

"It means he flew the coop," I added.

"How can you say that, Sonny?" Kayla asked. "This is all your fault. You never liked KJ. You probably wanted him to get away."

"I don't think so," I told her. "Your man here, Max—"

"Maxwell, sir," he interrupted. "Patrick Solomon Maxwell."

"Whatever," I said, exasperated. "Anyway, Kayla," I went on. "Max here got a little drunk, so he reached in KJ's cage."

"We do not call them cages, sir," he said, correcting me. "We refer to them as environments."

"Whatever," I said. "Max got tanked, he tried to grab KJ and KJ took a bite out of crime. KJ flew off like the witch in *The Wizard of Oz* and Max passed out like a pig at a pork festival."

"That's Max*well*," he reminded me.

"Check out his finger," I said, pointing toward him. "His flask is right here," I added, picking it up.

"Gimme that," he said, quickly grabbing the flask.

"You did this!" Kayla yelled, marching toward him. She then slapped him and he spun around and wound up on the rail of the deck shaking like a plate of warm Jell-O. Undaunted, Kayla edged closer to him and angrily said, "You tried to grab my bird. I should kick your . . ."

Before I found out exactly what she was going to kick, Kayla shoved Max. He flew over the side of the deck and splashed into the pool. Kayla grabbed Max's flask, which he had dropped to the deck, and tossed it over the side. Amazingly, Max reached for the flask just as it hit the water and wasted little time trying to finish it off. As he tilted his head back, KJ sprang from a tree in the backyard and swooped down toward Max's head. Water flew all over, like a garden hose gone mad, and Max panicked to cover his head while he yelled, "I'll kill ya, ya crazy bird," as KJ flew toward us on the deck. KJ gracefully flew into his new *cage* and gently dropped what appeared to be a tiny white rug to the base of the A-1000.

"You bring back my hair, ya crazy bird!" yelled Max, embarrassed.

"You get outta my pool, ya crazy drunk!" Kayla answered forcefully.

Max, of course, climbed out of the pool, reached for his flask, again tilted his head back and made his way toward the gate.

Kayla moved toward the cage, gently shut the door and then reached for my hand.

"I'm sorry," she whispered.

"Sorry about what?" I asked, concerned.

"I'm sorry for accusing you," she said softly. "I should have known you wouldn't do anything like that."

"Yeah," I said, smiling. "KJ's my man."

"Not quite, fat boy," KJ blurted out.

"KJ!" Kayla yelled.

"It's okay, Kayla," I said, reaching for his cage and taking it inside. "KJ's a bird, so he has a bird brain," I told her, laughing. "He probably doesn't know what's fat and what isn't."

"I know you're fat, fat boy," he squawked.

"KJ!" Kayla exclaimed.

"Don't sweat it, Kayla," I said, reaching for her hand. "He reacts when you react."

Then I looked her dead in the eye and, again, we caught fire as we had last night. We embraced and kissed. It was magic. Total and complete David Copperfield–style magic. She looked toward the ground and then up at me.

"I think I like you," she said, smiling.

"I *know* that I like *you*," I told her.

"I think I like you a lot," she said, stroking my hand.

"I *know* I like *you* a lot," I said, nodding my head.

She then kissed me and moved her lips toward my ears.

"Let's take this upstairs," she whispered.

"That's a plan," I answered happily.

And what a plan it was. I had stopped by 7-Eleven on my way to her place and this time picked up a pack of the blue Trojans . . . just in case. She stepped into the kitchen and returned carrying a shiny silver platter with a bowl of red, ripe-looking strawberries and another bowl with what looked to be smooth chocolate sauce. That actually didn't surprise me. I figured someone like Kayla couldn't even pull off a move to the bedroom without getting her eat on. As we walked toward the stairs I chuckled as I thought about how

KJ used Max's hairpiece as wall-to-wall carpeting in his new A-1000 *environment.*

Kayla pushed aside the door to her bedroom, stepped in and then hit a light switch. The blinds had been drawn and the lights were extremely dim so I could barely see a thing. This wasn't such a bad sign. I figured if we were going to be forced to actually look at each other naked with the lights on, it would be a turn-off of monumental proportions. She walked into the bathroom and said, softly, "I'll be right back, just make yourself comfortable."

I wondered just who was zooming who. Was I the man because I thought to pick up the Trojans . . . just in case? Or was she in control because she knew I wanted her and had everything choreographed? It didn't matter. I was where I wanted to be and with who I wanted to be. I sat on the side of the bed and wondered, as I had last night, if women the size of Kayla wore lingerie. I wondered what to expect and how I would react since it had been such a long time since I'd had any action. I wondered if the blue Trojans would still work for overweight guys as big as me, and I wondered if I could still get it up at the drop of a hat. A slow but steady rise in my lap gave me a quick answer to that question. But I had one more question that for now would go unanswered.

I still wondered if KJ tasted like chicken.

THE REASONS WE LOSE WEIGHT

Lame Reason

Seasonal Changes

I love women when the weather breaks. Swim-suits. Thongs. Bikinis. I'm with all that. My only problem with the summer is that there are way too many big-butt women who insist on forc-ing their flabby bottoms into something Twiggy couldn't even wear. Think about it—these women pig out on Thanksgiving, they eat everything in sight at Christmas, they drink, eat, sleep and drink even more during the New Year, go to Super Bowl *parties and stuff themselves so much that they couldn't tell you who won the game and then, they expect to force their cellulite-soaked tails into somebody's supertight, spaghetti-strapped bathing suit right in time for Memorial Day. Does it make any sense to you? Me neither.*

—*Chester "Chet" Melvin Stewart*

The Main Course

Chapter 12

Chicken, I thought as Kayla did whatever she was doing in the bathroom. You haven't had a good piece of chicken in nearly a week, I reminded myself.

Almost on cue, Kayla popped out from the bathroom, ooh-la-la! She wore a frilly satin red floor-length robe. It covered her just enough to keep me guessing about how big she actually was. Her toe and fingernails were ablaze with glossy red polish that tastefully accented the robe and her lips. She carried a matching red candle in one hand, which she placed on the nightstand beside the platter with the strawberries and the chocolate sauce. She then reached to turn off the lights (as if it weren't already dark enough) and sat beside me on the edge of the bed. The flickering light of the candle bounced off her chubby cheeks as she reached for my hand and smiled.

I used my other hand to reach for my pocket to get the blue Trojans . . . just in case.

"Are you comfortable?" she asked, smiling.

Who wouldn't be comfortable? I wondered.

"I'm all right," I answered, trying to appear cool.

"Good," she said, arranging some pillows at the head of the bed. "Why don't you just lean back here."

I had taken my shoes and shirt off the moment she hit the bathroom so I wasn't too worried about screwing up her comforter. I leaned back and played the role like a champ. I was very nervous. But she didn't need to know that. She turned on the radio, lay beside me, turned her face toward mine and kissed me with a newfound passion. Her tongue was as hot as a jalapeño pepper on top of spicy nachos. Her right hand moved across the flab that was supposed to be my chest and her left hand stroked my Jell-O-like side.

As Stevie Wonder's seventies dream-driven ballad "Creepin'" played on the radio, I thought, The only thing that could creep up in here is Free Willy.

The song kept playing and I kept trying to flip my leg over hers. It was like trying to roll a tree trunk up a hill with a pencil. We were still kissing like two teenagers who had been locked together by their braces when finally, I managed to roll on top of her. At that point our lips separated. I doubt even a giraffe would have had a long enough neck to keep kissing between stomachs as large as ours. Embarrassed, I kicked my legs back and forth, which only left me rocking on top of her.

You've never been with a woman this big; you must be using the wrong move. You gotta work your leg back to the side.

I tried desperately to again flip my leg to the side. Kayla, obviously concerned for her overall health and well-being, tried to gently push me off her. Between the two of us and Stevie Wonder sadly singing *"Why must it be that you always cree-e-e-p,"* we managed to finally roll me off. Unfortunately, it happened so fast that we held on to each other. She then rolled and ended up on top of me, and my hand somehow ended up in the bowl of strawberries.

I hurried to pop one in my mouth.

"Sonny," she said, chuckling. "I don't know if this is going to work."

"Why won't it?" I replied, reaching for another strawberry.

"Honestly," she answered, reaching for a berry of her own. "I've never been with a guy as large as you."

"I know what you mean," I told her, dipping another berry into the chocolate sauce. "I've never been with a woman who's nearly as big as me."

"So what do we do?" she asked, grabbing another strawberry.

We should lose some f-ing weight, I thought, ashamed.

"Maybe we should take our clothes off and then try to see what we *can* do," I answered, biting into yet another strawberry.

"You sure?" she said, finally deciding to do the romantic thing and feed me a strawberry.

"Yeah, I'm sure," I answered, excited. "Hey, could you dip that in some chocolate?" I asked, referring to the strawberry she was dangling over my mouth.

She dropped the berry in the sauce and then into my mouth. I bit into it and wondered exactly what to expect when we were finished undressing. I also wondered if she had more strawberries downstairs because we'd already knocked off the first bowl. Kayla flopped onto the bed and I knew it was time for me to take care of business. We'd already kissed like newlyweds and the strawberries were the best-tasting foreplay I'd ever had. I hadn't been with a woman since Marsha dumped me a year earlier, so I was plenty ready. Thankfully, the blue Trojan fit perfectly and after just a few unintentional pokes at her flab that made me *think* I'd found the right spot, I made my way inside her and was off to the races.

Unfortunately, "off to the races" was far too literal a term.

A year away from the strain and pleasure of sexual regularity coupled with an unexpected overwhelming surge of excitement put me into what many label as "early overdrive." The sexual experience I'd wished for and had even shown the foresight to pick up the blue Trojans for lasted a fat forty-five seconds.

Okay. So maybe it was more like thirty seconds.

I wanted it to last longer, and with me it usually does, but I was as out of control as a 2 Live Crew video. It reminded me of the very first time I had sex. I was seventeen and was dating a woman named Charlotte. She was a senior at George Washington University and we eagerly discussed our post-graduation plans. Charlotte was heading to law school. And I was considering "furthering my studies" in marketing with a concentration in sales. I had my rap down and she was as impressed with me as I was with her but I never quite figured out how to tell her I was only a *high school* senior. And I didn't think she would understand that my studies in marketing with a concentration in sales were directly tied to an application to work at Foot Locker at Landover Mall.

She wanted to celebrate on the night of her commencement. I had spent hours convincing her it would be a total waste for her to go back home to Texas without experiencing a *real* man. (As fate would have it, I wasn't about to hook her up with a *real* man, so her experience was going to be a big-time waste). I'm certain she was struck by that fact when soon after I clumsily found my way in, she gently urged me to "Slow down, baby, I'm not going anywhere."

"Slow down?" I said, panting. "I'm already done."

"Is that it?" I remembered her asking.

"Of course that's it," I wanted to tell her. "Doesn't the fact that I'm trying to sleep tell you that that's it?"

I couldn't believe I'd one day be forced to relive that experience.

"Is that it?" Kayla asked, sounding very much like Charlotte.

"Huh?" I answered, pretending to be exhausted.

"It's over?" she asked, annoyed. "I put all this together, negligee, candles, soft music, strawberries and chocolate," she was looking toward the ceiling, "and you give me thirty lousy seconds?"

I was feeling pretty bad. Just as I had when I'd lost it with Charlotte. Only this time I felt much worse. Charlotte didn't have strawberries. Kayla was out of strawberries. And all I wanted to do was I wanted sleep.

"Sonny," she said, sitting up and crossing her arms. "I'm

surprised you weren't able to handle yourself. I never figured you for that type." She smiled. "I didn't think that big, bad Sonny Walker would turn out to be a minute man."

"A minute man!" I shot back.

"Oops," she said, laughing. "I'm sorry, sweetie. I've got to give credit where credit is due. I guess I should have called you a thirty-second man."

What the heck was I supposed to say? She had me. As far as she knew I *was* a thirty-second man. Couldn't she tell I was just a little too excited? Didn't she know I hadn't done it in over a year? Did I actually last a full thirty seconds? Did she have any more strawberries in the kitchen?

"Yo, Kayla," I started.

"Hold up now, Mr. Sonny," she said, shaking her head and finger.

"Hold up?" I asked.

"Hold up," she repeated, laughing. "Don't hit me with that 'yo' stuff. 'Yo' is a term better suited for a *real* man. A man of control who is *in* control," she added, still laughing.

Jeez, I thought, embarrassed.

"Look, Sonny," she said, reaching for my hand. "I'm sorry. Jonathan and I haven't done anything in a long time." She sighed. "I guess I'm just frustrated," she said, slowly shaking her head. "I don't even know why we did this in the first place."

"We did it because we wanted to do it," I reminded her.

"I know that," she answered. "But we can't just do things solely because we want to do them."

The heck we can't, I thought.

"I want you to respect me," she told me. "I don't want you to think I'm a loose woman because I'm not," she added.

"I know you're not loose," I said, looking her in the eye. "I was here just like you. And I certainly wouldn't want you to think I'm loose," I said.

"That's cute." She sighed. "But everybody knows it doesn't work like that for men. Men can sleep with whomever they choose and no one calls them loose."

"You're right about that." I chuckled. "They don't call them loose, they just call them dogs."

"You're not a dog, are you?" she whispered, drawing close to me.

"Hardly," I confided. "That whole collar thing doesn't work for me."

She then kissed me and we fell back onto the bed. Our eyes seemed to meet at the same spot in the ceiling and she whispered, "Why don't we do something?"

"We just did something," I answered.

"*You* just did something," she said, laughing. "I mean, why don't we go somewhere?"

"Somewhere like where?" I asked.

"Why don't we go away for the weekend?" she said. "I think it will give us the chance to get to know each other."

"Let's make it happen," I said, reaching for her hand.

"Let's do that," she said, nodding her head.

"Yo, Kayla," I said, sitting up. "Let me ask you something."

"Let you ask me something," she repeated, sitting up and covering herself with a sheet. "This sounds serious."

"It ain't all that serious," I answered. "I'm just trying to find out one thing."

"What is it, Sonny?" she asked, obviously concerned. "Is something wrong?"

"Naw. Nothing's wrong," I told her, smiling. "I'm just trying to see if you have any more strawberries downstairs."

She just laughed, wrapped herself in a huge towel (which almost made it all the way around her body) and hurried downstairs. We fed each other strawberries dipped in chocolate and promised to stick with our FutraSystem plan.

I was hoping all this meant we were on our way.

I took two weeks off for my regular vacation, and on the last day called that no-good Andy and he told me I could be out a few more days. Jonathan James Leslie told Kayla he had plans and would be unavailable, so he paved the way for us to hang out. We drove to Atlantic City and spent two wonderful nights at the Tropicana. We walked on the beach, sat and watched the sun set, and later rise the next morning. We even made a huge sand castle.

"This is where we'll put KJ's cage" she said, pointing toward the rear of the castle.

"If that's the case I'm moving," I said, smiling.

"Not without me," she answered.

She was right. I wasn't going anyplace without her. Being with Kayla was better than a Wendy's triple-cheese with ketchup, mustard, pickles, onions *and* an order of biggie fries topped off with a Frosty (large, of course). We connected. We grew closer. And we made love. She found I was much more than a thirty-second man. And I found that "big girls" have a wondrous blend of sexuality, sensuality and good old-fashioned romance.

Before we left the Tropicana, Kayla made it clear she wanted to play the slots one last time. It didn't surprise me when she headed for the *jumbo* slots and she wasn't too disappointed that she didn't line up three cherries for a jackpot.

It didn't matter.

As we headed west onto Route 40 and back toward Maryland, I smiled. Who needs the slots? I thought, as she reached for my hand. We've already hit the jackpot.

Chapter 13

At least I thought we'd hit the jackpot. While we were in Atlantic City, I learned more about Kayla's company. She was her own CEO, accountant, secretary and everything in between, so she spent a ton of time on the phone arranging meetings, closing contracts and trouble-shooting computer systems gone wrong. I found that Kayla was *very* focused on her business. When we weren't eating or enjoying the shows in the casinos, she was working on her laptop. I usually made my way to the hotel's fitness center and did what exercises I could and would return to find her still typing away, downloading files, surfing the Net or advising clients about the programs and software she'd designed. They seemed to trust her and she told me that service and support were her strong points and that she was so committed to her clientele because she counted on them for referrals.

"Computers are computers, programs are programs, and software is software," Kayla casually remarked over a dinner-size snack one afternoon. "If your clients know you stand behind what you sell and that you'll be available for advice, upgrades and support, they'll beat a path to your door. And once I hook a big fish, I'll be cooking with Crisco," she added, downing her favorite drink, a Diet Coke.

She shared with me that she'd landed a major meeting with a company that could put her on the map. If she secured a contract with them, she'd double her already top-shelf income and would be open to even more business with even bigger companies. She felt it was important to dazzle them with an elegant suit that would put them at ease with her size, while at the same time taking the focus away from her waistline and putting it on her brain and her skills, where it belonged. We decided to hit a mall, where she could pick up an outfit that would carry her through the meeting.

"Nordstrom has a great women's department," she confided. "But I don't want to overdo it. I want something that's subtle, but that says I'm all about business. That's not always the easiest thing in the world because it seems like most of the designers still don't recognize that larger-size women want and many times *need* to look good too."

"That's not so much a problem for me," I replied. "I don't do the dress-up thing that often, so I just go with whatever's closest in the closet."

"I can tell," she said, smiling as we pulled into the well-maintained parking lot at Prince Georges Plaza.

"What's that supposed to mean?" I asked, locating a parking space near the front of the mall.

"I didn't mean anything, Sonny," she replied. "I just noticed that you have a really nice casual thing. Shopping for casual clothes is so much easier than trying to find dress wear and business attire."

"It wouldn't be so hard if we weren't so big," I said, laughing.

"It shouldn't make a difference," she reminded me, opening her door.

We walked into the mall and headed right for Weatherby's Northeast Emporium, a Collington Park, Maryland, department store that specialized in high-medium-range clothing and gifts. An escalator carried us upstairs, where we passed the juniors department, which was ablaze with brightly colored designer clothes, heart-pounding music, throbbing neon lights and well-placed TV monitors flashing the latest hip-hop and dance-music videos. The misses department, which had fashionable-looking clothes from size fourteen on down, was equally as nice. The monitors there were tuned to VH-1, which was running Michael Jackson's classic "Thriller" video. A bright-orange-neon light stretched across to the juniors department, suggesting a kinship of sorts. The salespeople, who doubled as cashiers, appeared to be attentive, friendly and were very attractive, and the tasteful displays and mannequins captured the energy and excitement the store undoubtedly wanted to pass on to its customers.

When we hit the women's department it was clear we were in for trouble.

No music.

No televisions.

And mannequins that appeared to be stunning size eights!

In a department for women cruising the size fourteen and up highway, these mannequins proved to be real dummies.

It didn't hurt that they had a guy in a bright-white chef's costume, with baggy shorts and white knee-high silk socks, waltzing about with a silver-plated tray of tiny, hot-dog-style snacks. Kayla, of course, grabbed a few and then made her way to the racks. She spent several minutes searching the racks, but the clothes were pretty pathetic. I couldn't imagine exactly who would want to be found dead in some of that crap. I saw frilly little-girl dresses blown up to monumental proportions, dull, monochromatic outfits with sewn-on appliqués that would have been outdated in the seventies and cheap-looking shirts and blouses that appeared to be little more than king-sized sheets with buttons and collars attached. Amazingly, Kayla managed to locate three outfits she thought had at least a chance of working. But she absolutely refused to let me see their sizes as she hurried to the dressing room. She did, however, promise to let me see her in the outfits before she bought anything.

That was a decision she would soon regret.

Moments later, Kayla slowly walked out of the fitting room wearing the first outfit. The guy with the snack tray stood beside me as she made her way to a three-sided mirror that showed all of us more than we needed to see. As she turned around to capture herself from all angles, I was having a hard time imagining how she squeezed herself into that blue pantsuit—it looked like it was suffocating her wayward body.

The salesperson, who was a young, reed-thin twenty-something with bleached-blond hair and snug-fitting black denim jeans, was in a state of disbelief as well.

"Doesn't do a thing for you," the salesperson said, smacking on some bubblegum. "Too tight across the backside," she added.

"Have a hot dog?" the snack guy asked me. He then looked at Kayla and shook his disapproval at the outfit.

I just shook my head no. Unfortunately, Kayla turned toward me at that very moment. It was obvious she thought I was saying no to her, but I was turning down a hot dog. She angrily walked in my direction and forcefully grabbed a tiny, cheese-covered frank from the tray.

"Those are pretty good," the snack guy whispered to me as Kayla headed back into the dressing room. "She's packing it in there, ain't she?" he asked.

He was right. But it was none of his business. I wasn't about to make a scene, especially since I'd dealt with idiots like him a thousand times before and knew he was too ignorant to waste time with.

After just a few minutes she returned wearing a modest navy-blue pantsuit that fit, but had even less pop and pizzazz than a generic jar of yellow mustard.

"That's a little nicer," the salesperson said, blowing a round, pink bubble with her gum. "But you might want to consider something a little more slenderizing."

"We had little cheeseburgers yesterday," the snack guy told me. "You ever seen big women put away baby cheeseburgers?" he added, laughing.

He might have thought it was funny, but Kayla sure didn't. She looked toward me and I didn't know what to do. If I nodded my approval, it would have been worse than giving her a gift certificate to a cabin on the *Titanic* because the suit was so bad she would have been sunk. And if I shook my head no it may have pissed her off, which would have left me sunk. My options were limited and time wasn't on my side. I looked at her intently, and tried all at once to raise my eyebrows, nod my head, shake my head, tilt my head *and* shrug my shoulders. The fact that I could manage only a crooked smile that fell somewhere between complete uncertainty and utter panic didn't help.

She simply raised her shoulders, let out a major-league huff and marched toward the snack tray, where she snatched up a smallish, dough-laced hot dog.

"If you guys hang around for another hour or so, I think maybe I can get you some cheesecake," the snack guy told me. "You a cheesecake guy? You sure look like a cheesecake guy to me." He grinned.

I didn't respond and didn't bother asking him what a cheesecake guy looked like. I guess I was just happy he didn't take me for a "two or three cheesecake guy," which is what I actually was.

I could tell Kayla wasn't about to give the third outfit a chance. She just walked away and did a really *l-o-n-g* double take as she passed the mirror. I didn't know what to do or what to say, but I could tell she was upset. Between that obnoxious salesgirl, the dumb and dumber snack guy, my complete lack of input and clothes as lame as crabcakes made with imitation, store-brand crabmeat, she had to feel embarrassed, frustrated and downright miserable. I felt so sorry for her because I'd never run into a problem like this.

I could get away with triple *X* and call it a day. Once I got really big, I didn't much care what my clothes looked like. As long as it was dark, it worked for me. During the day I wore a uniform to work and I gave up on clothes the very moment I started to gain weight. Foot Locker was the main source of my wardrobe. They didn't sell "meeting clothes" and since I wasn't meeting with anybody about anything anyway, clothes were pretty much a nonissue. But it was obvious that Kayla and women like her had a real problem. The plus-size clothes were cheap-looking and were always displayed on mannequins that were ten sizes too small. Style simply wasn't a premium that the designers or the stores usually attached to large women.

As Kayla worked her way into her own clothes in the fitting room, I couldn't help but overhear two other "before picture"–size shoppers move about the racks. I couldn't figure who or what was worse. The shoppers were pretty bad off. But the salesgirl, who was now engaged in a clearly meaningless telephone conversation, made their situation seem even worse.

"Why are these skirts so long?" asked one of the shoppers of her friend.

"Because after it stretches over your big behind it will barely hit your knees," the salesgirl said into the phone, making sure the shoppers didn't hear her.

"Why don't they have leggings here?" said the other customer to her shopping mate.

"You don't need leggings," the salesgirl said to her caller. "You need a chainsaw to chop off those tree trunks you call legs."

"I don't know why they don't have them here," the other shopper answered. "I've been trying to find me a nice red pair to go with my red sweater. You know, the one with the big snowflakes that I wore to the ski trip?"

"If she had snowflakes on a sweater for her big butt, they must have looked like a blizzard," said the salesgirl, shaking her head.

"Isn't this the cutest little dress?" asked one shopper of her friend, holding a bright-blue one-piece up to her body. "If I had one of those tiny pillbox hats, I'd look just like Jackie O."

"First of all, the dress *is* cute, but there's nothing *little* about it," the salesgirl said into the phone. "And second, the only Jackie O. you'd look like is Jackie Overweight," she added, finally finishing her call.

Both shoppers headed toward the register and the salesgirl greeted them with one of those "I shoulda been in pictures" salesperson smiles.

"How are you ladies today?" she asked, searching for the price tag for the rather large, bright-blue dress.

"Oh, we're just fine," answered one of the customers. "Is this on sale today?"

"It sure is," the salesgirl replied, scanning the price tag. "It's twenty percent off. You might want to consider a cute little pillbox hat to top it off." She leaned toward them. "It'll give you that Jackie O. look," she whispered, smiling.

They grinned like they'd won free groceries for life from Safeway and made a beeline to the hat department. Kayla walked out of the fitting room just a few minutes later and placed the suits she'd tried on on a counter behind the cash register.

"Sorry you couldn't find anything that fit today," the salesgirl remarked, smiling.

"I couldn't find anything I really cared for," Kayla replied, walking away.

"You might want to come back on the weekend," the sales-girl said, again reaching for the phone. "We're getting some larger sizes in on Saturday."

"Whatever," Kayla muttered, stepping onto the escalator.

"We're having ice cream on Saturday too!" the snack guy yelled as we made our way downstairs.

We hurried out of the store and headed back into the mall, where the sticky-sweet smell of a Cinnabon store quickly latched onto our nostrils. Kayla wasted little time ordering *three* full-size cinnamon rolls and, of course, a large Diet Coke. She located a tiny table and two tiny wooden chairs, where we sat and she attacked the rolls.

"Let's go," she said, standing up and walking toward a trash can.

"Hold up, Kayla," I said, reaching for her hand. "You can't keep eating like this."

"Not you too," she said, glaring at me. "I know you're not about to start pressing me about my weight like everybody else."

"I don't know who everybody else is, and I'm not talking about your weight," I stressed. "I care about you and your health, and you aren't doing yourself any favors by eating the way you're eating." I shook my head. "You can weigh what you want to weigh; that's not my concern. But I do care about your health and you've got to slow your roll."

"Slow my roll?" she asked, raising her eyebrows.

"Yeah," I answered, smiling. "You need to slow your roll."

"Explain that one to me, Sonny," she said, not nearly as upset as she was just moments earlier.

"You eat so fast you don't even have time to blink," I told her, starting to laugh.

She just smiled.

"Look!" I told her, pointing away.

"Look at what?" she asked, her head inching back.

"You missed it," I told her.

"I missed what, Sonny?" she asked.

"That's how fast you eat," I said, pointing toward her and nodding my head. "You blaze through food so fast I bet you don't even see it."

"I can't help it, Sonny," she said, sounding embarrassed. "I just like the way food tastes. I guess it's why I eat so fast. Is that so wrong?"

"There it goes again," I answered, smiling. "Look, I'm into you Kayla and your weight doesn't bother me like I thought it would. There's nothing wrong with liking the way food tastes. I should know, I *love* the way it tastes. But I just want you to slow down." I looked her in the eye. "If you eat a little slower, take the time to take more chews and get the chance to really taste what you're eating, maybe you'll eat a little less just because it takes more time."

"That works for you?" she asked.

"It has since I started this FutraSystem crap," I said, laughing.

"Speaking of FutraSystem," she said. "Do you realize we've missed a couple of meetings already?"

"How could I not realize it?" I answered. "Eleanor probably has my number programmed into her speed dial. She's called me a few times already—'You won't lose all that weight sitting at home, Mr. Walker. We need to see you before we lose you, Mr. Walker.' " I laughed, imitating her.

She laughed right along with me before hugging me and saying, "Thanks, Sonny."

"Thanks?" I asked, surprised. "Thanks for what?"

"Thanks for caring," she said, kissing me on the cheek. "Most men would only tell a woman to eat less for their own selfish reasons. But I can tell you're sincere about what you say, and that really means a great deal to me."

"Maybe one day I'll mean a lot to you," I said, grasping her hand and walking away from the table.

"Maybe," she said, leaning her head on my shoulder.

We walked through the mall and ended up in front of a store called Ashley Stewart that billed itself as a shop featuring "fashions for the beautiful, larger-size woman." As soon as we stepped past the entrance the differences smacked us like the cascading aroma from a spiral-sliced honeybaked ham. The music was live, the store was bright and well lit, and the clothes were like real clothes in real stores, only larger. To our surprise, the mannequins appeared to have the same type of weight issues we had and the sales force, each of whom was very attentive and *very* attractive, looked like they could stand to lose a few pounds too.

In a day of major minuses, Ashley Stewart turned out to be a big-time plus. Kayla found a beautiful black stretch-silk, wide-leg pantsuit created by her favorite designer, plus-size specialist Christina Covington. Kayla bragged that Christina Covington *had* to be a larger-size woman because her clothes and designs were simply too good.

"Whoever designs her clothes has been through the crap I've been through," she said, nodding her head. "The cheap fabrics, the lack of style and imagination and dresses that look like drapes," she added in a huff. "It's sickening."

The cashier, who had also helped her select the pantsuit, nodded her head in approval while wrapping up the outfit.

"If I were a size eight or even a size ten, I'd be able to find anything I wanted," Kayla continued. "So Christina Covington's clothes mean a lot to me because they're what I'm all about." She smiled. "I may have big curves but they're *my* curves and I want my clothes to reflect who I am. I work hard, I make *very good* money, I feel great about who I am, and Christina Covington's clothes allow all of that to come through. They're worth every penny and I'm glad someone finally decided it was okay for larger women to look and feel beautiful."

Before Kayla left the register she opened an Ashley Stewart charge account, was assigned a fashion "partner" who would help her manage and build upon her already sharp wardrobe and was invited to bring a friend to a special showing of the store's fall line of clothes, outerwear and accessories. They even gave her discount subscription cards for two different magazines that catered to plus-size women—*Belle* and *MODE*.

What impressed me most was that everything about Ashley Stewart almost seemed to celebrate being big. No one uttered a word about being overweight. They saw their customers as larger-size capable women and not overindulgent slobs. There were mirrors all over the place, which was something people with weight problems weren't used to, and the sales staff knew their stock and absolutely knew what would and wouldn't work on their clientele. They were brash. They were sexy. They were smart. And it was obvious they believed that if bigger wasn't better, it certainly could be beautiful.

It felt good, really, really good, to be in a setting where overweight, oversize people weren't made to feel like they were suffering.

In fact, it was as if the staff weren't going to allow us to feel like overweight, oversize, overeating, problem-riddled buffoons with pressures and attitudes tied directly to our waistlines and appetites.

They liked who they were and it was obvious that, besides favoring our business, they wanted only for us to be who we were.

People.

Chapter 14

We left the mall and I dropped Kayla at her place. Surprisingly, as she opened the door, she turned around, winked, and then hit me with a move I had avoided since the day Marsha lowered the boom on me. The dreaded "bye-bye" wave. Though being with Kayla made me feel totally at ease, a major jolt of tension rolled through me when she threw the "bye-bye" wave my way. I knew something I wasn't trying to deal with was about to happen and called my answering machine from the truck expecting the worst.

I had two messages.

"Yo, Chubbs," the first message started. "Where's your big behind hidin'?" There was a pause. "Anyway, big fella, I guess you ain't there, so give me a shout, dawg." It was Chet. And since Chet never calls anybody, I knew something was up.

"Hey, Sonny," said the caller on the second message. "I was just checking on you, pal. I wanted to see if you were sticking with your exercise program and how your diet was going. Give me a buzz when you get settled."

My man, E, I thought, smiling. I was on a high. No bad news and no major "bye-bye"-wave-style trauma.

I decided to call E first. I didn't want Chet to ruin my good mood.

"Hey, money," I said when E answered the phone.

"Sonny, what's up, buddy?"

"Ain't nothing," I answered, rolling down Central Avenue.

"How's the diet?"

"I'm taking care of business, E," I said, proudly. "I just went to Atlantic City and I barely ate a thing."

"What were you doing in Atlantic City?" he asked.

"I went down there with a lady friend," I answered, making a left onto Addison Road.

"What lady friend?" he answered, surprised. "Did you and Marsha get back together or something?"

"No, me and Marsha didn't hook back up or something," I told him. "I went up there with Kayla."

"Who's Kayla?"

"I told you about her a few weeks ago."

"You mean the big girl!" he shouted.

"Her name is Kayla," I told him flatly.

"Hold on, Sonny," he said, laughing.

I figured he was taking a call on his other line, but he wasn't. He was calling Chet on a three-way.

"Hey, Chet," E said, still laughing. "I found your boy."

"You found whose boy?" Chet asked, unimpressed.

"I've got Sonny on the line," he said. "And he just got back in town."

"Where's your big behind been?" asked Chet.

"What's up, Chet?" I asked, pulling into my parking space.

"Ain't nothing up. Where you coming from?" he asked, laughing. "The f-ing fat farm or something?"

"I went to visit your momma and her daughter on their chain gang and then I rolled up to Atlantic City 'cause they had already broken their rocks for the day," I said, laughing.

"That's cold, Sonny," E said, trying to hold in a laugh.

"He may be cold, but he's sure nuff a big m-f," Chet joked.

"Tell Chet who you went with," urged E.

"You went with somebody?" Chet said, surprised. "Don't tell me you hoodwinked Marsha." He paused. "It had to be Marsha. My man Chubbs, I knew you was gonna get back with that fine thing."

"I didn't go with Marsha," I told him.

"Who the heck did you go with, Chubbs?" he asked.

"I went with Kayla," I answered, turning off my truck.

"Who's that?" he said before pausing. "Don't tell me . . . "

"The big girl!" they yelled together.

"Her name is Kayla," I reminded them.

"I don't care if her name is f-ing Halle Berry in a platinum-blond wig," Chet said firmly. "She'll always be the big girl to me."

"What's up with you, Chet?" E interrupted. "It's not *that* bad."

"It ain't bad at all," I told them. "Kayla is like that."

"The big girl can't be like nothing but Henrietta Hippo on *The New Zoo Revue*," Chet said, laughing. "I guess you must be a big-boned Freddy the Frog," he added, laughing even louder.

"Give him a break, Chet," E said, trying to somehow contain Chet before he *really* got out of control.

"I don't need no break," I answered back. "His momma needs a break from that parole officer she's doing." I laughed. "But this here brother ain't in need of no break from nobody."

"That's too cold, Sonny," E chimed in.

"Shut up, E!" Chet and I yelled together.

"My bad," he answered, embarrassed.

"Look, y'all," I said, opening the door and stepping out of the truck. "I just got back on the scene, so I'll holla back later on."

"Later, Sonny," E said before hanging up.

"Whatever, Chubbs," Chet snapped.

I walked past one of my neighbors, who in true nineties suburban style barely acknowledged I was even there, and then made my way into the house and smiled. It was the first time I'd felt a sense of pride about anything in some time. I'd spent a wonderful weekend with a woman I really liked and knew I'd lost weight because there was actually a little room in my swimsuit.

After I dropped my bag at the steps I made my way to the pit and attacked it with a vengeance. I rolled through two sets of everything and did every single rep. Amazingly, I even managed to knock out ten full sit-ups and ten difficult yet fulfilling push-ups. My face again met the mat when my arms collapsed after the tenth push-up, but I felt satisfied. I knew I was on the way, just as I was with Kayla.

Sleep that night was followed by an early morning bout with the pit. The two sets I started with were a breeze. So I did a third for good measure. I still had a face-to-face meeting with the mat after my push-ups but it was cool because I managed to pump out fifteen! Afterward, I was starving, so I couldn't wait to eat breakfast. But I decided there was only one way for me to totally commit to my FutraSystem plan. I had to rid my kitchen of everything that didn't bear that big red logo I'd come to despise. And the only way to accomplish that feat was to have one last meal with real food. I figured I'd have my own personal last supper (with a breakfast-style twist, of course).

I unloaded a shrink-wrapped package of bacon into one pan, and in another fired up a mound of fresh home-fried potatoes with onions and some sassy Cajun seasoning. On the back burner, I started a pot of savory grits with cheese, and on the other sat a full pan of fried eggs with mushrooms and even more cheese. My house smelled like heaven. Though I was cheating, I knew it would be my last time. And taking in this scene one last time was sobering. The popping grease, sizzling bacon and near-hypnotic aroma of my breakfast feast sucked me in like a new Hoover vacuum cleaner.

Then again, it always had.

I slapped together two plates that gave new meaning to the phrase "heaping" and prayed for strength. Cheating at this level could be the start of the type of binge I wasn't trying to have, but it was as if my fork had jumped to my hand, ready to completely take over. I made the classic mistake of salting my food before I even tasted it and made sure there was a large pitcher of orange juice close by. I figured it would take me ten minutes tops to devour everything I'd prepared. The swirling aroma played pitter-pat with my nostrils. My napkin was neatly folded across my lap. My fork was poised to lift and deliver. And my mouth was willing, ready and able.

One problem.

The fork got stuck just as I tried to shove it into my mouth. I wanted it to become one with my mouth. I wanted to feel the eggs slide into my mouth and down my throat. I needed to experience the pork-filled pleasure of the hickory-smoked bacon. And couldn't wait to tussle with the chunky, onion-laced home fries. I wanted, needed and deserved to engage in this one, last wonderful culinary expedition.

But I couldn't.

I just didn't want to cheat. Your brain must have lost its brain, I thought, frustrated. This was a disaster. I was starving. I had a mound of food in front of me, but I couldn't eat. It was like I had two miniature Fred Flintstones pulling at me. One over each ear. A fat one dressed in a white robe and holding a harp hovered over my right ear. And an even fatter one over my left ear was decked out in red and had horns coming from his head. He had a pitchfork in his left hand and a juicy brontosaurus burger in the other.

"Don't eat, Sonny," said the Flintstone over my right ear. "You will only hurt yourself."

"You know it's just a one-time shot," countered the other Fred. "Get it over with and then you can deal with that FutraSystem crap."

I opened my mouth. The red Fred had to be right.

"No, Sonny," said the other Flintstone. "You're doing so well. You can't do this. You have to believe in yourself."

"The only thing you have to believe is that if you don't hurry up and eat, this crap is gonna be as cold as Marsha was when she dropped your big behind," said the other one, biting on his bronto burger.

I nodded and again moved the fork toward my waiting mouth.

"No, no, *no*, Sonny!" urged the white-robed character. "I simply won't allow you to do this to yourself."

He then smiled and started to strum an absolutely hideous verse of Elton John's "Rocket Man" on his harp. This, of course, forced his red-clad counterpart to cover his horns and bellow, "You know how much I hate that crap!"

And like the red Fred, I hated it too. It wasn't like I had something against the harp or anything. He just totally screwed up the song. It distracted me so much that I shook my head, blinked my eyes and prayed for the best. It took barely a second, but the dizzying aroma and mere sight of all that glorious food summoned to me with the force of a sheriff dragging a deadbeat dad to the courthouse steps.

The red-draped Fred won.

But in the long run I was the one who lost.

I attacked that food like a blue ribbon for the county fair's fastest-eater contest was at stake. Bacon was shoved down my throat four strips at a time and I slid the mushroom-loaded eggs into my mouth like they were a bowl of soup. The gooey grits with cheese and chunky onion-laced Cajun potatoes made a perfect combination as they collided before plunging into my happy stomach. The two plate-size pancakes shivered in fear as they were pierced by my fork and jammed into my mouth and forced past my teeth by a tall glass of orange juice.

I'd forgotten how good real food tasted.

But an equally dramatic leap into the next plate did even more wonders for my food-deprived memory.

As I glanced over the plate at the four yellow and red FutraSystem boxes sitting on my table, I broke into a wide, maniacal, uncontrollable grin. The lifeless boxes took on a stoic, almost overbearing presence. I literally had to shake my head and totally refocus on the boxes, which for some insane reason started to take on the semblance of a miniature-size

Mount Rushmore. With their arms crossed and each of them shaking their heads in varying degrees of disgust, Presidents Lincoln, Jefferson, George Washington and Teddy Roosevelt glared at me with the intensity of an overzealous department store security guard.

I couldn't believe that even *they* were pissed off by my obsession with food.

They may have been presidents, and merely their placement on Mount Rushmore definitely gave them some clout, but I could have cared less. Not even the most recognized, once most powerful leaders of the free world were getting in the way of my feast. And I was going to let them know it.

"What the heck are y'all looking at!" I yelled, still peering over my plate.

They just looked back at me, and were still obviously *very* annoyed.

"Y'all think I'm gonna just eat this FutraSystem crap?" I asked. "Look at this!" I shoved the plate toward them. "This is *real* food!" I went on, frantically moving the plate back and forth. "Look at you, Jefferson!" I focused on a box of FutraEggs. "You dag-on nearly wrote the Constitution by yourself and now you're on a stupid box of fake, slimy eggs with a dumb serving suggestion."

Just like any well-entrenched politician, he didn't seem to care.

"And what about you, Abe?" I asked, moving my eyes toward him. "One minute you're freeing slaves and the next you're stuck on a FutraMuffin box!"

At least he acknowledged me. He tilted and then slowly nodded his head.

"I got real muffins here, Abe!" I yelled. "They're dripping

with butter and they have big, fat blueberries!" I shook a muffin in his face. "Y'all can stare at me all day long," I said, lifting my fork, " 'cause Sonny Walker's gonna eat every last bit of this food and I'm gonna love every single minute of it!"

Much like the first plate, I bolted through the second like a first-semester college freshman on a trip home for Thanksgiving after suffering through a bland, wholesome, well-balanced meal plan. I was finished as quickly as I'd started. I slumped deep into my chair and it took very little time for the guilt gods to grab hold of me. I felt much more miserable than full, and I was plenty full. The meal had been fabulous, and I had truly reveled in eating real food again, but I also knew that binging was so, so wrong.

Had I listened to that non-harp-playing Flintstone and paid attention to the dead presidents sitting atop those hideous FutraSystem boxes, I'd have been okay. I'd still be on target and wouldn't be feeling so down about myself. But this was even worse than getting hemmed up between those mailboxes. At least I could blame that on the postal service—they'd obviously put the boxes too close to each other. But whose fault was this? I couldn't blame it on the red Flintstone, because the white one was pulling at me just as much as he was. And Kayla was nowhere in sight so I couldn't shove it off on her. It was all my fault, one hundred percent, and I knew it. The only person who got cheated was me. And cheating yourself is worse than a stale-shelled taco with unseasoned beef, limp, veiny lettuce and three-day-old, clumpy tomatoes.

Though my food hadn't come close to being digested and despite the fact that I could barely move, I forced myself up and slowly edged toward the pit. I stood over the bright-blue mat and, after considering just how hard working out would be, I lowered myself, curled up—as much as a guy my size can actually curl up—and quickly fell to sleep.

I don't recall exactly what forced me back up, but as soon as I awoke and got back to my feet, I hurried to the kitchen and threw every shred of real food that was still in my house into three huge green lawn-and-leaf bags. The dishes and pans were washed and tucked away, and I stocked my shelves with nothing but those yellow and red FutraSystem boxes and bags and FutraSnacks.

Cheating was no longer an option.

Though I felt worse than a pan of crusty, leftover Hamburger Helper and had let myself down even lower than the NBA's hapless Toronto Raptors, I hurried toward my truck so I could unload the three huge bags of food I'd accumulated. I dropped the bags at a local food bank and headed to work. Despite the fact that I didn't look forward to dealing with that no-good Andy or the loose balls section, I had no choice. My bills had to be paid. I started to park in my usual spot, which was about two steps from the store's front door, when it struck me that I had more to gain by parking farther away. After the meal I'd just scarfed down, I needed a challenge that wouldn't overwhelm me. If I parked at the far end of the lot, I'd have to walk a ways. I figured if I did that, I'd at least burn off a couple of calories.

And if I burned calories, I'd lose weight.

After I punched in, I headed for my department. Loose, f-ing balls, I thought, disgusted. What the heck am I doing? I wasn't sure, but it didn't matter because when I strolled past Helen in the tennis and bowling section, she stopped me.

"Hey, Sonny," she said, smiling.

"Hey, Helen," I answered. "What's up?"

"It's good to have you back," she told me, nodding her head. "You look rested."

I wondered why she thought I looked rested and why she didn't notice that I'd lost weight.

"So you ready for the big change?" she asked.

"What big change?" I replied.

"Oh," she answered, shrugging her shoulders. "I guess you haven't heard."

"Haven't heard what?"

"They're switching some things around," she warned. "So you might want to get to your shop before Andy totally screws it up."

"What's he doing in my department?"

"Who knows?" she responded, raising her shoulders and eyebrows all at once. "But you'd better hurry so you can beat him to the punch."

"Thanks, Helen," I said, turning to walk away. "I need to set him straight before he even starts to ruin my day—"

"Sonny," she interrupted.

"Yeah."

"He's really not all that bad," she told me.

"Whatever, Helen," I said, disappointed.

I kept moving toward the loose balls section and couldn't imagine why Andy would be in my department. When I arrived, it was clear he had a motive.

"Sonny, my man," he said, clutching the new white clipboard that marked his promotion. *"Que pasa?"*

"Why are you in my section, Mr. Martinez?"

"I just wanted to welcome you back, my man."

"Well, I'm back and I'm glad to be welcomed, so if you're done I'll take it from here," I said with an edge.

"*No problemo,*" he said, walking away. "Your section checks out okay and it's good to have you back, my man."

"Whatever, chump," I said under my breath.

"Hey, Sonny," he said, spinning back around.

"Yeah," I answered, hoping he hadn't actually heard me.

"You like this section, my man? Loose balls has gotta be a little loco."

"It's a lotta loco. But I can handle it," I said, trying to keep my edge.

"That's too bad, my man," he told me, scribbling on his clipboard. "'Cause there's an opening I thought you'd be interested in."

"And where might that be?" I asked, counting a row of new Wilson basketballs.

"Exercise equipment," he answered. "It'd be a good fit, my man," he said. "You could stand to be around the exercise equipment."

"I'm all right," I told him, focusing my count toward a row of footballs.

"Well, I already recommended you, so be on the lookout, my man," he said before again walking away.

Maybe Andy was right. The exercise equipment section might not be so bad. I'd be a world away from the stupid loose balls section. And I could use the equipment demonstrations to tone up and work out all at once. This could work. I just needed a way to make everyone think that a transfer out of loose balls was my idea and not Andy's.

I thought about it as I walked to the front of the store to find Mr. Matthews.

"Hey, Sonny," whispered Helen as I walked by her aisle.

She motioned me over and said she wanted to give me a heads-up.

"What's up, Helen?" I asked.

"Look, Sonny," she told me. "I just wanted to let you know that Andy put you in for a transfer to exercise." She looked around. "It may be a good move. You should consider it. I guess Andy's not so bad after all, huh?"

"Where did you hear this from?" I asked, concerned.

"It's just out there," she said, looking over my shoulder.

"Thanks, Helen," I said, walking away.

Andy had undermined me. If he put it out that he wanted to make the transfer happen, I wasn't about to let it happen. I'd starve before I'd let that no-good butt kisser hook me up with anything. There was no way I could let everybody think that Andy did me any good.

Mr. Matthews spotted me before I could turn around and head back to my section. I had already decided against talking to him about the transfer. Loose balls was going to have to do. I slowly turned and took a few light steps toward my section. Apparently they weren't light enough.

"Mr. Walker," he said, walking toward me. "It is indeed good to have you back. I know it's been a while, but I do apologize about the unfortunate incident in the tent section. But you did make quite a tent," he added, chuckling, then, recovering his more serious tone, "Anyway, Walker, I did consider your request for upward mobility and have elected to execute a transfer to the fitness equipment section."

"Excuse me, Mr. Matthews," I answered. "But I recall requesting a transfer to tents and outdoors."

"You most certainly did," he said, tilting his head. "However, that is now Andrew's department and you are his hand-picked replacement for the fitness section."

"What if I don't want to be his handpicked replacement?"

"I'm not certain that's an option," he answered.

"So why ask me?" I said.

"I didn't ask you," he reminded me. "You asked. You'll start in fitness in approximately one hour. In the meantime, you can bring Helen up to speed on your old section."

"Helen?" I asked, surprised.

"Indeed," he answered. "She has agreed to a transfer to the loose balls section."

Ain't this some crap, I thought, shaking my head. No wonder she all of a sudden believes that Andy "ain't so bad."

"By the way, Walker," he said, looking toward me. "The transfer should help you with your weight. I'm sure you wouldn't mind dropping a few pounds. And don't forget," he went on, "you should be grateful to Mr. Martinez. Thanks to him, you're in a new department *plus* you got the opportunity to impress the regional managers."

"I impressed the regional managers?" I asked, stunned.

"Certainly," he replied. "Thanks to you, we were able to properly situate our new jumbo, family-size tent and we were able to unload our stock in the very first week." He nodded his head. "Had Mr. Martinez not mentioned you and had you not made such a good tent, we would undoubtedly have more stock than we'd care to have."

Big f-ing deal, I thought, unimpressed.

I headed back to loose balls only to find Helen already taking inventory and totally revamping the racks.

"What are you doing?" I asked, walking toward her.

"Hey, Sonny," she said, writing on a clipboard.

"Don't 'Hey, Sonny' me after you took my department," I angrily stated.

"What are you talking about, Sonny?" she asked. "You didn't even want this department. You were always talking about how you wanted to get out of loose balls, about how you deserved a switch and about how you'd take a change to almost anywhere as long as it meant you were out of loose balls."

"And?" I asked.

"And you finally get out and you're upset about it," she said, shaking her head. "You're so consumed with Andy you can't see the forest for the trees," she added, still counting balls. "Andy may be a jerk to you, but his move up means opportunity for all of us. Think about it, Sonny, if Andy doesn't move, you're still in loose balls, I'm still in tennis and bowling and nobody's happy."

"I don't believe you, Helen," I said, ignoring everything she'd said. "Just a few weeks ago even you called Andy a jerk, so when you get what you want he's suddenly okay."

"Maybe I was wrong," she said casually. "I bet you didn't even know he totally retooled tents and outdoors and they sold out of that new jumbo-size, family tent in less than a week. That's incredible, Sonny. Maybe he's on to something."

"I could have pulled that off," I scoffed.

"Maybe you could have," she answered. "But he *did*, Sonny."

"Whatever, Helen," I said, walking away.

"Hey, Sonny," she said, laughing. *"Que pasa?"*

Chapter 15

I couldn't believe it. Helen was as big a phony as Andy and everyone else in Sports Authority. That's one of the worst things about work. The managers always figure out a way to keep the workers at one another's throats. They promote the wrong people, screw over the good employees, cater to the brownnosers like Andy and make sure opportunists like Helen are somehow satisfied. It's almost as if coming to work and doing your job's not enough. I did good work and where did it get me? Andy's work probably sucked, but he kissed more behind than a doorman at a five-star hotel. Now he had what should have been my department and I was his "hand-picked replacement." It just wasn't right.

But it could be a plus.

I headed toward the exercise equipment section and made a careful inspection of the aisle. There was a long row of new, gleaming equipment. Because Sports Authority was committed to carrying just about everything anyone could ever want or imagine, I had access to all types of accessories. Gloves. Knee wraps. Even pressed talcum powder was there for sale and I could get a lot of use out of the customers' sample box. The exercise equipment department had machines I knew absolutely nothing about, but I knew they'd come in handy.

With a pit here and at home I can't lose, I thought, walking toward a weight bench. I sat on the bench and picked up the two gray dumbbells sitting beside it. Before I knew it, I was doing the first set of alternating curls I'd done in years. Before I could finish, Andy waltzed by. He nodded his approval and kept moving. I'm sure he had been warned that I wasn't exactly thrilled with his recommending me to take over his old department, and the sight of him alone pissed me off so much that I knocked out another set before I rose to take stock of the rest of the department.

A women decked out in a bright-blue spandex aerobics outfit stopped me and asked for help. She was very fit and very cute.

Obviously, I was ready to help.

"I think I like this machine," she told me, walking toward a floor-based ab machine. "Do you know what time Andy comes in?" she asked, looking at her watch.

"He's already here," I answered, smiling. "But this is my department now."

"Oh, really," she said, looking me over. "Didn't you use to work over there near the basketballs or something?"

"Sure did," I answered, pulling the machine closer to us. "But everybody's got to move up sometime."

"Is that right?" she said, smiling. "This is a move up, huh?"

"Sure is," I said, lying down to demonstrate the machine.

The sit-ups I'd done over the past couple of weeks came in handy. I pulled off ten perfect crunches with a smooth, steady motion and talked to her the entire time.

"Impressive," she said as I sat up when I finished. "I hope you don't take this wrong," she added, looking me in the eye, "but you really move well for a guy like you."

"A guy like me?" I asked, knowing full well what she'd meant.

"You know," she said, shrugging her shoulders. "I guess what I meant to say is that I've never seen a guy like you actually do sit-ups so easily."

"A guy like me?" I repeated.

"I guess I'm not making much sense," she said, embarrassed. "Do you work out or something?" she asked.

"Yeah," I answered, laughing. "A guy like me works out almost every day."

"That's what I was trying to say," she told me, smiling. "You did those crunches so easily I knew you'd done them before."

"I know it probably doesn't show just yet, but I'm working out and watching what I eat. I'm really trying to take better care of myself."

"Keep it up," she said, smiling wider. "If you can pull off sit-ups that easily, it's really working."

"Thanks," I replied, getting to my feet.

"I didn't get your name," she said, reaching for my hand.

"I'm Sonny."

"It's a pleasure, Sonny," she said, nodding her head. "My name is Evelyn."

"Evelyn. How long you been working out?"

"Nearly a year. Andy really got me into it. I told him I was under a lot of stress, job stuff, you know," she said. "So he pitched me on a treadmill and the rest is history."

"What kind of job had you all stressed out?" I asked.

"I'm a broker," she answered.

"You're a broker?" I said, impressed. "I guess that would be kind of stressful."

"You mix that in with my crazy social life and stress becomes a major issue," she said, laughing.

"I think I get the picture," I replied.

"Well, Sonny, it was indeed a pleasure to meet you."

"Same back at ya," I countered. "Keep working out."

"Oh, yeah," she said, pointing her finger. "You did such a fine job with that little ab machine that I think I'll take one."

"You only want one?" I asked, smiling.

"That will do for now." She smiled back. "Thanks, Sonny."

We headed toward the front and, of course, ran into Andy. They hugged and he told her I was a really good guy. "If she gets out of hand, just give a call, my man," he said, winking at me.

I couldn't stand him. I'd have a rope around my neck and a bullet heading for my head before I'd call Andy.

Evelyn paid for her machine and quickly left. I felt an incredible sense of pride. Cute little Evelyn, who was obviously a workout queen, actually picked up a piece of equipment because of me. Everything was working. The only thing left to do was to firm up a date with Kayla. I couldn't wait to call her. I walked to the employee break room and sat down to use the phone.

I had no idea I'd actually *need* to be seated when I made the call.

"Hello," said a voice that obviously wasn't Kayla.

"Hello," I answered, surprised.

"Who is this?" asked the *man* who answered the phone.

"Who's this?" I asked, knowing it was probably Mr. Loser himself, Jonathan James Leslie.

"With whom would you like to speak?" he said, sounding like an old-school-style English teacher.

"I'm trying to holler at Kayla."

"You would like to *holler* at Kayla?" he asked, sounding totally repulsed.

"Yeah," I said in a huff. "I'm trying to shout at Kayla."

"Your vernacular is most interesting." He chuckled.

"So is that relaxer you use on your hair," I answered. "Can you just give the phone to Kayla?"

"She's in the shower."

"She's in the shower?"

"She's in the shower," he repeated.

"I bet she's in the shower," I said, frustrated.

"I don't need this triviality." He sighed. "Why don't you hold for just a second."

I hated that someone who was as polished as Jonathan James Leslie was such an a-hole. It was difficult being mean to someone who was so polite.

"Kay," he said, apparently walking into the bathroom. "You have a call."

"Who is it, honey?" she answered.

"I think it's that big fellow who came by the other day."

"What big fellow?" she asked, laughing.

"The really big one," he laughed back.

"Oh, my God," she said, sounding panicked. "That must be Sonny."

"I believe it is *that* big fellow," he said, still laughing.

"Sonny?" she said as he handed her the phone.

"Yeah," I answered flatly. "This is the really big guy."

"You're funny," she said, her voice strained.

"I ain't trying to be funny."

"Is something wrong?" she asked, sounding concerned.

"Does something have to be wrong for me to call?"

"I didn't say that," she answered.

"Then why did you ask if something's wrong?"

"What's going on, Sonny?" she asked. "You sound upset."

"Would you be upset if you spent the weekend with a wonderful man and you called his house on Monday morning and a woman answered?" I asked.

"I did just spend the weekend with a wonderful man, so I know what you're talking about," she told me, laughing.

"I'm glad you think this is funny," I countered.

"For God's sake, lighten up, Sonny," she said. "Jonathan answered the phone because he just happened to be here," she continued. "If it means anything to you, he's about to leave."

"You don't owe me any explanation," I said, shaking my head. "If he's there he's just there. It's not like I'm happy about it or anything, but that's your situation."

"Okay, Sonny," she said, sounding frustrated. "But I know you called for a reason, so why not get to the point."

"I just called to tell you that this weekend was incredible," I said, invoking lessons I'd learned in Guilt Trip 101. "I had such a good time and I can't wait to see you again. Being with you, just spending time with you, was so special and so vital that I couldn't even consider being in the company of another woman right about now," I told her, planting the final seed. "So if that's wrong, then I stand accused."

There was a long, long silence. It was clear my point had been made. She'd probably drop everything and make her way to Sports Authority before I could get off the line.

"You're full of it, Sonny," she said, obviously unimpressed. "You'll have to come stronger than that if you want to make me feel guilty," she added, chuckling. "I had a good time too but I know you called for a reason."

"You got me," I told her, breaking into a smile. "I really meant everything I said, but I called to see what you were doing later. My day is going so smooth I thought the only way to finish it off would be to be with you. So what time should I blow through?"

"Look, Sonny, I had an absolutely breathtaking weekend," she said. "And it really made me think about a lot of things. But I do have a life and unfortunately it didn't end just because you and I were able to spend a wonderful weekend together."

Jeez, I thought, frustrated.

"I'm really sorry Jonathan answered the phone," she said, sounding concerned. "That would upset me too. But like it or not, he is a part of my life. Like I told you before, we don't have a commitment or anything like that, but he's been there for me and I can't just dismiss him."

How in the heck am I supposed to respond to this crap?

"Anyway," she said, "I'd like to see you tonight as well."

"That's good," I said, relieved.

"I'm not so sure about that," she shot back.

"Why wouldn't that be good?" I asked, concerned.

"Because," she said slowly, "I'm kind of tied up."

"Well, we can get together when you're finished," I told her.

"I don't know about that," she said. "It may be kind of late."

"You meeting with a client or something?" I asked, wanting to snatch those words back before I even finished saying them.

"I'm doing the 'or something' part," she said, half laughing.

This sucks, I thought, worried.

Had I been a computer, I would have gone into sleep mode. She may have been pushing my buttons, but I wasn't interested in running her program.

"Sonny," she said cautiously. "Are you still there?"

"I'm here," I answered. "Where did you think I went?"

"It got so quiet, I thought the line had gone dead," she told me. "I thought maybe you had hung up or something."

"Why would I hang up?"

"I thought maybe you were upset."

"I'm not upset."

"You sure you're not upset?" she asked.

"I'm not upset," I repeated.

"So everything is okay?" she asked, obviously wanting me to take the pressure off her.

"Everything's fine."

"Maybe we can get together tomorrow," she said.

"Maybe," I answered, trying to sound like everything was okay when it wasn't.

"Good," she quickly replied. "I have to go to the store, Sonny. I'll call you when I get back."

"Later," I said, before hanging up.

I'd lied. I was pissed, hurt, upset and every other negative emotion I could muster. What did she mean Jonathan just happened to be there? What kind of fool did she think I was, anyway? How could she even have him around right after we'd hung out all weekend? I couldn't believe it. I would never play her like that. I really wanted to see her again. We'd started something that I was interested in finishing. I didn't like being cast aside so easily, but I should have known I'd end up getting screwed when we got back from Atlantic City and she hit me with the "bye-bye" wave. I hated losing out. Especially to someone like Jonathan James Leslie, who had me beat across the board. He had good hair, good diction *and* a good body. That chump had everything I didn't have.

Including Kayla.

Chapter 16

I sat at our shaky brown lunch table and tried to sort things out. Our poorly paneled break room was typical of companies that had to offer employees breaks when they really didn't want to. The turntable in the microwave didn't work and the television played one very hazy channel but had no volume. The radio was stuck on an all-Elvis-all-the-time station and even the light in the refrigerator didn't work. The vending machines rarely vended and the soda machine dispensed lukewarm low-fizz soft drinks. There were all types of "Safety in the Workplace" and "Fair Employment Standards" posters pasted to the walls, and the lock on the suggestion box had been removed and was rigged to keep the freezer part of the refrigerator closed. It wouldn't stay shut on its own. Ironically, the only thing that worked was the clock, which was situated over the top of the front door. Like many companies, Sports Authority knew that a working clock was one of the best ways to get employees back to work.

And when I got myself together and finally checked the time, even I was surprised to find I'd spent nearly all of forty-five minutes worrying and thinking about Kayla. I wondered what was really going on with her and Jonathan James Leslie. It had to be something. He walked into the bathroom to give her the phone and she again called him "honey." That had to mean something. A guy doesn't just walk into a woman's bathroom while she's in the shower unless he knows he can. And he doesn't know he can unless the woman makes it known that she's cool with it. The whole thing made no sense to me, but neither did hanging in the break room for forty-five minutes without feeling like I had a break. I was truly frustrated, but I knew I had to make a move.

"Yo, Sonny," said a voice I wasn't trying to hear. "You got somebody out here for you, my man."

Thankfully, someone was making the move for me.

"Whatever, Andy," I said, walking toward the door and pushing it aside. I rarely got visitors at work and wondered who it could have been. After just a second I smiled. It had to be Kayla. Maybe Jonathan James Leslie left like she said and maybe she came to her senses about getting together. It didn't really matter. She had rushed over and that's all I really cared about.

"Hey, Sonny."

"What's up, Chubbs?"

"What's up, y'all," I answered.

"You trying to duck us?" Chet said, laughing. "You roll out of town and don't even call. I bet you ain't been nowhere. Your big behind was probably sitting up in the crib sick 'cause you been trying to exercise and eat that FutraSystem nonsense at the same time."

"You sick, Sonny?" E asked.

"I'm sick of listening to y'all fools," I said, disappointed. "I'm all right. I been working out and trying to let go of some bad habits."

"I hope it's working, Sonny," E said, slapping me five.

"Yeah," said Chet, shaking his head. "'Cause you need to get it going on, dawg."

"Look, Sonny," E said, reaching for a dumbbell. "We slid by on our lunch break to see what you're doing this evening."

"Yeah, Chubbs," Chet said, looking around. "We plan on blowing through the Gardens so we can see how the other side lives."

"That ain't funny, Chet," I said, shaking my head. "You need to keep a lid on that 'other side' crap. You know I don't play that."

I couldn't play that. Especially in front of E. When Chet dared to mutter the "other side," he meant us. Black folks. Chet had a major, major problem with African Americans. He didn't appear to mind being one. He just had a problem dealing with us. Chet's life had been so wacky. Besides the obvious fallout from his jailed-up mother and sister, there was the very real setback he had faced from his ex-wife, Yvette. They were married right out of high school. Chet was as in love with Yvette as I once was with cheeseburgers. She had smooth brown skin, bright ebony eyes, a playful, toothy smile and a body that rivaled J.J.'s sister Thelma's from *Good Times*.

Yvette and Chet were happy until she announced she was pregnant. Chet didn't want anything to do with kids, so he was pissed. Yvette eventually presented him with a beautiful son, Chet, Jr., and they came to be inseparable. Chet, Jr. probably didn't know it, but he was his dad's best friend. To let Chet tell it, his son would one day find a cure for cancer, hit .400 in baseball, break all of Jim Brown's rushing records in football and have the world asking, "Michael who?" when it came to basketball. He would, of course, accomplish all of this between his presidencies and would be done in time to celebrate his eighteenth birthday. With his tidy little family, Chet's life was fulfilled and seemingly perfect.

Until Yvette met Lance.

Lance was Yvette's very rich, very smart, very connected and very *white* coworker. Together, Lance and Yvette conspired to buy out a very profitable car dealership. Everything was in Lance's name, so Yvette played the role of the downtrodden secretary who was canned when the "new owners" of the dealership took over. Chet didn't care if Yvette wasn't working. He was crazy about her because she brought a certain sense of balance to his life that his mom and his sister took away.

That's until she took Chet, Jr. away.

Apparently Yvette and Lance had made some pretty big plans. She had Chet served with divorce papers at their son's annual soccer banquet. Chet, Jr. had been selected as player of the year. While he was onstage retreiving his trophy, a burly white guy tapped Chet on the shoulder and handed him the papers that would change his life. When Chet, Jr.

made his way from the stage, Yvette scooped him up and jetted out of the building. Chet dropped his camcorder, read the
papers and nearly passed out. He said he was so stunned and
had been caught so off guard that he literally couldn't move.
His temporary state of shock gave Yvette just enough time to
collect her things and get out of town. When Chet made it
home, all he saw was her car speeding away from the house.
Actually, it wasn't her car. She took his three-week-old Benz,
which he'd purchased from (you guessed it) Lance.

She left him with the minivan.

She also left him with the mortgage, credit cards, which
she had maxed out, the utilities and the bill for Chet, Jr.'s
braces (even presidents who bat .400 sometimes have bad
teeth). When all was said and done, Chet had to pay Yvette a
grand a month, $500 for child support and $500 for alimony,
and was forced to pay the bank for the Benz, which Yvette
and Lance kept and *claimed* was stolen (Yvette allowed the
insurance to lapse, and since the car was in Chet's name, he
got stuck with the note). Sadly, he hadn't seen or heard from
Chet, Jr. since. For the past ten years, Chet had faithfully sent
a birthday and Christmas package to Yvette's mom's house
for his son (he knew he wasn't there, but was convinced that
she'd get the gifts to her grandson).

Sadly, he didn't know for sure if Chet, Jr. had ever received
any of them.

And thanks to Yvette, and to some degree his mom and his
grape-eating sister, Chet was as despondent and as screwed
up as a gambler without chips for a roulette wheel. He
thought "sistahs" were totally bogus, so he chose to date ex-
clusively outside of our race. In a weird way, I think he believed he was getting even with Lance and every other white

guy who ever screwed him. And in an even weirder way, he sometimes lost it and went off on one of his "those other people" tirades.

I'd long ago agreed not to bring up Yvette and little Chet. Since then, he'd never brought it up and I'd never pressed him about it. All I asked was that he drop that "other people, other side" crap.

"My bad Chubbs," Chet said, realizing he'd crossed the line. "I meant to say, let's go to the Gardens and hang out with the locals." He laughed. "Maybe we could down some malt liquor or something," he said, still laughing. "I'm trying to get back to my roots."

We both looked at him like he was crazy, which was actually fitting because he was—crazy that is.

"C'mon, y'all," he said, sensing our anger. "Can't a brother joke with his boys or does a brother have to have his hat on backwards before he can pull that off?" He flipped his hat around.

He just stood there with a simple look on his face.

"O-tay," he said, giving us a thumbs-up sign, while sounding very much like Buckwheat from *The Little Rascals*.

We, of course, burst into laughter.

"You are off the hook, fool," I said, laughing.

"You're just not right, Chet," E told him, shaking his head.

"My bad," Chet said, realigning his hat. "Look, Chubbs," he added, "let's just hook up at your spread after work and then we'll rush over to Republic Gardens."

"That's a bet," I answered.

"Sounds like a plan," E chimed in.

"We out," they said, slapping me five.

The rest of the afternoon was pretty blasé. I made some

adjustments to the row of workout equipment to suit my routine and actually sold a treadmill to a guy who I knew would never use it. I wanted to call Kayla back in case she had a change in plans, but that wasn't about to happen. She said she would call when she got back from the store, so that would have to do. Five o'clock arrived before I knew it, and I was out of work and back home in minutes. I made it to the house without much fanfare. And before I even thought about changing clothes for Republic Gardens I hit the pit and ran through two fairly easy sets. Even I didn't understand where the energy and inspiration came from, though I chalked it up to feeling so guilty about my breakfast smorgasbord.

The doorbell rang.

"What's up, Sonny?"

"What's up, dawg?"

It was E and Chet.

"Guess who we just saw over at the Safeway?" asked E, taking a case of Heineken to the kitchen table.

"Yeah, Chubbs," added Chet, sliding out of his jacket. "Guess who was looking so good, she made me think about hollering at sistahs again?" he asked, sitting on my rec room sofa.

"Let me guess," I said, smiling. "You saw good ole Marsha."

"Hold up, big fella," Chet said, surprised. "We kinda thought you'd be a little upset."

"Why would I be upset?" I asked, sitting in my super-comfortable cloth-covered recliner.

"Because you're pressed about Marsha," E said, grabbing a seat and popping open a Heineken.

"I *was* pressed about Marsha," I told them, laughing. "But that's history."

"If you had seen her today it wouldn't be history," Chet said, opening a beer of his own.

"Yeah, Sonny," said E, handing me a brew. "Marsha was looking pretty tight."

"It ain't all about looks," I said, checking the label for calorie content.

"You said that right," E chimed in, downing a swig.

"It ain't in the talk," said Chet, tilting his head back.

I had a feeling we were about to be in serious trouble. One thing we didn't do well was drink. Chet had the most tolerance. He could at least chug 'em down without getting sick, but he was pretty much done after his very first drink. I wasn't much better. About three quarters through my first brew, I was in buzz city. If I made it all the way through a beer, I felt I was no longer legally responsible for my actions. And E was a total waste. He'd get woozy over the fumes and be wasted halfway through the first sip.

We got drunk pretty easily. And we all had terrible drunk habits. Chet would constantly move his head about like he was looking for someone. I would rock back and forth like I was a human rocking chair and E would bat his eyes like he was caught in a wave of flashbulb-yielding cameramen. The only time we'd drink was when we collectively were pissed off at the world. Which, of course, led to some of the most ridiculous conversations ever known to man. Since we got torn up so easily, we sometimes got us in over our heads. Chet would become meaner than his usually mean self. E would somehow get some heart, which endeared him to Chet. And I would flat out lose it. Whatever was in me at the time—joy, pain, frustration, heartache—came out when I'd had too much to drink.

"Yo, check this out, Chubbs," Chet said, reaching for another Heineken.

"I'm checking it, baby," I said, slurring my words and starting to rock.

"Check this out, Chubbs," he repeated, his eyes moving from side to side.

"He said he's checking it," E muttered.

"Y'all with me on this," he said, looking about the room furiously.

"We're with you!" we told him.

"Check this y'all," he said, taking another swig.

There was a long silence. And we knew what was coming. If *Chet* was already wasted, things would be going downhill fast.

"Women suck!" he blurted out.

"Don't start that crap, Chet," I said, rocking slowly. "Women don't hardly suck."

"Why don't they?" E asked, his eyes blinking.

"Because they don't," I insisted.

"If women don't suck, why ain't you with Marsha, why is Carla with Snake instead of E and why did my f-ing wife take my son away so she could be with some f'ed up white boy?" Chet said forcefully.

"'Cause," E said, nearly laid out across his chair.

"'Cause what?" I asked, rocking as if some offbeat melody were leading me.

"'Cause women suck!" E said, plastered. "That nonsense Carla pulled on me, it ain't even right. She's marryin' my cousin, Sonny," he said, his eyes batting wildly. "My father lost his job because of her, man. She took me for five f-ing Good Humor toasted almond bars," he sobbed. "And now she's marryin' my f-ing cousin and they want me to be the best f-ing man!"

Surprisingly, Chet looked at him and blurted out, "I love you, man," just like that wacky guy in the Bud Lite commercials.

I knew we were in trouble then. Chet and E had never once said anything decent to or about each other. Now they *loved* each other and were hugging to prove it. This was going to be too crazy.

"Yvette should be locked up for what she did to me," Chet said, his head moving like he was suffering from a major case of paranoia. "She took my money, my Benz, my kid *and* the remote to the TV in the basement."

"That's why you have to get up to change channels?" I asked, sitting up.

"You know it, Chubbs," he said, his words sounding slurred. "I ain't seen my son in ten years, y'all. She took my f-ing son!" he yelled. "Yvette's mom won't tell me where he is. I don't know if he's dead, if he's alive, what he looks like, what he wants to do with his life. I don't know if he misses me, if he needs me, can he hit a baseball, has he had his first piece of tail. I don't know nothing, y'all," he said, his voice trembling.

He then looked toward the ceiling and sobbed, "I miss you, Chet, Jr. Please, please, please forgive me." He was shouting like James Brown. "I didn't want this, please know that I love you, son, please believe that I'll always be here for you!"

I couldn't believe it. Chet was on his knees crying like he'd won the lottery for a second time and E was right there with him. I didn't know what to do. So I grabbed another Heineken and rocked like I was on a mechanical bull with back spasms. Getting drunk was as silly as trying to use a two-dollar bill to pay for a three-dollar café latte at Starbucks.

"Y'all all right?" I asked, concerned.

"Yeah, man," they answered, almost in stereo.

"What's up with you, Sonny?" Chet asked, lifting his head and then a bottle to his lips. "What ever happened to you and Marsha, anyway?"

"Nothing," I told him. "Our time had come and we basically just drifted apart."

"You're nobody's fool, Sonny," E said, shaking his head. "Nobody just drifts away from somebody like Marsha."

"You outta stop," Chet said, looking from side to side. "Marsha probably dumped your big behind because you got so f-ing big."

Suddenly he wasn't sounding so drunk.

"So what *really* happened, Sonny?" E asked, nearly finishing off his bottle.

"You might as well go head and kick it," Chet said, wiping his lips.

"Okay," I answered between sips. "Marsha dumped me because I was fat."

"What do you mean *was!*" Chet said, laughing.

"She said I had no control and that she couldn't take it anymore," I told them, still rocking.

"Why can't you tell us what really happened, Sonny?" E pleaded.

"I told y'all," I said, laughing. "She said she was tired of me sleeping all the time and of my eating like I was a machine or something."

"I'm tired of that too but that ain't no reason to dump nobody," Chet said, sitting up. "What really happened between y'all, Chubbs?"

"What's up with y'all fools?" I asked, shaking my head. "I tell you what you wanna hear and you ain't trying to hear it."

"I'm not feeling you right about now, Sonny," E said, his eyes glazed but still blinking.

"Neither is Marsha," Chet said, laughing loudly.

"It don't even matter, Chet," I said, feeling drowsy and shaking my head. "I'm up with somebody new, so I'm all right."

"Here we go again with the big girl," E said, picking up his bottle of Heineken.

"We ain't even going there today, Chubbs," Chet told me. "If I ever find that you been with some big girl, you won't have to lose no weight because I'll whip the fat off your big behind."

I was sick and tired of Chet's fat jokes. Plus I'd had too much to drink. For a guy who gets especially angry when he's loaded, that's a lethal combination. I just shouldn't be held responsible for my actions. Especially the really screwed-up ones.

"Start whipping, chump!" I yelled, standing up. "You want some of this?"

"Look, fool," Chet told me, downing more Heineken. "You f with me and you ain't gonna have to worry about losing weight 'cause I'ma slap the taste out your mouth."

"Come on, punk," I said, walking toward him and clenching my fists. "You got a problem with fat people!" I exclaimed. "Come on and take a fat-boy-style behind whipping."

"Chill out, Sonny," E said, standing up. "We're boys. We don't have to go through this."

That Heineken was really talking now. I was feeling like I was a crazed middle linebacker on Super Bowl Sunday. Talking junk and halfway acting it out seemed *r-e-a-l* cool. Especially since the brew was doing all the talking.

"F you too, E," I said, pushing him aside. "I'm tired of hearing this fat crap all the time." I was sucking air. "Y'all parade around here like y'all square business got it going on just because y'all got some kind of physiques or something. Look at you, E." I pointed toward him. "What the heck makes you so much better than me? Your woman left you for your own f-ing cousin! And, Chet, you're so f'ed up I don't know where to begin," I yelled, turning toward him. "Maybe I should start with your fake-bookkeeping, inmate mother, or do you wanna talk about your trick-turning, grape-eating, stupid-as-a-flea sister Pauline?"

Being drunk put me in truly rare form. If I was blowing it, at least I could blame it on the Heineken. At least I hoped I could.

"My bad dawg!" I yelled, laughing. "Maybe we should just leave it at your white-boy-loving ex-wife, who took you for bad, took your ride, your bankroll *and* your stupid, spoiled son!"

The room got so quiet it made *me* afraid.

"What are y'all fools looking at?" I asked, staggering toward my chair. "Y'all think y'all are so much better than me. I tell y'all I finally met me somebody who I feel good about and all you got to say is she can't be about nothing 'cause she's fat? She's about something! It ain't about being fat, it's about being a person!" I said, anguished. "I'm fat and y'all act like something's wrong with me. Y'all think y'all are so much better than me, that you're smarter than me, that you want more out of life than me! Well, let me tell you one f-ing thing," I shouted, taking a long gulp from my bottle of brew. "Y'all a-holes ain't no better than me or nobody else who got a weight problem."

I fell onto my recliner and just shook my head and laughed uncontrollably.

"And you wanna know something else?" I said, sensing I was about to crash. "Women don't suck. Y'all fools suck!"

I had one last push in me. And since I'd already burned more bridges than a white-sheet-wearing Reagan Republican at a NAACP convention, I was taking it all the way.

"Get the f outta my joint!" I yelled.

"What's wrong with you, Sonny?" E asked, nearly in tears.

"He's a big fat slob," Chet said, standing up. "Except now he's a big, fat, drunk, stupid slob."

"Y'all know what y'all can do, right?" I said, laughing like a truly miserable fool and polishing off my Heineken. "Y'all can kiss this big, fat, drunk, stupid slob's big fat behind. And when you finish, then you can get up outta my joint."

In a matter of seconds they scrambled out the front door like rats running to a cheese festival. I felt terrible. Not because I'd told them off. The way I saw it, they had it coming. I felt bad because that Heineken had nearly 130 calories. And since I downed two bottles I had 260 calories to work off.

Just do it in the morning, I convinced myself, trying to fight off sleep. I was so out of it, my recliner would have to do. My good sense may have been gone, but I knew one thing. It was late and I still hadn't heard from Kayla.

She must still be at the store, I thought, dozing off.

THE REASONS WE LOSE WEIGHT

Lame Reason

To Get Someone's Attention

I've never had a weight problem so I can't relate to changing my eating habits just so I can get someone's attention. It makes me think of Sonny. He's my man but he's definitely got issues. What I'm trying to say is that sometimes he just flat out loses it. His weight works on his mind as much as it does on his stomach. If he decided he had to lose weight to attract someone, I'd wish him the best. But what if *he lost the weight and couldn't keep it off? What if the woman thought he was less attractive because he'd put on a few pounds? And if he wanted to keep the weight off and had to spend all his time working out, would he have time for a relationship anyway? This weight thing, it's gotta be a grind.*

—Everett "Easy E" Steven Casey

Intermezzo

Chapter 17

When I awoke the next morning, one thing stuck me harder than the headache that was pounding my head.

Kayla *still* hadn't called.

"I'll call you when I get back from the store," I thought, dragging myself from my recliner. She must think I'm a big sucker. Thinking like this is always a dilemma for big guys. You wonder if she thinks you're a big sucker just because you're big, but your common sense tells you she thinks you're a big sucker because you're a guy. Being big just adds to the anxiety.

I pranced around the bottles we'd left scattered on the

floor and somehow managed to drag myself to the shower. That's usually my first step back to Soberville. I was so gone, it felt like the water was slapping life back into my body and taste into my mouth.

I couldn't wait to eat.

I slid into my Sports Authority outfit and forced myself to the kitchen. I wasn't thinking about FutraSystem, but it didn't much matter. I'd thrown out all of my real food and had nothing but those god-awful yellow FutraSystem boxes lining my cabinets and counters. There probably wasn't an ounce of fat in the entire house that wasn't attached to my body. I couldn't believe it. I crammed two FutraMuffins into my mouth and washed them down with some bland-tasting orange-flavored FutraJuice. I made my way to the pit and forced myself through a truly agonizing set that had me see-ing double because my hangover had yet to wear off. In fact, it felt like it was just setting in.

It didn't help that Kayla hadn't called. And it bothered me because I imagined her "trip to the store" probably involved that no-account Jonathan James Leslie. After I finally found my keys and headed toward the door, the kitchen phone rang. I had a call. It had to be her.

So what if it is her? I wondered. She didn't think to call you all night. She was supposed to call when she got back from the store, but you can bet that creep Jonathan James Leslie probably screwed that up. Don't even answer it, I con-vinced myself.

I might have been pissed, but I wasn't close to being crazy. I'd spent the entire night drunk out of my skull, but I still managed to keep my thoughts on Kayla. I wondered where she'd been and why she was so wrapped up that she couldn't even pick up a phone. I couldn't stop thinking about whether she'd called Jonathan James Leslie when we were together in Atlantic City and grew angrier when I realized she probably had. So I couldn't figure out why she hadn't snuck in a call to me while she was marooned with him.

None of that mattered, though. I wanted to talk to her. I *needed* to talk to her. I just couldn't let her know it. I had to play it cool. She needed to know I wasn't pressed. That I hadn't thought about her all night. And that I was too busy to even be concerned.

"Where the heck have you been!" I said, with about as much cool as a hot ham and cheese sandwich. "I've been worried to death!"

"I've been thinking about you too," said the caller. "That's why I'm calling about tonight."

"Tonight?" I asked, trying to place the voice.

"Yes," she said, sounding like a cheerleader who'd inhaled a can of helium.

"What's happening tonight?"

"It's been more than a couple of weeks, Mr. Walker," she continued. "And we haven't seen you back at FutraSystem. I've called and left several messages, so I thought I'd try one more time before we gave up on you. We have a weigh-in tonight and it might be a good idea for you to come back and join us."

"Oh, yeah," I said, my voice falling flat.

"Well, I hope you've been sticking with your program and I look forward to seeing you tonight," she said. "I actually thought that you and Ms. Jennings would be two of our most successful participants, but she hasn't been back either, so I'm calling her next."

"She's at the store," I said sarcastically.

"Excuse me?"

"Someone's at the door," I said, surprised she'd even heard me.

"Well, I'll let you go," she told me. "See you this evening."

Eleanor was right. It had been "a couple of weeks" since I'd been to FutraSystem. I'd called Henry a few times and he'd hooked me up with more food, but I skipped the weigh-ins because I didn't feel I needed them. I knew I was losing weight.

I rode to work and again parked away from the front door so I'd have to walk. All the while I thought of Kayla and stewed because she hadn't called. I wanted to call, just to tell her to forget about calling me, but I knew I would look pretty desperate.

You don't have to tell her to forget calling, I thought, punching my time card. She's done a pretty good job of that on her own.

"Hey, Sonny, my man."

I didn't want to answer because I was in no mood to deal with Andy.

"Sonny, *que pasa*, my man?" he said, walking toward me.

"What do you want, Andy?" I asked, glaring at him.

"I brought this for you, my man," he answered, handing me a beat-up silver thermos.

"What's this supposed to be?" I asked, unscrewing the top.

"One hundred percent fat-free protein, with a couple of other goodies mixed in, my man."

"What am I supposed to do with it?"

"Just drink it, my man," he told me, smiling. "Sip a little here, a little there, and it will give you a little boost."

"What makes you think I need a little boost?" I asked, whiffing the thermos.

"You're on a diet, right?" he asked, nodding his head. "Well, check this, my man. Little calories and little carbohydrates means little energy. And little energy means little action," he added, winking. "They don't tell you all that when they put you on these diets. Think about it, my man." His eyes tightened. "You lose the weight, the señoritas, they want you, but you ain't got not pop, 'cause you ain't eatin' so you can look good for them in the first place." He slapped me on the back. "This will give you some pop, my man."

"Thanks, Andy," I said, downing a cupful.

"*Todo lo que,* my man."

"What the heck does that mean?" I asked, screwing the top back on.

"Whatever," he answered, smiling. "It means whatever, my man."

"*Todo lo que,*" I said, walking away.

Maybe Andy's not so screwed up, I thought, walking toward my section. The machines had been wiped down by the night shift and the accessory aisles were intact. The day breezed by, although my hangover didn't leave the building until early afternoon. Evelyn, the broker who'd purchased the ab machine, stopped through and bought a pair of workout gloves and some wristbands. I couldn't believe someone as tight as her was as stressed as she claimed to be. Kayla still hadn't called, but it didn't bother me as much as it had in the morning. I figured she was making a statement I obviously wasn't trying to accept, but that I needed to come to grips with. If I was this disposable, I didn't need her. I deserved better and wasn't about to settle for the crap she was serving up. She obviously was deep into Jonathan James Leslie and that was that. If she wanted him, she could have him. She just wasn't going to have me at the same time. If she wanted to have her cake and eat it too, she was going to have to get it done without me. That wasn't about to work.

Especially with someone who ate like her.

Andy's instant pep drink worked really well. I went through the whole thermos and found myself wanting more. Andy told me to hit GNC. "Ask for some Hot Stuff, my man," he advised me, smiling.

I forced myself through a quick workout before I made my way to FutraSystem. It was the only set I'd done since the morning and it was so crappy, it reminded me of the work-out I'd had at home when Chet and E first put me through the pit. I wasn't happy about going to FutraSystem because I didn't exactly look forward to running into Kayla. If she showed up, she was going to get dissed. She'd be ignored and totally blown off. I just wondered exactly how to pull it off so she'd know I meant business.

Sometimes a guy wants to ditch a woman but she's not ready to go. She may realize the relationship is in the crap-per, and she may want to jump ship herself. She just wants to do it on her terms. I couldn't say I was ditching Kayla be-cause we didn't really have a full-blown relationship. It was more like she hit and quit it and forgot to tell me she was gone. If I made it clear I was no longer interested, she'd probably really come around. She'd call. She'd make herself available. And she'd probably cook up something real tasty. Something with seasoning that was probably basted or, better yet, deep fried. It would be totally fattening. Completely decadent. And thoroughly delicious.

And then she'd dump me.

But that would be fine. If you have to get dropped, it's easier to deal with on a full stomach.

The parking lot at FutraSystem was full of activity. There weren't many guys, but there were a lot of overweight women in a wide array of colorful, leg-suffocating stretch pants who carried brown paper bags crammed with FutraSystem food. Like me they were chasing a dream. One that said losing weight would somehow make our lives better. We'd look slimmer. Get pep in our step. The way the dream was sold to us, we would even smell better. E explained to me it had something to do with the way fat interferes with sweat glands. That never made sense to me, but I bought into it like every other poor soul who was desperate to lose weight. Overall, our pursuit of the dream was supposed to make us feel better. Better about ourselves and the world around us. Maybe it was true, but it wasn't working for me. I'd lost weight. I could feel it. Others could see it. But it really didn't make that big a difference.

I still felt like crap.

It's amazing how great a woman can make you feel. What's more incredible is how quickly the very same woman can make you feel bad. You could feel like you're on top of the world one minute, and the next a woman could have you feeling lower than a slice of moldy wedding cake. I guarantee you that some Super Bowl MVP was brought crashing back to earth when his wife rolled her eyes and sulked before saying, "They only gave you a BMW. I wanted a Porsche." For guys like me who don't even get the BMW in the first place, getting trashed by a woman ranks right up there with wrecking your shiny new ride while it still has paper tags.

It hurts.

Thankfully, it took all of two steps inside FutraSystem's door to bring me some relief.

"Mr. Walker," said a voice coming from one of the front offices. Eleanor smiled and stood up. "You look like you've followed your plan."

"I sure tried," I told her, trying to suck in as much of my gut as I could.

"It looks as if you are on your way," she said, giving me a high-five. "See you in our meeting."

"Check you later, Eleanor," I said, walking away.

I felt a bit uneasy as I walked into the meeting room. I wanted Kayla to be there as much as I didn't want her to be there. It was a crazy feeling. Being surrounded by my fellow overeaters didn't help. Eleanor marched in and wasted little time in starting the meeting. She told us how happy she was we were there and tried to make us feel like we were worthy just because we showed up. Her roll call revealed at least five of those who proclaimed their desire to "part with the pounds" a mere three weeks ago had never again bothered to show up. "Classic underachiever," she said as she passed each name that wasn't present. She then told us it was common for people to drop out at the beginning. "Some people just don't have the wherewithal," she told us, with an edge. "They are the same types who would tell you they want a million dollars, and would purchase lottery tickets as opposed to consulting with a financial planner."

"I guess you're kinda like our financial planner," said a woman from the rear of the room.

"That would be correct," Eleanor answered, smiling. "You all have invested in yourselves and it is my intention to see that you make the most of your investments."

"What happens when I want to change portfolios?" asked a guy opening a bottle of water.

"That's not an option," Eleanor said, laughing. "Just consider this a mutual fund of sorts. We are all in this together and we will succeed as such—together."

This is such crap, I thought, remembering Kayla's observation about Eleanor right after our first meeting. It was clear Eleanor had spent no time lost in the abyss of fat land. I could tell she hadn't spent nights wondering how long she could hold out until she popped out of bed for a snack that became a meal. It was obvious she hadn't ordered seconds, then thirds and later fourths because she wasn't ready to accept that being full was a state of being and not a state of body. I think we all knew Ms. Eleanor could rattle off her dress size in a New York second.

The ladies in our group probably didn't know their sizes. Didn't want to know their sizes. And could most likely recite their eighteen digit driver's license numbers before they'd even consider what their dress sizes actually were. Like me, they were probably disgusted with their cellulite, repulsed by their flab and embarrassed by the fact that the only time they saw their shoes was when they were still sitting on the rack at the store. Eleanor was about as fit to lead us as she was the Green Bay Packers. And she'd probably have more luck getting them to the Super Bowl, because they'd at least get paid for their suffering.

We were paying FutraSystem for ours.

"Mr. Walker," Eleanor said, forcing me to look up. "Why don't you tell us about your first three weeks on the program? It appears you have had some measure of success. Maybe you can give your fellow members a few hints. Perhaps you can tell them about your favorite FutraSystem dishes."

"What's up, y'all?" I said, standing up.

"Mr. Walker," Eleanor said, shaking her head and waving her finger.

"Oh, yeah," I answered. "My name is Sonny and I have a weight problem."

"You can say that again," a woman in an off-white sweat-suit casually stated.

"Very good, Mr. Walker," Eleanor replied, giving me a thumbs-up.

"I don't have much to say," I told the group. "I've actually had a pretty rough go of it since the last time I was here. First, I got screwed over for a promotion at work because I was fat."

"*Was?*" said an unknown voice from the side of the room.

"Anyway," I went on. "They asked me to pose as a tent at work, and then they sold all the tents."

"What's so bad about that?" asked someone.

"Like I said, I didn't get the promotion, so the tents were sold in what should have been my department."

"Big deal," said an older guy sitting in the row behind mine. "You still have a job so you can still eat. That's what really counts."

"Good point," everyone agreed, nodding their heads.

"So I lose out on my promotion and then I hook up with a woman and we go to Atlantic City for the weekend."

"That sounds really terrible," muttered someone sarcastically. "Did you win anything or did you just hang out at the restaurants?"

"I barely ate," I told them. "Right before that my boys—well, I guess they're still my boys—anyway, they hooked my spot up with all this exercise equipment, so I got on this really tough exercise program."

"That's excellent, Mr. Walker," Eleanor said, again giving me a thumbs-up. "Nothing beats friends who are supportive."

"They ain't all that supportive," I told her. "They constantly run down people with weight problems. It's almost like they don't see me sometimes. They told me not to date my lady friend because she was fat." I shook my head. "I wanted to ask them, 'What the heck do you think I am?' "

"You're definitely fat," said someone from the left side of the room.

"That's what my friend's bird told me," I answered, shaking my head.

"What kind of bird is it?" asked one woman.

"He sounds like an intelligent bird," said another woman, seated beside her.

"I don't know what kind of bird he is, but he called me fat, these two idiots from Uncle Leon's called me fat, and between them, my so-called friends, my coworkers and just about everybody else, I got fed up and decided I *had* to do something."

"Uncle Leon's," said some guy, smiling. "Do they still have that two-for-one dessert special?"

"They had it last night," answered the woman sitting beside him.

"And how would you know that, Mrs. Jackson?" asked Eleanor, rising to her feet.

"Because I was there," replied the woman, lowering her head.

"So was I."

"Me too."

"I had a strawberry shortcake and a tapioca pudding."

"Wait just one minute!" yelled Eleanor. "Just how, please explain to me exactly *how* do you all expect to lose weight if you persist in eating food and desserts that are not on the program?"

"The food on the program isn't fit for human consumption," answered the woman sitting beside me.

"It's terrible."

"Wouldn't make my *worst* enemy eat it."

"It's just plain nasty."

"Would you all shut the heck up so we can get out of here in time to hit Uncle Leon's?"

We were in trouble.

"Ladies and gentlemen," said Eleanor, walking to the front of the room. "This simply will not work. You are only cheating yourselves and it will not be tolerated. We are a team. Look at Mr. Walker here." She pointed toward me. "He has made progress. He hasn't been to our meetings as he should have, but he's *clearly* stuck with the program. Let him explain it to you. It is not *that* difficult."

"Well, actually . . ." I said, again rising to my feet.

"Mr. Walker," Eleanor said, exasperated.

"Oh, yeah," I replied, embarrassed. "My name is Sonny and I have a weight problem."

"Thank you, Mr. Walker," she said, returning to her seat.

"Check this out," I said, turning toward the group. "Y'all are right *and* Eleanor is right. This FutraSystem crap is as useless as a beach without sand. But you can't win if you don't play the game. Last time I was here, each and every one of us had a horror story to tell about how our weight had screwed *something* for us. And look at yourselves now. You're even worse than you were three weeks ago."

"He's right," whispered someone two rows back.

"I don't know about y'all," I said, my voice cracking. "But I'm not going out like this. Like Eleanor said, nobody's getting cheated but us, and if y'all want to stay like this, y'all are doing the right thing."

"Listen to him," urged Eleanor, nodding her head.

"Losing this weight, it ain't all about being thin," I told them. "It's about your health. It's about you being able to run behind your kids and about being able to walk up a flight of stairs without resting after each step. Who in here wouldn't mind not being afraid to stop when you pass a mirror and not worrying about who's going to laugh behind your back when you leave a crowded elevator? This food may suck but you can't substitute it with stuff that's even worse for you and your health. Think about this," I summed up. "You paid for this crap because you wanted to lose the weight. I hate it so much I can barely eat it. But if you're not going to eat it and you're going to put on more weight, what in the world are you doing here, anyway?"

No one said a word.

Well, almost no one.

"I'm here because I owe you an apology."

I couldn't believe it.

"I didn't handle things properly and I don't want you to think the wrong things."

It was really her.

"I needed to sort things out. I knew I had a decision to make and I made it."

She actually showed up like I wanted her to.

"I only hope you'll give me a chance to explain," she said, walking toward me.

"Go ahead," said the woman in the off-white sweatsuit. "It would beat that speech he just made us sit through."

"This should be cute," muttered the guy with the bottled water.

"Could you kids speed this up?" asked a woman, looking at her watch. "Uncle Leon's closes in a couple of hours."

Eleanor was right, I thought, turning toward Kayla. This group is pathetic.

"Can we talk?" Kayla asked, reaching for my hand.

"Here?" I asked, surprised.

"Well, not exactly," she said, smiling. "Why don't we go to your place?"

"My place?" I asked, remembering how she'd done all she could to stay away from my spot.

"I think that would be a good idea," she told me. "Mr. Jonathan James Leslie is moving his belongings from my place."

"Really?" I asked, surprised. "Any chance of him taking KJ with him?"

"Who's KJ?" asked someone from the rear of the room.

"He's the bird," I told them.

"The one who calls him fat boy," said a guy in a dark-blue warm-up suit.

"The smart bird," added the guy with the water bottle.

"He ever eat at Uncle Leon's?" asked the lady with the off-white sweatsuit.

I didn't know if KJ had ever eaten at Uncle Leon's but it didn't matter. I still didn't know if he tasted like chicken, but that didn't matter either. Kayla had made a decision that hopefully included me. Jonathan James Leslie was breaking camp. And I was losing weight because I wanted to, and not for someone else.

Life was about to get pretty dog-on good and I couldn't wait to taste it.

Chapter 18

Kayla and I left the building and our FutraSystem buddies behind. I didn't bother weighing-in and didn't buy any more FutraSystem food. I'd snuck and bought enough from Henry to last at least two months over the past few weeks. Oddly, Kayla didn't weigh in and she didn't buy any food either. Eleanor again congratulated me and made it clear she was changing formats for the next meeting. "We're going to meet again this week, because I'm not convinced the every-week concept will work for this group," she said, sounding worried.

I had already decided that like it or not, I was sticking with the program. The food was so bad it had to work. I definitely wouldn't overeat as I'd often done in the past; in fact, I'd barely eat at all, which absolutely worked in my favor.

As we headed toward my truck, Kayla winked at me and told me she missed me. I missed her too, but she wasn't about to hear it from me. The way I saw it, she had put the ball back in my court, where it belonged. It worried me that I'd actually missed her as much as I had. It's simply not supposed to work that way. She was a woman. She was supposed to miss *me*. She was the one who was supposed to toss and turn and wonder where I was at three in the morning. She was supposed to pick up the receiver to make sure the phone was working because it had refused to ring. And she was the one who was supposed to swear *me* off and make pacts with herself that she'd never see me again and that she was better off without me. She was a woman. And that's how women operate. Not that guys don't operate much the same way. They do stuff like that too. In fact, they do all of it.

Because guys are so screwed up, women get more practice at it, so they just do it better.

My first duty was to stop at GNC like Andy said. I'd probably passed by GNC a million times in my life and not once considered what really went on behind their doors. I'd seen their commercials on ESPN and figured they sold stuff to bodybuilders and vitamin geeks. That essentially eliminated me from their desired demographic. As soon as I hit the door, it appeared I was wrong. I was greeted like I was a major stockholder.

"How are you today, sir?" the very fit guy behind the counter asked, smiling. "Is there anything I can assist you with?"

I could tell I wouldn't like him. He had broad shoulders

like me. He just didn't have the stomach to match it. His close-cropped dusty-brown hair was neat and combed to one side like Opie's from *The Andy Griffith Show* and his khaki slacks and stiff blue button-collared shirt appeared to have had major sessions on somebody's ironing board.

"Yeah," I answered, looking over the aisles of brightly labeled vitamins, minerals and other healthy junk. "I'm looking for something called Hot Stuff."

"Hot Stuff," he said, walking around the counter. "It's one of our best sellers."

"What does it do?" Kayla asked, following us down an aisle.

"It's a low-fat food supplement. Many of our customers utilize it to add mass."

"I don't think I need mass," I admitted.

"Well, sir," the salesguy said. "If you are trying to lose weight and it's your desire to tone up, this may not be such a bad way to go."

"It doesn't make much sense to me," Kayla said, as he handed her a cannister. "Why would someone want to add mass when they're trying to lose weight?"

"Well, ma'am," the salesguy started. "Many people lose weight and end up with an incredible amount of flab. They don't work out during the process and they don't anticipate that without tone, you could end up with sloppy, disgusting flab. If you go through the very real pain and sacrifice it takes to lose actual fat, you might want to build good, solid muscle as well. I know it sounds complicated, but trust me, neither of you really wants to lose weight without addressing the need of adding a little lean muscle."

He was right. It did sound complicated and like Kayla said, it didn't seem to make sense.

But I bought two cannisters anyway.

The way I saw it, it had to work. Over the years, each and every scheme I'd tried to lose weight had one thing in common: all of the diets were pitched as being easy. Nothing to decipher. Nothing to figure out. Nothing to worry about. "It's just so easy," they tried to convince me. I believed weight-loss programs worked because they were supposed to work. If an ad said I could eat and lose weight, like the Gut-Away ad said, I ate. That was always easy. If the ad led me to believe I could use the product at my leisure, I used it just like that, at my leisure, which basically meant I rarely used it. *Easy* is without a doubt the buzz word of the diet industry. The companies and ad execs nailed it right. They knew slobs like me liked hearing that *anything* was easy. Even if it didn't work.

The salesguy, who asked us to call him Josh, showed me some other "diet enhancing products." Josh convinced me I needed vitamins C, E and B-12. He sold me on something called Ginsana, which would help me to better utilize oxygen. "You'll need a good multivitamin and the Hot Stuff will give you the protein, carbohydrates and amino acids your body will be crying for," he advised. He gave me his card and told me to start slow. "If you work out too hard you'll get sore and that may just discourage you," he said, walking us out of the store.

If only he knew.

There was no way *anything* would have discouraged me. I had promised myself that I'd lose my weight and failure simply wasn't an option.

We didn't say much as we headed toward my place. All I could think about was where she had been and why she hadn't called. I didn't want to bring it up and it appeared she didn't either. I just hurried to get home so we could talk and she could confess. But, as women often do, she avoided the topic and kept the heat on me.

"You seem almost possessed about this weight thing," Kayla said as we pulled into my parking lot.

"And you're not pressed about it?" I asked, smiling.

"You know I care about it," she shot back. "But I don't believe I'm as consumed by it as you are."

"It's not a matter of being consumed," I said, parking my truck. "I'm just sick and tired of carrying around another person or two." I laughed. "Maybe if I lose all this weight, you'll be more attracted to me. And then we can really roll."

"Roll?" she asked, looking toward me.

"Yeah," I said, walking around to open her door. "*Roll.* Rolling is like moving in the right direction any way we can."

"I know what rolling is, Sonny," she said, stepping out of the truck and onto the sidewalk. "I just wonder why you choose some of the words you choose."

"I'm a guy and one of the things that makes guys, guys is that we can say just about anything we want to get our point across."

"Is that responsible?" she asked, walking toward my porch.

"Is it responsible for a woman to pick at the way a guy speaks when she gets his point and if he's not dissing her?" I shot back.

"It's not about getting disrespected," she said, shaking her head. "I'm not about to tolerate that, anyway, so respect is not the issue. I expect you to respect me because I'm going to respect you. I just don't understand why men go out of their way to inject so much slang into their speech when they know better."

"I get your point, Kayla," I said, opening the front door. "'Cause I'm trying to figure why it matters in the first place."

"What do you mean by that?" she asked, walking into the kitchen.

"I mean that Mr. Perfect Diction himself, Jonathan James Leslie, was probably a jerk, so isn't it more important for a guy to mean what he says and stand by it than for him to talk all proper and blow smoke up your behind?" I said, placing my bags on the counter.

"That's not fair," Kayla said, sounding frustrated. "This is not about Jonathan, it's about why you speak the way you speak."

"I talk how I talk because I'm comfortable with my rap," I said, unpacking the bags and placing the vitamins on the counter. "And this probably ain't no Jonathan James Leslie thing, but like I said, he talks better than a college professor and look where it got him. His proper-talking behind is moving his crap outta your joint right now and you're stuck here watching me chop up the language like I'm toting a samurai sword or something. I think I'm about to start talking *real* crazy since it got me this far," I added sarcastically, and walked out of the kitchen.

That was a mistake. Ragging on Mr. Grammar Machine himself, Jonathan James Leslie, wasn't a mistake because he had *F-O-O-L* written all over him. The mistake was allow-ing Kayla out of the kitchen. As soon as I clicked on the light switch, I hurried to click it back off.

"What are you doing, Sonny?" she asked, concerned.

"W-w-why don't we go upstairs?" I quickly answered.

"I'd actually prefer to stay down here," she said. "I don't want to rush up to your bedroom. You might think I'm easy or something." She laughed. "Besides, I'd like to see your place. I'd like to see how you live." She reached for the light switch. "You can tell a lot about the way someone keeps his place."

I was hoping she didn't really feel that way.

"Sonny!" she gasped, turning off the light even faster than I did.

"Yo," I answered.

"What happened in here? Are you some kind of closet alcoholic or something?" she asked, worried. "Is *this* how you lost your weight?"

"Nah," I answered, smiling, even though she couldn't see me. "Me and my partners—I *guess* they're still my partners—anyway, we just had a few brews and things got a little out of hand."

"A *little* out of hand," she said, concerned. "How often do you get a little out of hand?"

"Not often," I answered. "None of us handles liquor well."

"How did it get out of hand?" she asked.

"They got to talking about how women suck, then they started in on fat-this and fat-that nonsense and it just got crazy," I told her. "I got tired of it, so there was a little scuffle and then I put them out."

"And these are your partners?" she said, sounding like a true cynic.

"I guess they're still my partners," I said, shrugging my shoulders.

"You guess?" she shot back. "Was it worth it?"

"Oh, it was worth it," I answered, wondering why we were *still* standing in the dark. "I know the liquor was talking and all that, but they had it coming. I was tired of all that fat crap and they knew it, but it didn't stop them from riding me, so I handled my business."

"You handled your business," she said, clearly unimpressed.

"Yeah," I told her. "Look, Kayla," I said, before pausing. "Why the heck are we still standing in the dark?"

"Because you didn't handle your business," she told me, laughing. "This place is a wreck." She turned on the light. "Why don't you find me a nice big trash bag and something to clean with and find yourself a seat."

"I can get it later," I told her, walking toward the kitchen.

"You could have gotten it by now had you intended to get it," she said, rolling up her sleeves. "This won't take but a minute."

It took a little longer than a minute, but she definitely handled *her* business. While she cleaned, I worked out in the pit. I told her I would help, but she wouldn't let me. "Do another set of something and think of me while you do it," she said, pointing me back toward the pit. I didn't need to do anything to think about her. That was happening no matter what. I had to admit it was nice, really nice, having her there. Even if we were in separate rooms and in seemingly different worlds, we were together. She cleaned like my place was hers. It was like she'd decided she was there to stay. At least it seemed like she would stay. Until she slowed down enough to check out the top of my television.

"Interesting," she told me, picking up one of the frames. "Let me guess," she added, picking up another picture and then another. "Marsha."

I didn't know what to say.

"So this is Miss Marsha," she said, walking toward me. "This is the woman you can't let go of."

"You know Marsha's history," I told her. "You're the one who won't let her go."

"Right," she said, upset. "If I'm the one who can't let her go, why the heck are you the one with the cute little fine arts museum in her honor?"

"It's just some old pictures, Kayla," I stressed.

"If these are just some old pictures and she supposedly dumped you over a year ago, why do you still have them up?" she asked, holding two frames in her outstretched hands.

"I-I-I . . . "

"Don't stutter now," she demanded.

"It's-it's-it's not like I'm stuttering," I said nervously. "I just don't have a real good answer to your question. At least I don't have one I think will work."

"Why don't you just tell the truth, Sonny!" she exclaimed. "Why don't you just admit that you still aren't over her and that she could walk in that door right now and you'd drool like a sick puppy dog? I can't believe I'm wasting my time on somebody who's hung up on a no-good wench like her. She treated you like dirt and you're still hanging on to her pictures just like you're hanging on to her."

"I'm not hanging on to her, Kayla," I said, walking toward her. "I'm trying to hang on to you."

I then took the pictures and one by one tossed them into the trash bag.

"You missed one," she said, smiling.

"She's not in that one," I told her, picking up the first frame. "That's my boy Chet with his sister before she got locked up, and E and his ex, Carla, before she left him for his cousin." I reached for her hand.

"I don't think I got that right," she said, shaking her head.

"You got it right," I told her. "I'll tell you all about it one day."

We then leaned against the wall as she tossed another empty bottle into the garbage bag.

"Let me say something, Kayla," I whispered.

"Don't say another word, Mr. Walker," she said, turning toward me and smiling. "Just kiss me like you mean it."

"Sounds like a plan," I answered, nodding my head. "Sounds just like a plan."

She dropped everything to the floor and laid a kiss on *me* that was as gentle as it was firm. Everything suddenly became clear. Kayla was making a statement. Her cleaning up was making a statement. It was as if she were saying, I took care of this, so you would be advised not to have some other chick kicking up her heels in this spot. Especially some other chick you've got a bunch of pictures of. And her kiss. The message was simple—My lips + your lips = our lips. Kisses like hers were lasting and she knew it. Kayla understood passion and she used it like a chaps-wearing, tobacco-spewing cowboy uses rope. She was an expert.

We made our way to the sofa and just stared at each other. With our eyes, we asked all the right questions. And with our bodies, the answers were made simple.

Even though we tried to get comfortable, there was no way two people our size would be able to get it on, on that sofa. The Reverend Al Sharpton would wear a kinky Afro and a tailored three-piece-suit first.

We forced ourselves up and started to laugh. It was clear that almost at the same moment we imagined just how ridiculous we must have looked trying to wiggle and squirm so we could somehow fit on a sofa that had to be screaming for relief.

"Sonny," she said, laughing. "Maybe it's time we take this upstairs."

"Let's not," I replied, reaching for her hand.

"Why not?" she asked, surprised. "Do you have pictures up there too?"

"Nah," I said, sitting back. "I just figured we could talk."

"Oh, really. And just what would you like to talk about?"

"What happened with you and Jonathan."

"I already told you, I had a decision to make and I made it."

"That doesn't tell me a whole lot."

"What exactly do you need to know?" she asked, leaning her head against my shoulder.

"I'm trying to find out what really happened. I want to know why you went so long without giving me a shout and what store you went to that was open around the clock."

"What store are you talking about?" she asked, puzzled.

"You said you'd call me when you got back from the store, and last time I checked, you *still* haven't called a brother," I said, smiling.

"I think I get your point. Look, Sonny," she said, sitting up. "I tracked Jonathan down and told him we needed to talk. He dropped by and I lost track of time. I thought the conversation would be easier than it was, but he wasn't having it. Want a piece of advice?" she asked. "Never dump somebody at *your* place."

"Why?" I asked, looking toward her.

"You drop them at your place and they may not want to leave," she said. "They may start tripping and they might just start taking inventory."

"Taking inventory?"

"Yes," she said forcefully. "They may decide to remind you they gave you this gift and that present and then you're arguing about stuff instead of discussing what went wrong with the relationship."

"Maybe you have a point," I told her.

"Believe me, I do," she said. "If you ever dump somebody, insist on going to her place so you can leave when you're done."

"It's that easy, huh?" I asked.

"I didn't say it was easy," she answered. "I just said that's the way to do it."

"So it's done?"

"It's done," she said slowly. "And let's just leave it at that."

"It's left," I assured her.

We then leaned back against the sofa and she said she envied me.

"Why?" I asked, surprised.

"You have so much willpower. You've already lost weight and you're positioning yourself to lose even more," she said, playing with my fingers. "I want to lose my weight, I really do. But it's just not a big enough issue for me."

"Well, I can't make your issues for you, but I'd imagine

your health is an issue you care about," I said, looking her over. "If your health isn't important, I hope it becomes important, because it may be the only thing that really counts."

"I know you're right, Sonny, I really do," she admitted. "But I'm okay with me and who I am. Don't get me wrong. I'd like to be slim and trim like Eleanor, but I don't *have* to be that way to be happy. I have a career, a beautiful home, the car I've always wanted." She smiled. "And I've even met a wonderful man who can *handle his business,*" she said, shaking her head and moving her shoulders with each word. "I'm happy Sonny. You know I exercise and that my health is in order. Being overweight hasn't stopped me from doing anything besides fitting into a bikini."

"You're too much," I said, shaking my head and smiling.

"You are too," she whispered before kissing me. "Sonny," she said, as we pulled apart. "This evening has been very special."

"It really has," I told her, smiling. "I really didn't expect this."

"Why not?" she asked.

"I guess I thought you had run off with Jonathan or something," I admitted.

"I didn't run off with Jonathan or anything," she whispered, reaching for my hand. "But I wouldn't mind running off somewhere with you."

"Somewhere like where?" I asked.

"Somewhere like upstairs," she said, standing up. "Let's go."

"Sounds like a plan," I answered, leading the way. "Sounds just like a plan."

Chapter 19

Suggesting that we go upstairs was the best thing she'd said all night. The weekend we spent in Atlantic City was great. The night we spent in my bedroom was *incredible*. She was different. Very, very different. She held me tighter, caressed me with more passion and moved with a deep, deep sense of purpose. Much like when we kissed on the sofa, it was clear she was making a statement. I felt she wanted to convince me that she was interested in taking our situation to an entirely different level.

When we woke up the next morning, I was convinced.

"Good morning, handsome," she whispered, trying to reach her arm across my midsection.

She would have had to have arms as long as Lurch from *The Addams Family* to reach that far.

"How did you sleep?" she asked, smiling.

"I slept great," I said happily. "I didn't even have an urge to eat."

"Wow," she said sarcastically. "And I was just starting to believe that maybe I had something to do with your fantastic night."

"You had a lot to do with it," I said, sitting up. "If you hadn't been here, I'd have probably been awake thinking about you," I admitted.

"Really?" she asked, sounding surprised.

"Yeah," I told her. "I'm really into you. I like it when we hang out and I want to know more about you."

"I'd like to know more about you too," she countered.

"Let me run to the bathroom real quick," I said, stepping away from the bed.

"Do you have an extra toothbrush?" she asked.

"I'll leave one on the counter," I told her. "I'll use the bathroom in the hall."

I checked my watch as I made my way to the bathroom. It was only seven and I didn't have to be at work until eleven. I blazed through my "lucky enough to have a woman at the crib in the morning" routine—brush the hair, brush the teeth, brush the hair *again* and generally convince yourself that the woman really wants to be there—and then hurried back down the hall into my bedroom.

"What are we going to do about breakfast?" she asked, buttoning up her blouse.

"I'm not really hungry," I answered. "But I'll throw something together if you're hungry."

"As long as it's not that FutraSystem junk," she told me. "Those FutraEggs didn't come from any chicken I've ever heard about."

"They are pretty crappy," I agreed. "But they're on the program, so what do we do?"

"We should be able to eat like regular human beings," she answered.

"That's the problem," I said, laughing. "We don't eat like regular human beings."

"Touché," she answered, reaching for my hand.

Then she kissed me and said we should go downstairs. She wanted to eat. To her surprise, there were nothing but yellow and red FutraSystem boxes on the kitchen counters. She was really upset when she flung open the cabinets, only to be confronted with rows of neatly arranged boxes of FutraSnacks, FutraFoods and other FutraGoodies. Kayla was on the prowl like a junkie in search of a quick hit. She needed food. I didn't have any. And she couldn't deal with it.

"We've got to get out of here," she said, reaching for a seat.

"Why?" I asked, concerned.

"We need to get some food," she replied, fanning herself with the morning paper. "Let's just go."

"Are you okay?" I said, offering her some water.

"I'll be just fine," she answered, nodding her head. "Thanks for the water. It was right on time."

"I'll run upstairs, throw on some clothes and we can roll out," I said, heading for the stairs.

I decided to put on my Sports Authority gear so I'd be ready for work. If we were going to eat, we'd be out awhile. Especially if she had an appetite. We ended up at BET's exciting, new Sound Stage restaurant in Largo. Huge TV screens and an impressive collection of contemporary Black art, movie and music memorabilia gave the dining room the type of inviting atmosphere we needed, because she was inviting a bunch of food up into her mouth. Kayla started off simple. A cup of coffee, a glass of orange juice and a nice fluffy cheese Danish lasted all of two minutes. Then she downed two king-sized omelets, one stuffed with shrimp, crabmeat, scallops and cheese and another with shredded chicken, mushrooms, green peppers, cheese and onions. After that, she had a plate of chilled honeydew melon and cantaloupe, and she finished her feast with another large cup of coffee and, of course, a large Diet Coke.

"You barely ate," she said, sipping her coffee.

"I told you I wasn't that hungry," I reminded her, smiling. "I had an English muffin and a nice glass of juice. That was enough for me."

"O-k-a-a-y," she said, again sipping her coffee. "You want to talk?"

"Sure," I answered, nodding my head. "What did you feel like talking about?"

"I'll leave that up to you," she told me. "You push the buttons and we'll just go with it."

"All right," I started. "I know you said you wanted to leave the whole Jonathan thing alone, but after last night, I can't help but wonder what happened."

"What happened last night that has you wondering about him?"

"You just seemed so different," I said, tapping my fingers on the table. "You rolled out big time."

"I rolled out big time," she repeated, slowly stirring her coffee.

"Big time," I said, smiling. "You were so excited, I thought I'd hit your G spot or something."

"And why do you think that is?" she asked, looking down.

"Why don't you tell me," I said, looking toward her.

"Okay." She sighed, took another sip of coffee. "I was different because I felt different," she said. "I felt different about you, I felt different about Jonathan—everything just seemed so different to me. It just seemed so right."

"It seemed so right," I repeated.

"It seemed really right," she said, smiling. "It was like I was free, Sonny. I'd been stuck for so long and last night was the first time I felt free. I was relieved."

"Relieved because you'd dropped Jonathan?"

"You got it," she said, looking down at her coffee. "I met Jonathan nearly three years ago. I told you my dad represents athletes, didn't I?"

"Yeah," I answered. "You told me that."

"Well, Jonathan was supposed to be one of his star clients," she said, looking away. "Jonathan James Leslie was the next can't-miss Olympic gold medal hurdler. Jonathan didn't believe he had to work hard, so he didn't train like he should have. My dad had lined up some pretty lucrative endorsements that would have set him up for life."

"So what happened?"

"He didn't even qualify for a bid to the Games," she said. "All he had to do was make the team, which was pretty much a given. But he was disqualified for false starting three times in a row. The race went on and he just stood in his starting block and watched his dreams, his endorsements and every-thing he'd worked for run down that track without him."

"I thought you said he hadn't worked hard," I reminded her.

"He didn't train hard for the Games because he'd lost his son," she said, again looking down at her coffee. "His coach tried to push him, but Jonathan couldn't concentrate so he'd just go to the track and sit in the stands. Before he knew it, the trials were there and he just wasn't ready." She shook her head. "He hasn't run competitively since."

"So how did y'all hook up?" I asked.

"I was just there for him. My dad pretty much dropped both of us at about the same time, and we chatted on the el-evator while we were leaving the building," she said, starting to smile. "We went out and found that we had a lot in com-mon."

"Like what?" I asked, looking toward her.

"We were both kind of loners and we hated my dad." She laughed. "He ditched my mom and we've never heard from her since, and he dumped on me all my life because of my weight," she said, her mood quickly changing. "He was ashamed of me and he did all he could to embarrass me into losing the weight. He said I was a fat, lazy, slob who couldn't keep friends, just like my mom, and he threatened to run me out of his life just like he did her. He'd dumped Jonathan, so we just started hanging out and got kind of involved. My roommate got married and left, and Jonathan had lost his apartment, so I told him he could stay with me until he got back on his feet and, three years later, he's still not on his feet. We didn't really have a relationship, but he was a decent guy, plus he came in handy."

"What do you mean he came in handy?" I asked.

"I was starting my own business and I had to get out and socialize," she said, looking toward me. "Showing up with a well-dressed, handsome, articulate man like Jonathan was a plus—even if I had to pay for all his clothes."

We both laughed at that one.

"He encouraged me and I think he really believed in me," she said. "I really believed in him and thought he was being totally straight with me. But I found out he was seeing someone else and there wasn't much I could say because we'd never really discussed a commitment. So I confronted him, he told me he wanted me and we *supposedly* started a relationship."

"Supposedly?" I asked.

"Like I told you before," she said, smiling, "Jonathan has issues."

"What kind of issues?"

"Women like Jonathan," she said, looking me in the eye. "And Jonathan *loves* women. He did it all." She sighed. "Slept with my ex-best friend, took women out in my car, used my MasterCard to send flowers to some bimbo, and he even had the nerve to escort some young twit to a reception for one of my father's clients. The only thing he didn't do over the course of three years was bring a woman into my house. And knowing him, he probably did that too."

"Dude is a trip," I said, shaking my head.

"Dude *was* a trip," she said, pointing at me.

"If he was rolling like that, why did you stay with him?" I asked.

"I think, in my mind," she started, sounding stressed, "I really believed Jonathan was almost doing me a favor. He was a fine, fine man with a soul, a spirit, and a sense of goals and of accomplishment. And I looked up and he was with *me*. I'm no fool, Sonny, I'm realistic about my weight and I know how people feel about it. But I convinced myself that any man who would deal with me would at least do so because he was into me and not my body or anything superficial like that. I always knew Jonathan was out of my league, so I started to believe his just being around when he *was* around was a big deal." She looked down at her coffee. "I thought he gave me credibility as a woman. Even though I was supporting him, I still believed that someone as smart and as handsome as Jonathan was doing me a favor by spending any time with me at all." Kayla wiped a tear from her face.

"Here you go," I said, handing her a napkin. "I don't mean no harm, Kayla," I added, reaching for her hand, "but you gave *him* credibility." I smiled. "You made *him* relevant and he's the one who really needed *you*. You may have wanted him but he *needed* you. He'll be crawling back before the week is out. I just hope you're strong enough to tell him it's too late when he shows up."

"That you don't have to worry about," she said, looking up. "Jonathan is done."

"He's toast," I said, nodding my head.

"Toast," she repeated, slapping me five.

"That's one order of toast," our waiter said, reaching for one of the plates Kayla had left in front of her.

"That's okay," Kayla said, smiling. "I think we've already had enough."

"Your companion barely ate," the waiter reminded her.

"I'm aware of that," Kayla answered, giving him a stare that would have sent Hitler into retreat.

"The toast will be on the house," he acknowledged, realizing he'd said something she didn't care for.

"So what about you, Sonny?" she asked, looking toward me. "What little demons would you like to exorcise?"

"None," I said, smiling. "You know all about Marsha. And I told you about my boys. Well, I guess they're still my boys."

"They're still your boys. If they were ever your boys, they'll always be your boys," she said, nodding her head. "So since you can't tell me much more about them, why don't you tell me about your family."

"There's not a lot to tell. You already know I was born in Detroit, but my parents sent me out here so I could be raised by my aunt in the suburbs."

"How did you deal with being away from your parents?" she asked.

"It was tough at first, but I made friends pretty quick, plus I got to go back to Detroit every summer. Detroit was pretty rough back then, so I knew they were doing the right thing, even though I wanted to be at home. I loved my parents, but my aunt was cool. She was a teacher and the schools here had a good reputation," I said, smiling.

"Did she have children of her own?"

"Sure didn't," I answered. "But she treated me like I was her very own. My aunt Bunny was the best. She passed about eight years ago and I still miss her. The house we just left, it was hers. She left it to me."

"I'm sorry about your aunt," she whispered. "I didn't know."

"It's okay," I said, looking toward her.

"What about your mom and dad?" she asked, looking back.

"My father worked on the line at the Cadillac plant until he could buy himself one," I said softly. "And he passed a month later. My mother said he had a heart attack when he got his payment book and realized what the car note would be. Cadillac was real decent. They let my mom keep the car and it's been parked in her garage for nearly twenty years."

"So your mom is still in Detroit?" she asked.

"Heck, yeah. She's there with my baby brother, Tayvon. Tayvon is dad's son by his other wife, Coreen."

"Your dad had two wives?"

"Coreen sure thought so," I said, laughing. "She showed up at the funeral and sat right next to my mother and they cried like they were sisters. They rode in the hearse together and greeted friends and family at the house. And they basically helped each other get over my father's death." I smiled. "Two weeks later, Coreen showed up and introduced us to our new family member, Tayvon."

"Are you serious?"

"Very," I answered.

"Here's your toast, ma'am," the waiter said, sliding the plate onto the table.

"Thanks," she said, reaching for a knife and a packet of grape jelly.

"So Coreen stops by with Tayvon," she said, reminding me where I left off.

"Yeah," I said, looking away. "She stops by with little Tay and says she has to run to the store. My mom had already dealt with Coreen being his mistress; she accepted that pretty well, I thought. But then Coreen pops up with a four-year-old kid and drops him off like my mom was just supposed to baby-sit my old man's illegitimate son." I shook my head. "That was too much."

"Did your mom know about Tayvon?"

"If she did she never let on. Coreen went off to the store just like she said. And twenty-something years later, she's still there," I told Kayla, looking at my glass of water. "We took Tayvon in and my mother raised him as if he were her own. I guess the fact that he looked exactly like my dad and had all of his mannerisms, right down to his having to have ketchup on literally everything he ate, didn't hurt."

"That's why you jumped on me about going to the store?" she asked, reaching for my hand.

"You got it," I answered, looking toward her.

"So how did you feel about having a new brother?"

"I felt great. Tayvon turned out to be a straight-A student, plus he's responsible and he takes good care of mom. He's an attorney back in the motor city and he's about to get married. We don't get to talk a lot, both of us are pretty busy, but we are definitely brothers. He's a lawyer, I work at Sports Authority and we still compete about who *really* has it going on."

"What about your mom?" she asked, chomping on a piece of toast.

"My mom is as cool as they come," I said, smiling. "We talk maybe once a month. Moms is so busy nobody can keep up with her. If it's not her mall-walking club, it's her bingo trips." I laughed. "When she's not at a bingo table, she's pulling slots in Vegas or jetting to the islands to catch up with her other newly rich widow buddies."

"Your mom is rich?" she asked, opening another packet of jelly.

"My mom is smart," I told her, downing a sip of water. "Mom had four different insurance policies on my old man. After my dad died, she admitted to me that she suspected my dad had at least three other women, and if they came calling, or showed up with some kids like Coreen, she'd be ready for them."

"She'd be ready?"

"Yeah," I said, nodding my head. "She'd sit and have tea with them, share some old 'Tiger did this' or 'Tiger did that' stories."

"Tiger?" she asked.

"Tiger was my father's nickname. Anyway, she said if they showed up, she'd listen to their crap, smile politely and then give them what they really came for," I said, shaking my head.

"Which was?" she asked, downing another piece of toast.

"Money," I answered. "Before Coreen broke camp she and my mom were so close it scared everyone else off because they figured if there was any money, Coreen had already tied it up. If there were some other women, they never made themselves known, so Moms kept Tayvon, she kept the cash and she's living the life."

"So with your family back in Detroit, what kept you in Maryland?" she asked, smiling.

"I wanted to get a degree but it didn't work out," I admitted. "I started back over at P.G. Community College, but after Marsha I kind of gave up on that."

"Do you plan on going back or are you going to let Marsha impact on that too?"

"I'll probably go back. But right now the only thing I'm thinking about is losing this dag-on weight," I said, laughing.

"I know what you mean," she shot back, grinning.

The waiter returned and slid the check toward Kayla. I guess he figured since she'd eaten enough for just about everybody in the restaurant, she should pick up the tab.

"I got it," I said, reaching for the red-and-white-striped check.

"That's okay, Sonny," she told me. "I wanted to go to breakfast, so this one's on me."

"You can get dinner the next time we go out," I said, smiling.

"Okay," she replied, nodding her head.

I pulled out two twenties and left another $7 for the tip. Kayla had managed to devour $33 worth of food, and I felt with all the running around she put him through, the waiter absolutely earned the tip. We looked at each other and she reached for my hand.

"Yo, Kayla," I said, cautiously. "Let me ask you something."

"Yo, Sonny," she said, mocking me. "Go right ahead."

"I'm trying to figure out why you like me—like, what do you see in me?" I asked.

"What do I see in you," she repeated. "First, you're such a nice, nice guy. You're funny, I like your confidence and your perseverance," she added, smiling. "You seem honest and you know what you want. And I must admit I find you quite handsome, not to mention the fact that you're a sensuous and attentive love. To top it off, you also have a little street in you and I definitely find that alluring. And I like the way you dance."

"I *love* the way you dance," I told her.

We grabbed hands and headed toward my truck and went

back to my place. I had just enough time to run in and knock off a set in the pit. Kayla went back where she'd left off cleaning the night before. I felt so good I downed some vitamins, drank some Hot Stuff, swallowed some Ginsana and went through another set. I hurried to change clothes and then walked to the rec room toward Kayla.

"I'm about to go," I said, looking at my watch.

"You have anything to hide, Sonny?" she asked, throwing a bottle in the huge brown trash bag.

"Nah," I asked, shaking my head. "Why would you ask that?"

"Well, if you don't mind," she said, sitting on the sofa, "I'd like to hang around and finish cleaning up here."

"I think I can deal with that," I told her, smiling. "Just lock up when you leave."

"You got it," she shot back. "And, Sonny," she said, blowing me a kiss, "I think you'll be surprised when you come home."

"Surprise me," I told her, walking away.

"I plan on it," she said as I closed the door.

I drove to work and knew I was in for a good day. Kayla had given me a night to remember, plus she was cleaning my place. I couldn't lose. I had no idea what her surprise would be but it didn't matter. I knew I was ready for just about anything she could dish out.

Work was totally awesome that day. I hit Andy with my question. "How many?"

"Fifty, my man," he answered, referring to the amount of push ups he'd done before work.

"Get real, Andy," I said, punching my time card. "I did two hundred and that was before I had breakfast."

I worked out all day and when I wasn't pushing, pulling, grunting or counting reps, I sold machines and equipment, downed Hot Stuff and vitamins and searched the paper for anything I could find about losing weight. That was the luxury of working at Sports Authority. If your department looked good and your inventory was moving, work was a wonderful place to be. I quickly learned how Andy stayed in such good shape. Eight hours around workout equipment with little else to do would give anyone an excuse to work out.

Except maybe Kayla.

That night, Kayla's big surprise was made known before I even hit the door.

Before I even made it to my tiny square porch, the smell of honey-dipped fried chicken, freshly chopped collard greens and seasoned macaroni and cheese hit my nose with the blunt force of a full frontal assault. I stood there, traumatized. In the past couple of weeks I had successfully kept away from food because I'd not really been confronted with it. All I'd seen were those horrible yellow and red FutraSystem boxes, and the sight of them alone made me mad.

It was then that I figured out FutraSystem's whole move.

They made sure their food was so bad, you didn't want to eat it. If you didn't eat, but you'd actually paid for it, you'd most likely not pig out on other foods. After all, you had an investment to protect, plus you didn't want to be the only fat guy in a room full of people who were losing weight. We all knew diet food was pretty awful.

"It's an acquired taste," Eleanor had warned us.

Finding diet food that had any level of taste wasn't impossible, but if you did find some, there were usually two major problems. First, the portions were so small you'd have to eat at least two to satisfy your hunger. And second, and perhaps most important, the food would be loaded with so much salt and other seasoning that any health benefits you may have realized were lost before you sunk your teeth into it. It was a crapshoot either way, and FutraSystem used it to their advantage. You'd buy more FutraSystem food, which basically squeezed just enough from your budget to keep you from buying other food, and the cycle was complete. No money, no eating. No eating, you lose weight. Besides the food, what's not to like?

I pushed the door open and walked inside. Amazingly, Kayla had done a wonderful job on my place. The walls were even brighter than when I'd last had them painted and the hardwood floors looked better than the trees in a redwood forest. I stumbled into the kitchen, almost in awe of the haunting aromas swirling about my nasal passages.

"Here," she said, handing me a tiny plate with miniature franks enveloped in slices of juicy bacon and flaky, golden-brown twist pastry. "Wash your hands and grab yourself a seat."

"What are you doing, Kayla?" I asked, downing one of the mini-franks without giving it a thought.

"I made dinner because I don't think you've had a good meal in at least three weeks," she answered, leading me into the dining room. "So just sit down and maybe you can force yourself to eat this one last good meal before you melt away to nothing," she said, laughing.

"I'm not trying to melt away to nothing," I replied, spreading a napkin across my lap. "I'm just trying to lose some weight. What's so wrong with that?"

"Nothing at all," she said, scooping some mashed potatoes

onto my plate. "But you're going about it all wrong," she went on, sitting across from me. "Just how long do you think you'll last by working out without eating? Your adrenaline is driving you now." She grabbed a chicken leg. "But you need protein, real vitamins and not that bottled stuff. And more than anything," she said, pausing, "you need a good woman who will stand by you, who will support you and who will be with you regardless of what your weight may be."

"And you know where I can find somebody like that?" I asked, holding a crispy chicken thigh in my right hand and a wing in the other.

"Looking doesn't have to be hard," she answered, smiling. "But let me give you a bit of advice," she added, licking her fingers. "Don't go looking for a sistah while she's sucking on a chicken bone."

I knew she was right. As much as I liked Kayla, there was no way I'd ever try to track her down while she was eating anything.

Burger King would sell Big Macs first.

Thankfully I didn't have to wait that long. Kayla, with a chicken leg in one hand and my hand in the other, dragged me to the rec room, where she demanded I sit on the sofa.

"You like?" she said, her fingers pointing inward.

"You mean you or the chicken?" I asked, smiling.

"Either!" she shot back.

"Well, I really do like the chicken," I admitted, reaching for her hand. "I like it a lot. It beats FutraSystem any day of the week," I went on, laughing. "But if I have to make a choice, I choose you."

"You sure?" she whispered, her head edging closer to mine.

"I'm sure," I answered, our eyes meeting.

"I choose you too," she said, pressing her lips against mine.

I reached to dim the lights and couldn't help but smile when I heard something hit the floor. As she ran her hand across my chest I opened my eyes for just a second to see if my suspicions would be confirmed. Thankfully, they were.

Kayla had actually let go of her chicken leg!

It struck me then that I really was her main course. And I knew she'd be mine.

I just couldn't wait for dessert.

THE REASONS WE LOSE WEIGHT

Lame Reason

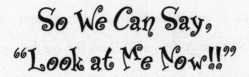

#5

So We Can Say, "Look at Me Now!!"

It's been over a year and I've learned a lot. I wonder sometimes what it would be like to run into Marsha now that I'm not "two tons of fun." At first, the only reason I could see to lose my weight was so I could get back with her. That was stupid. Then I wanted to show Chet and E that I was just as good as they were. That was dumb too. I admit it. For a while there, in the back of my mind, I would exer-

cise knowing that I'd run into any one of them and I'd be able to say, "Yeah, look at me now, fool!" And I wouldn't even have to say those words because their expressions would give it all away. They'd know I'd gotten past the weight and that I was better for it. It took me some time, but I figured that was pretty ignorant too. Losing weight was something I had to do for me. I needed to feel good about myself regardless of what my waist size was. If I had let somebody beside me dictate my weight or my size, I'd have really blown it. Don't get me wrong. It would have been sweet to stare those clowns down so they'd know I had some willpower, but it wouldn't have necessarily made me acceptable to them—it woulda been all wrong. It took me a long time, but I finally realized that even if I'd lost every single pound I'd put on since Marsha dropped me, if I ain't happy with me, nobody else will be either.

—Sonny Walker

Dessert

. . . *One Year Later*

I never went back to FutraSystem and instead elected to join the Sergeant's Fitness Program. The program is run by a guy named Patrick who was once a Marine Corps drill sergeant. To let Patrick tell it, his program was worse than any boot camp anywhere. He was right. I never worked so hard in my life and can't remember ever feeling so good about myself. I hated getting up at six every morning so I could get yelled at and told what to do, but it worked. It really, really worked. I liked exercising and it helped to be around others who wanted to do something about their weight and their health besides waiting for some crazy diet to work. I lost so much weight I had to revamp my wardrobe.

Gone was the sweatsuit that had me looking like a police SWAT van and in came outfits that at least allowed people to know I was human.

Losing weight never became a big issue to Kayla. Every night after dinner we took a long walk and Kayla figured that as long as she exercised moderately and felt healthy, her weight was of little consequence. She even confessed that FutraSystem had given her more than she could have ever asked for. "I got you," she told me while eating a sandwich.

The meeting she'd bought the Christina Covington suit for was a big success and, like she'd said, her business took off. Things were going so well that she called her father and they reconciled. Well, they almost reconciled. They met several times and she so impressed him that he hired Kayla to set up a computer network for his offices across the country. She bought the hardware, the software and tapped him into every sports-related database in the land. He took us out to dinner to celebrate one evening and his credit card was denied. Three days after that, the check he'd written to Kayla bounced.

While watching the evening news about two weeks later, we learned that Mr. Jennings had lost many of his clients and was forced to file for Chapter 11 bankruptcy.

And just as I predicted, Jonathan James Leslie came back into Kayla's life.

At least he tried to.

He *just happened* to be at the Cheesecake Factory in Rockville when we were eating out one evening. He came right up to our table and asked, while I was there, no less, "Why won't you return my calls?"

"I already told you," she said between bites of smoked salmon. "I have a man in my life."

"Just like that?" he asked, bewildered.

"Just like it," she answered. "Would you pass the salt, honey?" she asked, reaching my way.

"No problem," I replied, standing up. "Look, Jonathan," I said, extending my hand. "She's not interested and it ain't like you just gonna stand here and disturb me and my lady, so you need to get to steppin' or something."

"Yeah," he said, reaching to shake my hand.

I had waited for that opportunity since the day he blew me away when we first shook hands. The Sergeant's Program had served me well. He trembled, *his* knees buckled and he walked away feeling like Michael Jackson.

He knew she was out of his life.

Andy was nearly fired from Sports Authority because he wrecked one of the district manager's cars after he'd just finished washing it. He crashed it and left it running in the middle of Greenbelt Road while he ran off. Andy had washed, detailed and driven just about every bigwig's car in the company. He just forgot to tell them he didn't have a driver's license before they handed him the keys. Mr. Matthews was about to can Andy, but I convinced him I'd help Mr. Boot Licker get his driving permit and that Andy was too valuable to lose. And the district manager wanted to keep him around so Andy could work to pay for the damage to his car.

Luckily, Matthews cut him some slack. And thankfully, he hurried to promote me to the department I'd wanted since my first day of work, tents and outdoors. Helen quickly tired of loose balls and was relieved when I recommended her for the exercise and fitness section, which I'd managed and received the Store Department of the Year award for. After four thoroughly pathetic attempts and equally embarrassing failures, Andy lucked out on his fifth try, aced the test and was presented with a valid Maryland driver's license.

He is now our loose balls section team leader.

And he still kisses even more tail than the leather-mask-wearing "gimp" in *Pulp Fiction*.

My brother, Tayvon and his lady split up. "It just wasn't happening," he confessed. "She's nice and all that but she can't cook. And she doesn't even like sports, Sonny. Who wants to marry somebody like that?"

My mom actually considered remarrying but she got cold feet. "I don't need any man telling me I can't go to the islands when I'm ready to go when I'm the one who pays the bills," she told me.

Sadly, Coreen still hasn't come back from the store.

Evelyn, my favorite customer from my exercise equipment days, finally told me the source of her stress. "I've gotten myself mixed up in a love triangle," she confided. "It's absolutely crazy. One of the guys is just a regular guy. He drives a bus, but he's a real sweetheart. But the other one, he's a typical white-collar brother. Nice suits. A real sense of class. I don't know what to do," she said, worried. "Sometimes I feel like I should write a book or something."

I just laughed. I figured one of them should write a book about *her*.

Kayla called me at work one day and said she was going to have some friends over.

"Can you make it home by seven?" she asked, sounding concerned.

"I'll be there," I assured her. "You gonna take some clothes out for me?" I asked, counting cans of Sterno. "Is this one of those client things?"

"You could call it that," she told me. "I'll make sure to put something out that shows off that incredible body of yours."

"See you at seven, sweetheart," I said, hanging up.

I made my way home and I let myself in. Surprisingly, there was no one in the living room. When we entertained her clients they usually lounged around on the sofa and were both mesmerized and repulsed by KJ.

"She's upstairs," KJ told me.

"Thanks, K," I answered, walking toward the staircase.

"No problem, fat boy," he squawked.

Some things simply never change.

"What's up, Kayla?" I asked, walking into the bedroom. "I thought we were having company."

"We do have company," she said, walking toward me. "And our company is already in the basement, so why don't you go on down while I change."

"Like this?" I asked, referring to my Sports Authority outfit.

"This is *my* show," she reminded me. "You look just fine." She kissed me on the cheek and adjusted my collar. "I'll be down in just a few."

I walked down to the basement and the surprise was all on me. Nobody said a word. We just shook our heads and hugged.

It was Chet and E!

We caught up so easily, it was like we'd never lost touch. Chet was still Chet. Big. Bald. Bold and brash. "You look like a different person," Chet remarked. "Your big behind don't even look like a big behind no more," he said, slapping me five.

He told me he was dating a lawyer. She'd filed custody papers because he'd had enough. He wanted his son back.

"We were about to go to court when Donna, that's my lady," he told me, "Donna got some info on Yvette and Lance. They were mixed up in some kind of embezzling scheme or something, so she made a deal and I got little Chet back about a month ago," he said, beaming. "You've got to see him, Sonny. He's big-boned, just like you used to be. Maybe you can give him some pointers."

I couldn't believe it. God did indeed work in mysterious ways. Chester Melvin Stewart, who made me feel so bad about being overweight that I literally had to cut him off, had a fat kid.

"And you won't believe this," Chet told me, excited. "Donna is a sistah!"

His mother and sister are still doing time, but now he and Donna and Little Chet visit them at least once a month. That was pretty amazing because Chet hadn't visited them since they'd been thrown into the slammer. Arranging the visits had to have been Donna's work. It's amazing what a good "sistah" can do for a guy.

Even one as screwed up as Chet.

E was much more somber. But then again, E was always more serious than he needed to be. I just knew I was in for some bad news.

"Well, I guess you heard about Snake," he said, shaking his head.

"What about him?" I asked, looking toward Chet. He just lowered his head and tried to hide his face.

"Some guy caught Snake sneaking around with his old lady so he freaked out and deep-sixed Snake, but he showed his wife some mercy. He let her live," he told me.

"Snake is dead?" I asked, surprised. "Your cousin Snake is f-ing dead!"

"Old Snake is pushing up major daisies," Chet said, grinning.

"Anyway, Sonny," E said, standing up, "I came by to ask if you'll be the best man at my wedding."

"What!" I yelled. "Who the heck you getting married to?"

"Carla!" he answered proudly.

"Carla!" I yelled. "I can't believe it! You're marrying Carla after all these years?"

"I kind of have to," he admitted, smiling. "We're about to have a baby."

"Ain't no way," I said, shaking my head. "This fool went from not getting any at all to having a kid." I slapped Chet five. "This is incredible."

They told me they thought Kayla was "great" and they actually apologized for all the crap they'd said about her.

"We were just plain stupid," E said regretfully.

"No doubt," Chet added, nodding his head. "Kayla's all of it just like you said she was."

I knew that all along. Kayla was definitely all of it, but I wasn't going to rub their faces in it.

Not yet, anyway.

I told them I missed them. And I really did. It felt good just being around my partners and it was like Kayla had told me, "If they're your boys, they'll always be your boys."

One day while I was talking to Andy in the parking lot, a stunning woman in dark shades and a black skintight bodysuit approached me.

"Hi, there, Mr. Sonny Walker," she said, smiling and extending her hand. "I can't believe how good you look."

Ironically, those were the same words she'd hit me with when I had that crazy dream after I'd passed out when Chet and E first forced me to exercise.

"Thanks, Marsha," I answered, smiling. "You look good too."

"I'd ask how you've been, but it's obvious you're fine," she said, leaning her head to one side. "I mean it's obvious you've been fine." She giggled.

"Thanks," I said, still smiling and nodding my head. "It looks like you're still doing well too."

"Actually, I'm having a little problem with some things around the house. Maybe you can drop by and give me a hand," she said softly. "I think it would be worth your while. I'll make that cheesecake you like."

"You're *still* having problems with some things around the house?" I asked, raising my eyebrows. "I told you that the last time we saw each other."

"What are you talking about, Sonny?" she asked, sounding confused.

"I told you way back then that there was something wrong with your scale!" I said, laughing.

"There wasn't a thing at all wrong with my scale," she replied, her head moving with each word.

"You know something, Marsha," I remarked. "You may be right on target. Maybe there wasn't anything wrong with your scale, but there was definitely something wrong with you!"

I walked toward my truck and then turned around and smiled. Before she could say a word and even *try* to tell me off, I hit her with it.

The dreaded "bye-bye" wave!

I hadn't felt that good since Kayla hit me with *her* peanut butter cheesecake, which blew Marsha's to bits.

Eventually, Kayla convinced me to go back to school, and thanks to her encouragement and support I earned my associate's degree in management. I'm finishing up at Maryland this fall and have been accepted into law school at Georgetown University. After all the crap I experienced while I was totally overweight, I decided to help other fat folks who may have been discriminated against.

Carla and E's wedding was beautiful. Kayla had that crazy look in her eye that women always seem to get when they're at some other woman's wedding. She didn't really need to, though.

We'd gone to see our very favorite jazz band, the Pat Metheny Group, two weeks earlier. They were playing at the Capitol Jazz Fest at the Merriweather Post Pavilion amphitheater in Columbia and the evening was incredible. A light breeze swayed and carried the music for what must have been miles as the band played and Metheny's sultry guitar flowed throughout the packed audience. The moon was so clear and inviting and the air was so thick with romance that I'd have paid franchise fees for a Cupid's Arrow concession stand.

"We'd like to play one last song before we leave," Pat said, walking up to the microphone. "When I wrote this tune," he added, his guitar at his side, "I felt that if someone truly loved someone else, that he would follow her to the end of the world."

I knew what Pat meant. I was feeling him just as much as Kayla's soft hands, which were wrapped up in mine.

"You've been a wonderful audience," he told us, smiling. "And we'll close out with a number from our new album. I hope you enjoy it. The album is called *We Live Here* and the song is 'To the End of the World.' "

The song was beautiful. I loved Kayla and I knew I wanted to be with her and near her at all costs. Even if it meant I had to follow her to the end of the world. As the tune played on, I turned to her and proposed. And before the song ended and the audience rose to give Pat and the group their sixth standing ovation, she accepted.

Kayla goes on and off diets that never work but it's okay. She doesn't eat quite as much as she once did, and I convinced her that I wanted her to live to a ripe old age. Her weight goes up and down, but at least she's watching it and taking better care of herself.

And me. The weight comes and goes. Mostly it comes. But it's cool. Gold's Gym opened a beautiful, equipment-packed workout facility in the very same mall as Sports Authority, so I work out a couple of days a week at lunchtime. My doctor's given me a clean bill of health and I feel great. My cholesterol is down, I've cut back on the fat and the calories, my blood pressure is okay and I'm just not all stressed out anymore. Kayla and I walk hand in hand every evening and our love, respect and commitment grow with each step. She's made my life complete. I still may be a little overweight, but it's not a problem like it once was.

Being a fat guy ain't so bad.

Especially when you're as happy as me.

BEEPERLESS REMOTE

A Guy, Some Girls, and His Answering Machine

Beeperless Remote is Van Whitfield's tale of one man who has been thrown into the dating pool and is struggling to get out. Meet Shawn Wayne. He's single, employed, hard-bodied, a former All-American, and looking for his ideal woman. His search for the woman of his dreams leads to misadventures ranging from nightmare blind dates and underage flings to encounters with married swingers. Held hostage by today's technology, which has made dating a complex web of answering machines and cell phones, Shawn finds the rules have changed, and that he now has to contend with all types of modern women.

Fiction/0-385-48934-X

ANCHOR BOOKS

Visit Anchor on the web at: www.anchorbooks.com
Available at your local bookstore, or call toll-free to order:
1-800-793-2665 (credit cards only).